EUTOPI

EUTOPIA

SUYASH

Publishing Facilitation: AuthorsUpFront

The Write Place
A Publishing Initiative by Crossword Bookstores Ltd.
Umang Tower, 2nd Floor, Mindspace, Off Link Road,
Malad West, Mumbai 400064, India.

Web: www.TheWritePlace.in
Facebook: TheWritePlace.in
Twitter: @WritePlacePub
Instagram: @WritePlacePub

For:
Sharkleaves

.

.

Contents

Destiny Calling

The dawn waits on him. The sun is delayed by one fifth of an hour. Descartes sits on a black rock in his garden, with his chin on his knees. He peers into a hole, in which lies a drop of water. Under his gaze silver markings appear on the drop; powered by his imagination, they form a circular pattern. A web, not dense, or overshadowing the original sparkle of the liquid, but embellishing it.

He wills the droplet to float up in the air. The night's crickets grow silent, and the first light of day shines on this suspended prism. Colors fill the field, and with a smile Descartes realizes this to be the prettiest droplet of its kind, the best he has yet designed. It then floats on its own, drifting free, and settles on the trunk of a tree.

The tree, too, a thing of marvel. Its canopy green like any other, but much thicker, no light has ever passed it, and no bird may dare nest in it. Its branches are hidden behind a curtain of leaves, which are interwoven together in such a deep green, that it isn't possible to tell where the individual ones end and begin. The trunk's surface, too, is concealed, covered with large drops of a watery liquid, with silver patterns on them. Each unique as a snowflake, none alone capable of keeping an observer's attention, forcing the onlooker to see the very tree as a single masterpiece.

Descartes watches it for a while, analyzing his new addition to the tree, admiring it; knowing the like of such doesn't exist anywhere else in Eutopia. Then he hears her call, a telepathic realization in his mind. It's not a sound; it's not of words, nor is it imagery, but closer to an emotion. Unlike a memory, it carries the essence of her present self; it raptures Descartes, reminding him of her touch and those nuances that make her Destiny. She calls him from the other side of their world, from the opposite end of their Bubble of Perfect Existence. There is no thinking twice for Descartes, she is all that matters. The best among the countless number of 'them' he has ever known.

In childish excitement he jumps off his seat, but chooses not to land on the ground; instead, he floats a couple of inches above it. He uses the skills he had acquired in his younger days, back at the Academy, to tune into existence a path under his feet. It's narrow as a single file alley, made of platinum bricks placed on nothing but earth. A design starts to appear on the bricks, depicting all the floral life Descartes loves, whether creation of his own, of others or of mother Gaia. Similar to the droplets of the tree, each brick alone is a wondrous piece of art, encapsulating a chapter of a story, but still Descartes' creativity flows from one brick to another painting a bigger picture. He slowly descends on the road, wondering whether his works are beautiful enough for her.

By the tree, on the hill is Descartes' cottage, a rudimentary structure with its front door facing west, and opening to a vast expanse of grasslands. Standing there all one can see is a boundless lush ocean of green. In the east from his backyard starts a patch of tall gray slender woods, beyond which lie many older sceneries, caves, castles and mansions; forgotten places where Descartes lived and wandered in his younger years.

Descartes has designed his half of the Bubble of Perfect Existence with immense care, charting its every aspect; for instance on a clear day, the sight from his porch is adorned by a distant tree line, which ribbons the horizon beyond the grasslands.

Descartes commands the sun to follow him as he walks on, and bring forth the day. He watches the illustrations on his platinum path grow finer with every step. His entire will is bent upon elaborating it. Not once does he get the chance to look up, never does he notice the approaching forest.

In a moment he realizes all he needs to do to hide away the flaws in his novel creation. He must make the path glow. An addition to the natural shine of platinum, a distraction to keep her from noticing errors caused by his quick-handedness.

Adding on this new feature to his road, Descartes looks up to notice the forest a few footfalls ahead of him. He breaks into a run. He hasn't seen her for a while. He misses her. He knows that time spent with her is worth much more than anything else he could be doing this morning. Only ten more strides, he is inside, and the transition begins.

The forest is an invisible boundary between Descartes' and Destiny's halves of the Bubble of Perfect Existence. A vibrant blend between the skills and the taste of the couple, reflected in its every beast, tree, bug and blade of grass.

Now inside he can see Destiny's influence grow around him. In the little things, those that are dear to her, light suggestions of her imagination, much like a red leaf popping out of a green bush. The forest has always been the greatest interest the two share, and the only part of the bubble where they work together, and that has been contrived by their collaboration.

Behind the many films of foliage there is a sudden break in the pattern that governs the order of this forest. It's a large wooden structure, a house that could be mistaken for a maze. Its walls are as thin as paper, barely a little more than soggy sheets of wood. It has no roof but is, instead, open to the sky; still it never endures a drop of rain, as if the very clouds bear in mind to leave it alone.

They call it 'The Attic', an apt name for the purpose it serves. It's the place where they keep relics, souvenirs dear to their ancestors, some even dating back to the Earth of Old. These objects of mass were bounded by the unbreakable laws of physics, and could not be literally carried into Eutopia. Though their architecture, outlines and blueprints easily crossed over, and their replicas were forged in Eutopia.

It's not all junk. The Attic plays a crucial role in Destiny and Descartes' lives. Where they as Newman talk to the wind and feel the steps of a lonely ant on a leaf from a mile away; where they know all that happens in this world of their making. Only here in the Attic are things they do not wholly know. It's a library, a museum, a place of mysterious secrets that allure them again and again to its maze of knowledge.

Destiny visits often, as many as three to four times a week, habitually looking for memories, in search of little somethings that happen to pass through her thoughts. Her belongings include intricate clockwork mechanical devices. A giant gothic pipe organ, whose pipes spread across the entire Attic. Its five keyboards wait for her to strike their notes, and the music that ensues fills every corner of the building with voices. Wind-up toys, which mimic animal behavior; there are scorpions and snakes on the dark side and cats and birds on the good. She may spend hours glaring into small, curious globes of glass, whose inner workings are only known to Destiny; they each keep a glimpse of the worlds of her ancestors, of their bubbles, and the landscapes they had shaped and inhabited.

Descartes can live contently in the Attic for days; there is simply too much to learn. His personal collection, a random assortment of art, literature, music and fantasy, will take more than a gross full of years to unravel and imbibe. Yet, there is more, for the many small steps of technological evolution have reached much closer to their eventual end in Eutopia, but it's the lore of the past that Descartes finds more mysterious than the coming future and the end of times.

It is here that they access the data marked public by other Eutopians. If tagged as 'freed knowledge' by their holders anything can be called upon to present itself. Irrespective of where the data is stored, in a personal Bubble of Perfect Existence, or in the collectively owned City. Yet there isn't much of it to go around. Newmans are known to be very possessive of their work, ever shy of sharing their inventions and imagination with others. Most consider their work sacred, and to them allowing the interference of others would only mean breaking its sanctity, even when others may help refine their talents and creations.

Descartes enters one of its many chambers. For a moment he feels lost, for the Attic is truly a maze. Its walls and everything in them move on their own at night; it's a new puzzle every day, solving which is one of Destiny's favorite sports, and as for Descartes, well, he has never complained.

Descartes feels luck favoring him today as the room he walks into reminds him of a tune. A soft slow jiving tune, with a sweet voice blabbering in the beautiful confusion of love called 'Sorrow'. This room, just as other rooms of the Attic, doesn't have a roof and the morning sun shines through.

However, unlike other rooms, in here are kept many layers of records, Compact Discs and Bedtime Storytellers. All organized in alphabetical order covering every inch of its three walls, while the fourth is stacked with ancient, outdated electronic gadgets. Descartes walks in and without hesitation presses a tiny button; the tonearm on the record player slides away, he picks up the vinyl and walks out again. A couple of minutes later the album cover flies off a shelf and follows him.

Forest Queen

Yes, the forest is truly shared by Descartes and Destiny; only here do their thoughts and shades of creativity mix and mash in real splendor, yet it's evident that they have their separate spheres of influence. One where Descartes is its creator and maintainer and the other where Destiny is queen.

Across the Attic begins her half of the forest. It's much more explicit; breaking away from the limitations of green, it blossoms into a chaos of colorful flowers and golden leaves. There are many nasty insectivorous plants here, who judge their victims by their visual appeal. Their poisons and set traps more efficient against the viler creatures. It's nothing more than an imaginative way for Destiny to get rid of ugliness, which evolution, at times, does mistakenly produce.

Descartes walks slower now, his steps are softer. He is observant, which is usual for him in these parts. In barely a murmur he tells himself, *"It almost feels as if I have walked into a painting."*

There are yellow hummingbirds with red beaks and insects with beauty of a kind only found in ladybirds and butterflies. He can feel the stare of a million eyeballs, the very forest is aware of his presence and by them is Destiny.

The soft warm sun is still climbing up the sky, it's not yet noon. Descartes is weary of walking; he wishes to linger here longer. He misses his yellow straw hat, and so he finds it placed on the stub of an old tree. Wearing it, he decides to rest a while and appreciate the much comforting sun.

He feels a change in this place, not an evident one, but noticeable. The wind blows swifter than it used to, and the ground seems softer. Musing, watching a spider carry a tied up struggling ant upon its back, up a tree, Descartes makes up his mind to investigate.

To speak with the world around him, to communicate with the bubble, he must call upon an inert, and for ages unexplored capacity of the human brain.

His conscious grip on his imminent surroundings starts to fade. A wave of information plights his mind, much like in a dream; his eyes half shut, and rapidly move behind their lids. It's tiring, but Descartes is used to it. The bubble lets loose all that it has to tell, an exact record of every event of the land in recent days, however pertinent or irrelevant they might be.

Waking of one thousand nine hundred and ninety-two butterflies, twelve times over blossoming of ten million and seven flowers, shedding of truly innumerable leaves and an unnatural storm, the cause of the change he feels.

As Descartes draws closer to discovering the source of the storm she calls him again. Faint is her presence at first, but the mere thought of Destiny is capable of willing Descartes' heart to abandon any errand and seek her instantly. Her call is much more than a bare thought. It grows louder, stronger, and under its spell the world changes. She brushes away all his calculations, all his ideas and speculations. She envelops him.

He is back on his feet. She is closer than he had earlier presumed; she does not lurk on one of her far away beaches but hides somewhere in the forest itself. He well-nigh willingly gives way to her enchantment, and breaks into a haphazard run. He must find her, but it's as toilsome a task as the queen bee's search for the sweetest nectar of spring. *"Where is she?"* A soft voice whispers in his head. He trips and falls only to rise and stumble again. *"Where is she?"*

He sees a light, a glimpse, through trees and shapely curves of long leaves, a gleam he can only associate with her skin. *"Could she really be there or do my senses fool me?"*

He runs in her direction even though he knows the shine was an illusion, he can't help but hope to find her. Reaching the spot where she seemingly stood a moment ago, he hears a sudden rustle of bushes on his right, though no footfalls or her voice preceded their movement.

And there she appears right in front of him, but he can't fully see her. She is a blur. She is close enough for him to notice her smile, yet further away than a hand's reach or even a few swift strides. She beckons him with a nod; her hair that hides her shoulders follows her one gesture tardily.

Her image turns around and walks away, and Descartes sprints after her. He can hear a voice "It's not enough Descartes." It's her voice. "Do you think I am happy?" With her every light step the spiky undergrowth turns to soft grass. "Why aren't you with me?"

Descartes is well aware that it's not really she who teases him. He knows he pursues a shadow image of her real self, and those are not her words, but an impression of his own imagination cast upon a dreamy vision of Destiny.

Then she disappears, the charm breaks, and all of Descartes' senses are restored. He is now where Destiny wishes him to be, in an open glade by a silent grey pool. *"Strange."* He considers this place, it isn't usual for him to be lost in his own bubble.

He stands there trying to peer inside, attempting to fathom the secrets the pool seems to hide. His sharp green eyes fail to pierce through the opaque water. The force underneath is far too strong and will not wither so easily.

He smiles, amused by the works of Destiny; he runs his hand through the black of his hair, which reach his knees. Now he knows the importance of the pool and would wait here for her to turn up, and show him all that is new.

Playing With Curtains

Concealed, underneath the surface of the pool in a bubble of air, is where she waits. Dry and safe in a blue world of her Absolute Defense, Destiny plays and tosses around three feather-light balloons of water. They drift about, defying gravity, yet never going astray or too far, staying limited between her fingertips.

She has been here for hours, waiting for Descartes, and had planned to reveal herself the instant he arrives. "There is so much I have to tell him, so many things he hasn't seen," she breathes, but Descartes never hears a word. Even now she suppresses the urge to be with him, for rarely she gets a chance to eye him in secret, and in his waking.

She watches him, as he runs his hand through his hair. A trickster's smile appears on her lips when he gets restless and starts walking around the pool in circles. She wonders of his thoughts when he settles down on the grass and stares at the water.

Then all of a sudden she gives herself away, emerging out with a splash, she catches Descartes unguarded. The liquid walls of her Absolute Defense concave outwards, forming a fountain that sources from the pool, and makes a pedestal for Destiny to stand on. The water flows softly underneath her feet. Descartes lies on the ground, wet and shaking. She wears a dress crafted of white, made of silk. Surprised by Destiny's sudden appearance and lost in her fair presence, he can only see her. See the light of the sun, and the wind play with the flares of her dress as they may do with curtains. Precious stones in her hair – red, amber and blue – much like prisms split light to all its seven shades, creating the most delicate aura around her. Descartes does not appear shocked and confused to Destiny. His plot has worked. Destiny couldn't see it all from her hiding place. The platinum path he had designed at the start of his day's walk has traced him till here. Now out of the pool, Destiny witnesses the intricacy of its pattern. Her eyes follow the path, which cuts across the forest, goes through the Attic and melts away into the darkness of the woods. Its surface bears a vivid reflection of their world's floral wonders.

She looks down at Descartes, who is still on the ground, drenched, and cold. No, Destiny doesn't find his balled over fall laughable. She can barely manage a smile. The humor of her well planned joke is eclipsed by the brightness within him, by his extravagant capacity of creation. Nine years of being coupled, and another two decades of knowing each other from before, hasn't been enough for her to get used to his teal skin with dark freckles, which shimmer in and out of existence with his every motion.

The sand trickles ever more slowly in the hour glass as she extends a hand. Descartes lifts himself up and takes her hand in his. He gives into the temptation of kissing it. He steps up and joins her onto the fountain; with locked eyes they linger there for a moment and then disappear into the pool.

Descartes knows nothing of what's beneath the grey pool, for he has never been inside before. He doubts any of this existed a week ago. *"It wasn't there, neither the glade, nor the grey pool."* Destiny leads the way as they descend deeper, and Descartes follows, unaware of the tunnel's depths, or of what awaits at the other end.

It's a labyrinth, with countless passageways and burrows bifurcating in every which direction. Soon, the water chokes up the fractured little sunlight that had followed them inside, leaving them in darkness.

"May I make light?" Descartes asks her. But Destiny holds his hand tighter and pulls him further. They go straight down until they reach the floor, where they enter a cavern leading west.

This passage is lit with green torches burning in small slots carved in its stone walls. "It's bright enough, don't you think? And the best part is, they are not my doing," she tells him merrily.

Her words trigger a pause in Descartes' casual stream of thoughts, and revoke his worst nightmare. He knows the illuminants aren't his either. *"Someone else is here, or was here, in our Bubble of Perfect Existence. Is Destiny letting someone else in, in secret? But I have been cautious; no Newman can visit or leave the bubble without my knowledge. Who is he?*

"No it couldn't be, I am being irrational, she wouldn't. Besides, who would she want here anyway? She has no friends left, and hates visiting the City almost as much as I do."

"So whose are they?" he asks her a little later.

Destiny draws her index finger to her lips, and tells him with a sharp, "Shh! You will see."

In silence as they move down the passage Descartes begins to notice a change. The lights and their carved slots are more than simple torches; the flames appear to spread onto the wall of the tunnel, and stem across as channels of fire. These streams form symbols and images around the burning torches. They seem to evolve with his every step, turning more refined with each slot that they pass.

"It's a kind of calligraphy, but I don't know the script," Descartes wonders out loud.

A single syllable, "Wow," is her only reaction to his cerebration, a sufficient clue for Descartes to solve the puzzle.

They have discussed it before; he has tried to convince her against it. Many a time has he warned her, "But Destiny, don't you feel the Elders would intervene?"

But every time she has averted his worried looks and concerns with, "Well, why should they, it's not as if I am doing something illegal." The conversation always ends in this fashion. Descartes can never win an argument with Destiny.

Still, his silence is not one of concordance; he knows the time is near when he must breach the harmony they share, and have a talk.

It is unacceptable. There are few laws that Eutopians are expected to abide by in the comforts of their personal Bubbles of Perfect Existence. The Elders are not pleased when one creates a creature of near human intelligence; much as the forbidden fruit of Eden, it is the one and the only thing out of bounds in the Newman world.

Descartes always thought it was silly of Destiny to count on a legal loophole. He knows the Elders will ignore that her creation was a natural occurrence of evolution, and not the result of a single premeditated act.

Guessing the origin of the symbols, Descartes tries to read them again, but just as everything else Destiny does, they too outwit him. They move on, traveling west, deeper in the passage, and all this while the calligraphy on the walls continues to evolve. The tunnel then abruptly ends, right when he feels he could recognize a few of them as letters.

Jellies Bloom

Water has always been Destiny's favorite element. She, too, as most Newman who are lured by the vast blue depths, grew up with a taste for salt, and for all creatures who can breathe without air.

The tunnel has brought them far beyond the forest and Destiny's beaches, into the open, to the sea, where all of Destiny's underwater fascinations thrive. Where long before her mimicry of evolution first began.

Descartes smells change. A presence, a fragrance, which he knows is not of Destiny. Perturbed by it, in a much accusing tone he asks her, "Someone's here?"

"It's been long since you have been here," she replies calmly.

Descartes has been here a gazillion times, in Destiny's sea, but the magnificence of her imagination has never failed to amaze him. The sea is alive. It embraces them with warmth, driving away the cold, still dread of the tunnel from their minds.

Both Destiny and Descartes appreciate the night and the secrecy of darkness; still they have a magnanimous moon, forever set to light the world with all the generosity it can muster. Yet, all its might is not sufficient to light up her underwater world adequately. Their moon is not alone, the seabed is coated with a special microorganism. An ancient life form remembered by only a few but Destiny. Its unique capacity of soaking the daylight and emitting a part of it at night gives the sea a light of its own.

Only a dozen miles into the sea, several species of squid, starfish and octopus ease in a coral reef that runs unabridged along the full length of the coast. This reef is characterized by the peculiar absence of fish and is, instead, bestowed with the mysterious creatures of Destiny.

There are elephantine naked marine snails with robust tentacles, who have mastered the art of sloth, and proudly display their toxic colors. Descartes even sights a Blue Water Dragon, the King of her ocean. It swims with the elegance of an eel, breathes with the majesty of a whale and kills as viciously as a crocodile.

Usually, Destiny would spend hours here, lost in the love of all her creations, content by Descartes' passive presence; but in her haste she scarcely acknowledges the wonders around her. No, they can't distract her, for she is finally ready to share her secret with him.

Further on beyond the reef they are greeted by missionaries of the twilight zone: jellyfish. They appear first as bright multicolor polka dots to the dark mute waters of the ocean, and in time they environ Descartes and Destiny.

In the midst of a jellies bloom, in a smooth spread of orange and a whisper of blood red, Descartes' insecure mind is still bothered by his fantasies.

"Who is it Des?"

"Who is it Des..." She mocks him, repeating his words, imitating him in a baby's voice. His impatience irritates her, but she isn't angry. There is little that Descartes can do that would hamper how ecstatic she is, not here, never at sea.

He can see through her playful charms; he feels her discontent, and is reminded that he mustn't speak his every thought aloud.

"I must keep my cool, and besides, she would never..."

Dwarkoids

Descending deeper, leaving behind the twilight zone, Descartes expects nothing but a pitch black void. A desert concealed from light, where only shadows of Destiny's imagination dwelled: ill-formed creatures that were never to be truly alive.

The sea used to end here, in the desert. A place Descartes has seldom ever ventured on his own, yet Destiny leads him forth into its darkness. Where once there was nothing but shadows, now there is more.

The way, back in the era of the Earth of Old, the first men in space perceived the dark side of their planet: sprawling with humans who clustered in little beacons, the city lights, announcing to all who cared to look, "We are here, this is our world." Upon a vertical scale, on the wall of an underwater crater, created not by a fallen fireball but by the will of Destiny, live a folk who too announce their existence by illuminants brightening the surface with the allusiveness of stars.

Moving on, reaching the center of the crater, Descartes can grasp some of the lights' mysteries. Lamps to light a city, a city carved out perpendicularly in the wall. It is equipped with every detailed structure: streets, boulevards, houses, plazas, tunnels and giant halls. The lampposts protrude out, each bearing a pair of glass lamps; they emit a glow identical to the microbes', which coat the seabed, closer to the shore.

"Electric blue and green, jars filled with bioluminescence. Aren't they so bizarre!" are Descartes' words of appreciation. "No more can I contain my curiosity," he admits with a sigh and asks her, "Who lives here?"

"Can't you see already Descartes?"

Descartes strains his eyes, he might have seen a shimmer but he isn't sure. It happens again. In unison they sparkle gold and disappear.

"Look closer."

At his command, delicate slim sheets of glass cover his eyes, lenses for far sight. Descartes strains them further, zooming in, scanning the underwater city. The architecture: alien, designed for those who don't walk, but swim. He can see them. Limbless yet agile, faceless but crowned; their skin black but occasionally glittering gold.

"Dwarkoids, they fancy calling themselves, and their city they call Dwarka. Has a nice ring to it, don't you think?" A rare fondness fills her voice.

"Sure it does, Destiny," he reassures her, and they share a smile.

A small phalanx of Dwarkoids advances toward them, moving together in a close military formation. As they approach, Descartes is better able to fathom the peculiarities of these deep sea beings.

They are clad in metal, their helm covered by a classical Greek warriors' headgear. Their body is hidden in a mail of gilded chains, which curtains their anatomy and the mechanics behind their crabwise motion.

"Ah! No wonder you have been buzzing about primitive human armor all month," he teases her, laughing with every word. "I knew something was fishy, so unlike you to care for my beloved dry history."

"Descartes, look at them," she says, gently tilting her head to the right. "They are the most unusual of all those who breathe in my world. They have my soul, but your heart."

The platoon of Dwarkoids comes closer. They seem familiar to Descartes, as if he knows them from before, maybe from childhood or a half forgotten tale of myths.

The centurion of the Dwarkoid platoon, an officer of rank, marked by a necklace bearing a purple gem, steps forward, and stretches out an open palm. Descartes stares deep into its circular eyes. A multitude of colors with streaks of beige, falling into a black oceanic pupil enchant Descartes. He never notices the absence of a face. Dwarkoids only have eyes.

"Take it," Destiny whispers to him. There is something in the centurion's palm.

"What is that?" he asks her, still spellbound by those eyes.

"Just take it," she tells him again, moving closer to him. He picks it up, it's a transparent capsule, Descartes can see through it. He can see the quiet discipline of the phalanx, the sea, the far off city of Dwarka, its light, and its lively clamor.

In a flash it's all clear to him and he pops the pill. The moment it's inside, the drug erupts, and a wave shudders inside Descartes.

He takes a few dreamy missteps; it echoes as it would in an empty wine bottle. Borders smudge, colors leek and join the water. He turns around and he can see a blurry image of himself standing in front of the centurion. Descartes has left his own body.

The centurion is holding his hand. Every motion is taking twice as long as it should. A long spiny finger darts out from the Dwarkoid's chain mail. The pointed nail hovers over Descartes' wrist, as if hesitant of touching him. Time stands still. Everything stops.

Behind his physical self stands Destiny, peeping from his shoulder. She is attentive and frozen. *"She is beautiful"* is his last thought before he plunges into the unknown. The Arrow of Time returns, the Dwarkoid's finger makes contact with his skin. He begins to draw symbols, slow at first, but with an increasing velocity. Its touch, the smooth flow of the nail upon his hand and every figure traced upon his skin, is as coherent to Descartes as spoken words.

As the centurion's finger rolls faster and faster on his palm, the words fill him up. They turn from being merely sounds, to images and finally film. They tell him the tale of the Dwarkoidian past. Lost in time, a journey through the lives of these strange beings; selective glimpses of secondhand vision teach him all that the Dwarkoids know. He experiences their sorrows and joys. He knows how it is to eat an eel alive, the pain of a Blue Sea Dragon's sting, and the warmth of the invincible fire that burns purple underwater.

He fights their wars, and watches them grow from being cave dwellers to builders. He witnesses their first attempts with mathematics and geometry till they master the art of architecture. Descartes frowns at their barbarism, but later delights at the nuances of their complex society. The knowledge of a thousand years, cramped in the time for one, is not enough to satisfy Descartes.

It's waning, the drug's grip loosens, and Descartes' mind is returning to reality. He fights it. His time in Dwarkoid memories was amazing; he wills it not to end, but knows not how. He slips further away from the realm of the unconscious mind.

The story hasn't ended yet, there is more to be told; the last that's shown to Descartes is from the eyes of the centurion himself, who now Descartes knows by name.

Centurion Boomer shivers, standing at the head of the welcoming party awaiting Destiny and Descartes, hoping all goes as planned. Descartes can feel his anxiety and the fear of what he has been taught from childhood: the legendary wrath of Lord Descartes.

"They have my heart but her soul. I know what you mean love. They revere their ancestors; they forge swords and fancy shields. Their culture is burdened by elaborate customs; they churn myths and stories for breakfast, lunch, dinner and sleep. They are my children, and I will love and father them."

Descartes can see himself and Destiny coming toward the Dwarkoid city, and toward Boomer and his platoon. Slowly, his consciousness leaves Boomer, and slips back into his body of the past.

"How long have I been lost in my thoughts?" are the first words that find his lips.

A relieved titter escapes Destiny, "Not long, hours in this part of our bubble but only a few minutes for the two of us."

Missing a Loop

Gushes of water, spiral trails of bubbles follow Descartes and the Dwarkoids as they make their way to the surface. Boomer and Descartes play as lion cubs, like brothers; Destiny swims along, but a distance apart.

They play a sport, an addiction for the Dwarkoids, in which two teams race to the top in coordinated formations. The gameplay is simple: swim right through the opponent team, tear them apart, and gain the lead while they regroup. The winner is determined in a heartbeat, the first intact formation to reach the surface.

The heavy copper taste of adrenaline teases Descartes' tongue; he can feel it rush in his veins. No more can he communicate with Boomer in words, but with solely intuition and feel. They are nearing the end, the finishing line, the air.

Descartes is not the one to cheat, neither are his skin and bones any match for the scales and tails of the Dwarkoids. In all fairness, only to compete, he recalls his past strengths, when he did swim and learn their ways. He remembers what his tail could do and the agility of his multitude of arms. Descartes calls upon the bubble, twists time and is head to head with Boomer. He then fools space, takes the lead and breathes air.

He bursts out of the water, laughing, with Destiny not far behind. He turns around and stares at his newfound friend's beautiful bright circular eyes; soon a pair more appear, and then more, but the sea dwellers are bound to water, and no further can they follow their masters.

"Don't worry, I will be back soon," Descartes tells them in English, willing them to understand.

The moon reigns the sky. Destiny and Descartes have lost the evening and the better half of the day to their oceanic adventure. At such a late hour, far away from dry land, they have but one option.

They rise from the ocean, hand in hand, and comet toward a crowd of clouds, while a twin tail of blue and red taints the air behind them. Their sky is an optical illusion, crafted to appear infinite as on the Earth of Old. Here it's only a two-dimensional dome, cupping their world.

They hop on a cloud, which, though not entirely substantial, easily supports their weight. "To the Moon," Destiny commands it, and they set sail.

Crafting a throne of white, shaping the cumulus cloud by hand, Descartes asks Destiny, "Ah! Once more on a cloud, I keep forgetting how slow it is, yet how exhilarating and fine. When last were we here?"

"Maybe a month, maybe two, but never mind the clouds, tell me now what you truly think."

"What, about the clouds?" Descartes plays the fool.

Destiny rolls her eyes, "No, not the clouds. The Dwarkoids! How do you like them?" she says, speaking a little louder than she had intended.

Resting on his white chair that moves to take his shape even as he moves, Descartes looks away, at the far off faint radiating bolts of lightning, and replies before the thunder reaches their ears. "They are wonderful."

He looks at her, smiles, and waits for the heavens to be at peace again, "I am sorry I doubted you. I couldn't believe it was possible to create a being of such delight without breaking the law. I never imagined that the natural course of evolution could be this graceful. Oh, you should have seen them Destiny; I can't begin to retell their tales, their notions and ideas, or their..." His voice trails off into silence, leaving alone the glitter in his eyes. Destiny isn't smiling, her face is taut, and worried. "No, that's not entirely true," she tells him timidly, as their cloud anchors itself to the moon.

Their moon is no celestial rock, but a place for spirituous drinks and comfort. Empty, but for a pair of stools for a snowy bar table. A moist haze laces the air as Descartes and Destiny step on its silvery surface.

They scurry to the bar together, and in a snap of Destiny's fingers the torso of an exceedingly large man appears. A hollow man made of mist. His face round and ballooned, his lips heavy, his toothless smile stretching from ear to ear. His voice booms, "Welcome back my lord and lady, what would you have tonight?"

"The usual," they answer in unison, and the bartender pours their drinks with a flare of his hands. Descartes and Destiny dive deep into a conversation about the Dwarkoids and how having them is to change their lives. Destiny tells him of how years ago she had first conceived the Dwarkoids in a dream.

Their talk streams from one thing to another. Until, eventually, Descartes brings forth the dreaded question of the Elders. "Do you think they would intervene?" he asks her.

"You know how complex the law is; I don't know if I have breached it, I have done much to help my children." However much she tries, she can't morph the fright in her voice.

Descartes holds her hand and calmly interrogates her, "What do you mean? Have you modified them, bred them, or helped them mutate?"

"No, but I have altered the world for them, made our waters safer for them," she confesses with doubt-embedded eyes.

The warmth in their clutched hands disappears, he lets hers go. Descartes looks away and mumbles, "They may intervene, and if they do; all would be ruined. How then will we keep the balance of our Bubble of Perfect Existence?"

Silence fills the space between them, and every moment passes painfully slowly, until the cloud steward speaks, "May I serve you another, my lady?"

A nod of consent, and he pours her a double single malt from a pearlescent crystal bottle. Destiny cups the lowball glass, preventing him from adding ice to her drink and rises; in reverie she floats away from the moon, toward the vaulted sky.

"*Who is she?*" Descartes contemplates as he watches the trail of her kirtle, blowing gently in the nightly wind. Nine years and rarely ever can he tell her thoughts, "*How can you be this carefree Destiny? Don't you see we are on the brink of losing everything?*"

Descartes resists following her for a while, until he sees the stars gather together; high as the noon sun they form a perfect circular oculus in the darkened sky, and together they outshine the moon.

She is unaware of Descartes, even when he comes up behind her. Soundlessly he spies her; curiosity keeps him from disrupting Destiny, while she plucks the studded stars from the midnight blue sheet of a sky. She turns around and adds the cold star to her whiskey. "They have the shine of diamonds, but they float like ice," she tells him with a smile "Would you try some?"

A fumbled out of breath laugh, he hands her his glass, she turns around, and reaches out for the stars once more.

A mute toast, their glasses clink, and to Destiny's delight it starts to rain, an unusual rain with music and voice, a shattering feminine voice.

Descartes bows, "A dance, my lady?" In a light embrace, they twist and wriggle. They skid in the air with every blue verse, while rain drops burst into sound. Swinging to a song Descartes knew would uplift Destiny, the one he handpicked hours ago, the one called 'Sorrow'.

Yet he recognizes a subtle tension in her moves, he spots her missing a loop, he can discern her wistful dispositions, he knows she wishes for something more. The stiffness in her steps: it's fear, a fear of expectations.

He holds her close, "I will build a ship by hand, and sail it across the five true seas of the Earth of Old, if I could, only to fetch you a cluster of Picard grapes, if they were to please you."

"I am here with you Descartes," she reassures him, then she laughs her pleasant laugh and asks him, " Promise me you wouldn't stop being you, even when I were to ask you to."

Message in the Bottle

She sleeps. She is calm, in the sand, in a dreamless slumber, in the warmth of darkness, of pitch black, until she feels a tender grip on her index finger. Crouching beside her, Descartes watches her with a reassuring gaze, the kind that wakes her beaming. Descartes then leaves her to herself, knowing well how slow Destiny's mornings are.

It usually takes her awhile to rise. She first stretches, twists, yawns and stares at the sky. Thin clouds sprawl across it and she plays with them. Still lying in the sand, she lazily traces new contours for them, she shifts the miniature sand dunes, and the clouds do their best to imitate their shapes.

When Destiny gets up, the pressed sand against her body slides off as if it was never there at all, leaving her skin clean. The memories of last night glow as gems within her.

She finds Descartes afar, but not out of sight. A tiny figure at the shore; she can see that he hasn't bothered to get dressed yet. "It's such a sunny day after all," she muses. He is holding something glistening in his hand. Getting closer, she recognizes it, and winces in fright. It's a glass bottle, within it is a rolled up parchment tied with a red ribbon. It's a message; the ribbon signifies that it's for her. If it were to be blue, then it would have been Descartes'.

He waves over the bottle and entwining cracks appear on the glass. A little tap and the limp frame breaks, the glass shatters and falls harmlessly on the sand, leaving only the scroll in his hand.

"May I?" he asks Destiny before he opens the knot, and she consents with a nod. Descartes reads the letter, a letter that Destiny has dreaded for long.

"It comes from the City," he informs her.

Descartes' face stretches into a grimace as he reads on.

"What is it?" she asks, hoping it's to do with anything but the Dwarkoids.

"They have been observing us, why don't you have a look," he says coldly, pressing the parchment in her hand.

Mr. Descartes and Mrs. Destiny

How have you been? It's been long since you last paid us a visit. Why don't you attend one of our monthly get-togethers, you are sure to find many old friends and maybe make some new ones. We have worked hard over the last few years to make our events hospitable, inviting and attractive for all.

There is another reason why we wish you come soon to the City. Lately, strange reports have been coming from our Observatory. They claim that the intelligent life in your Bubble of Perfect Existence has far exceeded what is considered normal. We do not consider this possible, for it can only happen when there are many millions of individuals living in your bubble. We would truly be obliged if you could confirm our observatory's observation as false. If, however, some urgent matter keeps you, or you are wary of leaving home, we ourselves will pay you a visit in 7 days.

Hope to see you soon.

The Warden of the 27th Hive
Elder Machiavelli
Maintaining Perfection

The letter is no surprise to Descartes, he had long foreseen it. He had anticipated its arrival, yet he had gulped down Destiny's reassuring words, he had brushed aside just worries and embraced ignorance.

Destiny can't take to a single word of what the letter said. It is all pretense, and a rude, blatant threat. In simpler terms, as she understands it, it's an ultimatum. "You better turn up, and come clear within a week or we will pay you a visit, and that surely won't be pleasant."

While Destiny reads the message, Descartes falls in an unsettling turmoil. Anger never has a form; it has no kindness, but a life of its own. Descartes' wrath has a foul reputation, the kind that prevents him from thinking. Anger has no art, nor wisdom. It won't let him pick his words and it rarely if ever lets him speak, but at times it overwhelms him, becoming him.

"You promised you would be careful, how could you let this happen? This was so stupid of you," he accuses her, with disdain, his voice shaking with rage.

"So I am stupid now, am I?" Destiny retorts, taken aback.

"Sure you are. This is your doing. It's your battle Des; I am not coming with you. You know how little I enjoy the City. I won't be humiliated this way; I shall not sit there as they interrogate us."

"All right." Aghast a moment, and composed once more, "I am not asking you to accompany me. I can tackle them alone."

Whether in the jungle or the ocean, animals quail away in fear, distancing themselves from Descartes and Destiny, fury fills the air between them. They both recognize the real tension embodied in every fragment of their bubble. They look away in shame; arguments between those coupled are an absolute taboo in the Eutopian society.

A shaft of sunlight breaks through the clouds; Descartes regrets losing his temper and attempts to make amends. "I will come along, if you so insist," he tells her, wishing she would forget their little quarrel, but Destiny isn't there with him anymore; her mind wanders in daydreams of uncertainty.

"No," she speaks softly, "I will face the Elders alone."

Descartes stares at her in disbelief, waiting for her say something more. His offer rejected by silence, he finds an excuse, "I better get along then, still have much to do."

Disruptions are not a part of Descartes' life, he has labored long to keep tranquility in his bubble. He walks away with a heavy heart, full of guilt; he should have kept his nerves. He is apprehensive of the time to come, and knows nothing good will ever come of Elders meddling in their private affairs.

The Yonder Land

The white sand beach gently rolls into the sea, and the massive waves are dwarfed by the time they reach Destiny. Alone, she tries her best to soothe her mind, to keep the tense thoughts at bay, and imbibe the presence of the ocean.

She takes her time; the world turns still, the wind static, and the waves die out in murmurs. She calls him now, the invisible gondolier. Seemingly on its own, a distant mirage boat steers to the beach. The currents that carry it ashore are calm as a soft stream.

Destiny looks not at the vessel as it approaches, but she broods in worry and disappointment. She hopes she hasn't angered the Elders beyond reason. She is yet shaken by Descartes' hesitation to accompany her, his vehement disapproval of the letter, and how easily he blamed her for a mere coincidence.

Once ashore, Destiny boards the boat. In its felze: a cabin made of glass and black wrought iron, she rests upon a red velvet cushion, her fey legs crossed. If she had so chosen, she could have galloped across the sea to the last island with the high winds. She could have already been in the City; instead she bids her gondolier to steer slowly.

The water is clean, a peep reveals the ocean a mile deep. She watches the oar's graceful paddle; the submerged plank adorned by a starfish is a matter of great amusement for an orange fish. The fish swims around it, nibbles on the star, flies in fear of the rapid movement of the plank and returns again with earnest curiosity.

The gondola takes Destiny to the very end of their bubble, to a bare green island. They call it the Yonder Land, kept concealed, leagues apart from the mainland where the two reside. Here they entertain the few guests they ever have.

The master of this island is a one-horned metallic green scarab beetle. Years ago, upon the first day of Descartes and Destiny being coupled together, Descartes had blessed the beetle with near immortality, and entrusted in him a serious responsibility. Descartes' touch had made the master beetle wise; from then on the beetle keeps a watch on the island and is the doorkeeper of their bubble.

Destiny hovers over the memory of that day, how young and naive they were then. She barely knew him, yet how blatantly had she questioned him, "Why a beetle, Descartes?"

"I remember little of my father," he had told her. "He did his best to teach me all he could in those first years. Things the Mentors at the Academy tend to ignore: old legend and myths, most of them not more than bedtime stories, of how Newman created Eutopia. I still keep the shades and emotions of his tales but I forget his words." Descartes paused in a forlorn silence. "I remember the beetle," he continued, "my father would always speak of it, 'This is who you are, a beetle. Each father to son, we the Beetle hearted Newman.' He would remind me often."

"Ah, the beetle is your family insignia, isn't it?"

"I reckon it is; it took me years to fathom its significance."

Destiny had looked at him with kind eyes; she had known Descartes' parents had abandoned him, leaving him to the Mentors when he was only a boy of nine. She still wonders how such cruelty was permitted. She resents them on his behalf, even though Descartes holds no grudge. In his mind he explains it away by accepting that it wasn't his upbringing alone that they had lost interest in, but life itself. Why else would they forsake their bubble, and instead choose hibernation sold in the bazaars of the Sleepy Suburbia. All she can do is her best to prevent Descartes from dwelling much on thoughts of his parents.

"Why, have I shown you my family's emblem? Do you want to see it?" she had asked in an attempt to distract him.

"Sure I do." But his voice had never reached Destiny. She leaped in the air, came down fast, and a tremor shook the island as her fist struck the ground. In the brilliance of all the colors of fire the land lit ablaze. It spread rapidly, the grass crackled and hummed.

Descartes was dumbfounded and hoped Destiny knew what she was doing. The fire branched out in three different directions following an elaborate defined path, in circular spirals, burning the rear but leaving the middle intact.

Quarter of an hour of despair, the flames veiled Destiny; Descartes knew the hazards of playing with fire; his concerns were fair, for Destiny wasn't known to be careful. Nor was her Absolute Defense that of flames, as was his, but instead one of water. It was ridiculous, the fire kept growing, higher than Descartes could see; it engulfed the entire island.

He was relieved when it vanished, as abruptly as it had erupted. The fire never touched Destiny and she stood there within the blue of her water shield, with her hands raised, yet her white dress glowed with a faint new taint of red.

"Can you see it?" Destiny asked him, breathing fast.

It took a while for Descartes to realize what Destiny was referring to: the fire had burned the turf that covered the island, and it had left nothing in its path, not even ash. He could see bits of it first, but, much as a crop-circle, it wasn't possible to see it in entirety from the ground.

Descartes bounced off, and floated away "Yes I can, it's the ancient ruin, the Triskelion symbol. Is that your insignia?" Descartes yelled, as he landed yards away from her.

"Is that what it's called, 'Triskelion'? I didn't know that." Destiny had blushed, embarrassed at how little she knew of her own ancestry.

Nine years later, walking on the spiral path she had crafted,

Destiny considers how innocent they were then. She knows those days are gone. She misses them.

At the core of Triskelion, which still remains, where the three paths converge, Destiny finds the Master Beetle. She picks the beetle from the earth, holds him close to her lips, and speaks a message in her cupped hands. "When he comes looking, tell him I am gone."

She walks on to the other side, where the island ends, but the sea doesn't begin, a place where the arch of the domed sky eventually rests upon the land. Little ice prisms float in the air, they shine through the mist and have more than once been mistaken for fireflies. It's the end of the realm of Descartes and Destiny; here all things lose their form, and order relents to chaos. No word in Newman tongue can justly define this portal that leads to the City and the rest of Eutopia.

The ill shapes of this unformed land are cordoned off by a high fence, and are accessible only through a little gate. The gate is shut. It bear's metal work of artful precision; its double doors are carved, they depict an image of Descartes and Destiny holding each other. The slightest push, barely a tap, and the gate comes to life. Its many mechanical hinges and the network of gears twist and turn, the doors part and the two-dimensional sculptures of the couple are separated from one another.

Their hands fall in grief, and their heads hang low as Destiny steps out of the bubble, into the sky and the City.

Mentor Zen

They sit in a row on the fallen trunk of a dead tree, camped for a moonless night. The only sound other than their breathing is the crackling of the fire. The three companions sit close together barbecuing pieces of the day's game on the flame, occasionally biting into one, tasting to see if it's cooked right. No one has spoken for well over an hour.

They know they must part ways tomorrow, and their silence is a product of their dreaded goodbyes. Days of bickering and arguments have not yielded a solution, still their leader Mentor Zen runs his hand through his wise beard and tries once more to broker a peace. "I do know you are uncomfortable talking about it, but we must. Today is the last day of your being in my care, come morning and I will be gone. I shall ask you once more, have you received any word from the Academy?"

Damon, the fairest and the most prickly of them replies, "No my Mentor, for a millionth time we haven't, and that's why you can't leave us." His distress is noticeable.

Broad and short as a dwarf, Zen rises up before addressing Damon, "Trust me, it is good. Our separation was always inevitable. There are a few..."

Damon interrupts him, "You have insisted that it's merely a delay on the part of the Academy, but how could it take so long? Never before have they left us at sea, always forewarning us seven days prior to a Mentor's departure, and letting us know in whose care we would be in next. They would even detail the learnings the succeeding Mentor is to bestow upon us. I refuse to believe they forgot, that it's simply an error." Damon turns to his co-traveler and friend, "Why don't you say something Diablo, Zen is about to abandon us."

The dark eyes of Diablo mirror the blaze of the bonfire; he is familiar with this conversation, and has seen it in his thoughts. No scenario in his mind leads to a solution, and so he chooses not to add his voice to their quarrel.

"No, no Damon, no one has forgotten you, nor am I abandoning you. There is no need to panic. It's all been inten..."

"Why then won't they keep us in the loop? Perhaps it's something more sinister. Mentor Zen, hasn't it been you who all along have lead us to believe that the Academy shall not lead us astray."

"Yes, you must trust the Order of Mentors, we only hope good for you, and have meticulously planned your future."

"You are abandoning me, and now we must travel alone, are we to join the strange lonesome ones, who say they refused to grow up? They wallow and brood, and carry nothing but melancholy with them. Is that the future you speak of?"

Diablo grabs Damon's arm firmly. "Calm down Damon, have a breath of air, take a gulp of water, and let us hear out our Mentor Zen. I think he is trying to tell us something."

"Thank you Diablo," says Zen.

Damon lets Diablo pull him back down onto the trunk again. He places his chin on his wrist, and says, "Go on old geezer, and tell me what you have to say."

Zen smiles, "In all honesty I am glad you haven't received any word from the Order of Mentors. It only means I have done well at teaching you how to tap into the Eutopian flow of energy. Your time here at the Academy is done. You must seek the mountains of Olympus."

Both friends, Damon and Diablo, stand up. "We are going to the mountains of Olympus?" they exclaim together, but while

Damon speaks of the highest mountain range within the grounds of the Academy with foreboding, Diablo does so in excitement.

"Yes, you are, and there are many places I recommend you must visit on your journey there. On the banks of the river the New Nile you will find the replica of the complex of Giza; you won't miss them, perfect pyramids of white, a wonder of the Old Earth, a sight to behold. It would frighten you how much our ancestors were capable of doing with such frugal technology.

And don't you forget the moss gardens on the foothills of Olympus; if you are in luck you might meet Old Mali Bhagat Big Hands, a keeper of many stories. Time in his company will have your mind wandering across all ages of humanity."

"But Mentor Zen, what of the Incident of White? No one made it out alive at the graduation convention last year. They say it takes only one schizophrenic among the thousands of scholars who gather there, beyond the mountain, to go rough, turn into a demon, and kill us all. Was it not you my mentor who had barred us from getting close to the mountains in the aftermath of the incident? Besides, it's not as though the dreadful tales coming from the mountain's shadows are encouraging," Damon complains.

Diablo wonders out loud, "Yet, Damon, there have also been rumors of a land of never ending bliss, a place where you can mold weather and each one of us would be a God."

"Does that not sound too good to be true to you Diablo?"

"No Damon, it isn't. The reality is far better than your wildest imagination. You shall have everything you have dreamed of and more."

"You are mocking me, aren't you Elder Zen."

Mentor Zen shakes his head in disappointment and replies, "I shall dispel the rumors and let you know the truth, at least as much of it as I am permitted to. Seeing is believing in Eutopia, and there is much you haven't seen. I shall try and tell you in a manner that you understand."

Mentor Zen sits back again, and carefully picks his words, "Do you remember where you were Damon, before you were a Scholar of the Academy?"

"Yes."

"You shall go back to where you once came from. Where is it that you are from Damon?"

Damon is taken unaware by Elder Zen. Talk of parents and the home before the Academy is unusual among Scholars, and often discouraged by Mentors.

"I once lived in a Bubble of Perfect Existence," Damon replied stonily. "Will we be going back to our parents?" The idea sounds too far-fetched to Diablo even as Damon says it aloud.

"No, but you shall become one. You shall have your own Bubble of Perfect Existence. The rumors of the Incident of White are overblown. Miss White was sick, not a schizophrenic. No lives were lost, but a handful were injured. They are well, and today are proud residents of Eutopia."

Over The Olympus

The High Mentor Ananta sits on a throne on the wall of the City. Older than most who walk the earth, he takes pride in his thick gray hair and his gently meandering wrinkles.

Aging is a matter of choice in Eutopia, and many Newman never take to its unpleasant hardships. Ananta, on the other hand, thinks of it as an art. To him, if people were to age with grace they would find serenity in thought, and perceive the world in a caring loving hue.

Wrapped in a saffron stole, his eyes shut, he patiently waits for the Scholars. He can feel the anxiety in Elder Pax who sits on his right, way before the representative of the Elders musters the courage to word his worries. "How many are we expecting this evening my High Mentor?"

Ananta can sense their presence, a horde of many thousands descend upon Mount Olympus. "They are here," he announces softly.

The fifty-two watchtowers on the mountainside keep a lookout over the vast grounds of the Academy. Their beacons burn bright through the clouds of Olympus, guiding all those who seek the gates of the City.

Ananta smiles with pride as his flock gathers; for nearly twenty millennia he has watched able Newmans cross over to the City, and embrace the Eutopian way of living. Generations after generations have passed on, but he has remained.

The scholars who cluster together under the orange stroked

clouds of the evening have spent years here in the Academy. Where some of them mature early, and leave the grounds when in their late teens, there are others who live here for decades.

They trickle down into the valley; the first to arrive are the 'vagabonds': the ones who turned quiet, grew fearful of others, and are lonesome. They are followed by the 'many': groups and packs of scholars who travel together. They are the slow learners, but are known for their kindness, beauty and merrymaking. The last are the wandering 'pairs' and 'trios': they move with their chosen companions, never more than three at a time, and are inseparable from one another.

Diablo and Damon descend through the pine woods to the valley on foot. Damon, the curious, has to explore all of it. After all, none who make this journey today have been over Mount Olympus before.

Diablo is spellbound by the virtuosity of the Elders. Their work stands in heartfelt perfection; the woods to him seem truly enchanted. Whichever way he may run, the trees block the sun, yet the forest is immersed in its red warmth. Every pair of eyes that peers at him through the bushes beckons him to come closer. A perfume rides the wind, it grows as he walks on, luring him to the pastures below.

Clearing the woods he finds himself in a field that must have been green a few hours ago, but is now tainted in rich radiant pastels. Damon isn't with him anymore. He took a different route in the woods, but Diablo isn't concerned. He is transfixed. He can't take his eyes off them. How they talk to each other, their laughter truthful and clear. He observes them, as they play as children, some running free, and the others who chase them. A league or two around the field, and more often than not they crash into one another, tangle together and fall to the ground, still laughing and joyful.

A wave of innocence breaks upon Diablo's soul. "So many people, so many, many people," is what Diablo can't stop repeating.

He dawdles around, watching every passerby. He wonders how they all seem at such ease. Is he the only misfit in this scene?

Where is the pool that sources their happiness? Diablo wonders why strangers smile at him, why his face flexes one in return. He wishes he could stop them, only to observe them, if he cannot mold them.

Then it dawns upon Diablo. They are individuals in their own right, they have independent wills, and they do as they please. Their thoughts are not simulated. Their actions are unpredictable; every inch of them is real. Newmans can't help but be in high spirits when at such grand get-togethers. There is simply way too much beauty around for them to ignore.

Under the mist that veils the high wall of the city, the pasture buzzes in excitement, turned into a living breathing suburbia. A landscape where creativity abounds and manifests in unsustainable ever-changing ways. A pair, a girl in white and a boy teal of skin, pose a demeanor that as much as says, "I warn you, don't you disturb us." They work a small patch of daisies and purple perennials with silver trowel and sickles.

Their neighbor, a very talkative lanky fellow, is committed to build the tallest, the thinnest glass palace on the west of Mount Olympus. He speaks not to the people around him, but only to his reflection. Periodically he melts the mirrors, unhappy with them or perhaps in discontent with his own face; it's impossible to tell. Diablo is certain the boy's structure won't even be two floors tall before sundown.

Walking on, Diablo encounters a bunch of fire breathers and opera singers. Their disagreement is renowned in all of Eutopia, and they argue here as well. Their voices rise in melody and fall in querulous fire.

He scurries away from them as quick as he can, and soon finds himself in an empty clearing. Diablo wonders if he will meet anyone worth sharing the delicacies of a conversation with. He is lonely, and misses Damon. He tries to search for a friendly face in the crowd but most of them are too dynamic and loud.

He decides to approach the gardening pair, the turquoise-skinned shapely man, and the miss by his side. Her features by their softest movement warn him; if he ever had a chance to kiss them, he shall forever be at her mercy.

Diablo barely reaches them when he hears a BOOM, which drowns his thoughts of how he shall introduce himself, and also all the hullabaloo of the rest of the crowd. There are growing whispers that mention the speech that is to begin, and then there is another BOOM.

"Welcome! Welcome! Welcome! Children of men. I have long expected you, and I know how eagerly you have awaited this day. Some of you may recognize me, others might have heard of me, but for those who haven't, I am the High Mentor of the Academy: Ananta."

Raised in the sky, leaning over the pastures, above the mist on the west looms a face that Diablo isn't entirely sure is human. It's crumpled, lined and wrinkled, with expressions that change slower than the words.

"First, I would like to congratulate you for making it so far. I am proud of you. I believe you are all aware that we have been watching you very carefully. The Academy judges it to be your time to leave our grounds. Where some of you might have taken longer than others, here, today, you are all prepared for the rest of your lives."

The crowd's response is confused. Some cheer, a few clap reluctantly, but most gasp, and are honestly surprised. Not because a giant in the sky is talking to them, but by how old he looks.

"I have heard the distorted hearsay many of you have believed to be your future, but what awaits you will far surpass your most wonderful dreams. You have nothing to fear." He sneers, pauses, adjusts his cloak and continues, "No there are no monsters beyond who wouldn't do as they are told, nor do you have to go back to your parents. That would be ridiculous." He smiles and surveys the silent crowd.

"These are the gates of the City, and once you cross them, I assure you none of you would ever wish to return."

He waves his enormous hands, clearing the mist upon the fields below. The blinding fog recedes to reveal a sky-high stone wall.

"Beyond, you will face the last hurdle in achieving perfection. Yes, you still have a lesson to learn, but don't let the task dampen your spirits." His voice grows strong, and echoes off the mountains, filling the valley below. "None that have come before you have failed, nor would you. Today I invite you to a party that never ends, where you will discover many new hearts, though you won't remember three quarters of anyone.

"Welcome to your coupling season. A tradition immemorial, kindled by the architects of Eutopia such as I, from the days before the beginning of our reckoning.

"All we require of you is to stay in the City a while. You may ask why; you want a reward in return, and you demand so justly. You will find the answers for all that you are looking for: you will know the meaning of existence. You will have the answer to life, universe and everything." He chuckles, and his smile is mirrored by Elder Pax.

The silence breaks, and every trumpet, bigul and drum in the crowd is sounded. "Hurray!" is the common word of cheer. Many begin to dance. Some rush toward the stone wall in a mad frenzy, some embrace whoever they might find closest to them. Others cry.

Ananta elates in his success, for he has got the response he had expected. "Go forth, my children," he shouts loud and clear. "Your destiny beckons you." His voice drops down, and his last words to them are, "Just remember, do not panic."

With the will of thousands of Newmans the City wall begins to crumble. The grounds below Ananta and Elder Pax shake. Done with his speech, Ananta turns around to find Elder Pax glowing pink. "I am scared of flying," he squeaks.

Anata yawns with near formal elegance. "A pity. We were having so much fun." He unhurriedly walks up to his throne, enjoying

Pax's agony. The wall beneath them gives way, but the topmost stone slab upon which they are seated doesn't.

To his annoyance, Elder Pax somehow overcomes his anxiety. "Alas, so few answered our call this year, O beloved of Eutopia. I wonder how many of them stayed away; did they get wind of the truth of the Incident of White?"

Boulevard Amsterdam

In puffs of smoke and debris the wall disappears and the crowd floods in an empty space beyond. There is nothing here, but white. White is the earth, and so is the sky. Powered by their collective inertia, the crowd has trouble slowing down. It takes a while for them to spread and ease in this newfound void.

Before one could properly begin to ponder their whereabouts Diablo and many others spot a cluster of color pixels from afar. "That way... Further on...? Where...?" are some of the calls of the crowd, and they start moving again.

In a while, as he gets closer, the image starts to clear, and mere smudges start taking shape. It's a street divided by iron lampposts with benches in between them, a little closer and he can see pedestrians. As he nears the Boulevard Amsterdam the plain white beneath his feet fills up with the red and brown of cobblestones. In awe Diablo watches an invisible brush paint into existence a line of identical blue buildings. Their wooden windows open to the street below, a street canopied by yellow shower trees.

Diablo looks up through the flowers at lucky balconies wrapped in the morning sunbeams, from where most of those who gaze down seem to be looking for nothing more than to be. He can comprehend the purpose of this boulevard. He can imagine the years of careful deliberate design and the grand collective effort of generations of Elders that formed everything around him. Below, gentlemen in coats and hats of every fashion tuck into a lavishly spread breakfast on a leisurely moving tram. Only one of them has ignored the breakfast buffet. He leaps off, and makes to where Diablo is.

Still imbibing the street, Diablo turns around, but only to be further surprised by green hills and the trickling waterfalls of the far off horizon. He can hear the distant sound of the water smashing on stone. The flapping of wings in the sky, and the roars and grunts of the beasts in the valley below. This vast green is more to his liking, it inspires him. He makes up his mind to have a mountain to call his own one day. He reveres the work of the Elders, but is certain of his own capacity to match them.

A man wearing a coat of many colors, smoking a pipe, stands about half a dozen paces away from Diablo, looking straight at him. They stare for an awkwardly prolonged period, until the stranger breaks into a knowing smile and introduces himself. "Machiavelli. Elder Machiavelli; and you must be Diablo."

"How many years to this day?"

Machiavelli takes his time to reply, his smile still constant. "Welcome to the City Diablo." He then turns around and walks away, expecting Diablo to follow.

His nose up, and with an uncaring air Machiavelli leads the way, as well as the conversation. "It's splendid isn't it? Far outstrips the ruins you must be used to at the Academy... and no, you haven't seen anything yet."

Diablo hears half of all that's being said and comprehends only a quarter. He is distracted. The buildings along the avenue, they don't have doors but are open to the street; from within them spreads aromas of feasts and beats, laughs and cries of joy. Where in some the occupants sing and dance and make love, there are others where they do nothing but idle.

"It's been nineteen thousand nineteen hundred and eighty-nine years since the conception of the first conclave of the Architects; this City has been there from the very beginning of our reckoning. The history of the days before are vague, and it very well might have been there even before." Machiavelli fails to notice when Diablo starts to lag behind.

The avenue is crowded, there is a constant sense of urgency; a few sprint but everyone's hasty. Diablo the newcomer means to follow Machiavelli and his words, but a pleasant fragrance of spice and cooking weakens his will. They urge him to turn left and walk into an unnamed yet fine establishment of Boulevard Amsterdam. Then there are the abandoned heaps and heaps of treasure to reckon with: vases, cutlery, paintings, mirrors, candles, perfumes, toys, statues, crystal balls, watches, kaleidoscopes, compasses, eyeglasses, telescopes, jugs, chests and locks and keys, to name a known few.

Diablo hasn't been much the one for clothes, but there are enough here in every material and fashion for him to wish to try some on. There are robes, trousers, shirts, shoes, vests, shawls, bandanas, scarves, raincoats, swimsuits, night suits, and, sure, hats. Not to forget the kind Diablo is very unlikely to wear, there is much more of those: gowns, dresses, stockings, blouses, corsets and petticoats all in a gazillion colors, available in any perceivable texture and material.

Machiavelli rolls his eyes and sighs when he finds Diablo trying to wear a feathered headgear the wrong way on. "Oh! These freshers, how can none of them keep enough nerve for such a short walk?" Diablo manages to wear the headgear somehow, still the wrong way on, successfully blinding himself.

Before helping Diablo, Machiavelli channels the air in such a way that nothing but his voice reaches Diablo's ears. "Diablo, it's vital you pay heed to what you are about to hear, your future depends upon your deeds here in the City. Listen carefully Diablo, it's expected of you to live here for at least for an entire season. You will meet many strangers, most of them wonderful, at times amusing. You will learn their names and faces, later you may tend to search for them in any crowd you ever come by. You very well might fall in love, but beware, don't be deceived by false desires.

Always remember, we the Elders know better. We care for you, and will find you the one who will be true."

"Do you follow Diablo?"

"Yes... Yes, I do my Elder Machiavelli."

Reckless Fresher

It's hot. It's bright. Diablo struggles and can barely open his eyes. There is sand in the harsh wind. Elder Machiavelli is with him. In a white cotton robe, covering his face in a scarf, Machiavelli stands on a dune watching the sunrise.

"Are you uncomfortable Diablo? Thirsty perhaps?"

Diablo down in the sand manages a nod.

Machiavelli chuckles. "Make it rain Diablo, ask for the moon. Give us shelter, and a bathing pool. Why must a Newman suffer a desert?"

Diablo is slow to compute the things being said, and once he does, he concludes Machiavelli is mad. He has no such powers; such acts aren't possible in the City or the Academy.

"Remember your childhood Diablo. You have seen others do it. Oh! At least give it a try."

A delayed epiphany, a sudden burst of energy, and Diablo jumps up in excitement. "I am in a Bubble of Perfect Existence."

"Well, not exactly." But Machiavelli's response is drowned by the deep rumble of the shaking earth. The sun stumbles and falls off his throne. It pours so hard that Machiavelli crouches in fear of the very sky falling on his head. The dust settles and the wind cools, but the earth erupts and stone and rock rise up.

THUD, CRASH they sound, rising to engulf Machiavelli and Diablo. Not a piece breaks loose or brushes by them. Untouched, without a notice the world transforms, and the two find themselves in an oddly comfortable cave.

Stones protrude out of walls to form crude chairs. A hot spring streams on the deep end of the cave. Machiavelli twists his neck with a crack, and rests his chin on his right shoulder, his eyes bulge as he gazes upon Diablo. His stare makes Diablo uncomfortable, he feels Machiavelli's eyes sneak within him, as though they are able to see more than what general visibility permits. Hesitantly he says, "The best I could do in an instant Elder."

"I took the time to glance through your report, it mentioned your quick handedness, but this is extraordinary." Machiavelli's signature smiles and giggles have all but disappeared. He knows now that Diablo must not be taken lightly. He must be led carefully.

Machiavelli reaches in his coat's inner pocket, and draws out a rolled up parchment. "Here are the rules of the Coupling Season Diablo, I wish you to read them out loud."

Diablo unrolls the letter and reads it...

Dear Participant

I hope you are finding your accommodation comfortable. Before you ask, you are not yet in a Bubble of Perfect Existence, but a Room of Boulevard Amsterdam. The room is to demonstrate how things are to be in the near future, of how your life would be once you are coupled. Being only a demonstration, the room has several shortcomings, and I deeply apologize for its natural limitations.

Your room will be welcoming for only 8 of 24 hours, post which it will eject you. You may then go mingle out on the street and the town square, or you may choose to visit a friend. Though I must warn you, rooms tend to be even less welcoming for secondary guests. Your friend's room won't have you for a moment more than 4 hours. Manage your time carefully.

We encourage all participants of the Coupling Season to spend as much time with their peers as possible, and try as many new things as they can. Drink every potion except poison, and eat everything but each other. Do not fear. The Elders are watching over you. This is the time for exploration and adventure, go out and find them.

Faithfully Yours
The Keeper of the Tranquility of the Boulevard Amsterdam
Elder Pax

"Good, now I presume you are eager to explore the possibilities of your room, and if you have no further questions, I will take your leave and get back to the City."

"But Elder, how will I find my way back to the City?"

"Oh! How can I forget, it's easy, split open the air and look for an exit," Machiavelli beams at Diablo.

"Like this?" A sizzling buzzing tear cracks up the air, and within it is a corridor with red wallpaper.

"Why, yes," Machiavelli replies softly.

Diablo walks through, leaving Machiavelli behind. Machiavelli paces around the cave mumbling, "The folks at the Observatory are getting sloppy; one must be warned about such reckless kind. How could a fresher leave an Elder in their room?"

Machiavelli too tears himself an exit.

Coupling Season

Soft whispers coming from the wall follow Diablo wherever he goes. The corridor walls bear detailed illustrations, a hint of what might be found behind and beyond them. They depict a world of possibilities, of beasts and men as friends and as enemies, at times bundled together close, at times roaming free on the vast landscape of imagination.

With his ear upon the wall he hears them talk, the chit chat of young girls walking their dogs down the boulevard. A step away to the right and within the other wall a pod of whales hum their songs of the deep.

The illustrations go on to embellish the doorways that pass him by at irregular intervals. The light that seeps through their edges is at times warm, seldom freezing, but more often than not, comforting.

Until black paint spreads upon the wall, and only the colors of the moon and stars break the monotonous background. The rustling of leaves, the wind and the occasional hoot of owls is all that's left for him to hear. Diablo comes upon a black door, its darkness so absolute that it's all but invisible to him.

When he tries to find the doorknob, his hands surprise him: they touch water instead. A splash. He retraces his steps and waits. Then slowly he approaches the door again; in a snap of his fingers he summons a flame, and the artwork is revealed.

A cold lonesome lake with no rivers and streams to feed her. A leftover child of a long gone winter. Composed with no waves, nor a ripple to disturb her. She is mastered serenity. She spreads upon the surface of the door, her irregular embankment form the corners of the door.

"This is the one." He dives in her head first. He must swim, but within a stroke or two he reaches the other side, as if the entire facade of the door was designed only to drench him.

From under a rock, and behind a curtain of water, Diablo steps forward into the night. At the shores of the lake Diablo surveys his surroundings. The water as depicted on the artwork upon the door is very still. The waterside quiet, except for the chirping of crickets.

Here is anchored a thousand ton galleon. The darkest of all black, so pure that the painted wooden stem of the ship is reflective. Through every opening of its gun deck juts out thick rugged old roots that reach down to the water. Where there should be masts and sails, the galleon boasts tall Snow Queen Trees, with their brilliant white slender trunks, and illuminated green canopies.

Diablo wishes to have a closer look and decides to swim to the galleon, but as he takes his first step in the water, a harbor begins to emerge to support his feet. He walks on, and plank by plank the harbor appears, not with the purpose of showing him the way, but only to support him to wherever Diablo might wish to go. He makes straight to the galleon, and the harbor crumbles behind him, returning back to the water it came from.

Diablo apprehends the true enormity of the ship only when he is close enough to touch its stem. He stands in the shadow of the galleon and no more can he see the deck, but only the dim reflections of the lights above on the lake's surface.

He walks along the ship, looking for a way to climb up, or a way in. Sure, Diablo can will his leap to land him on the deck in an instant. He need not go through the trouble of finding a physical route, but he is a guest here, in this room of Boulevard Amsterdam, and such an act could easily be taken for a slight by his mysterious hosts.

So he searches on, but finds no trapdoors or ladders, only a lone thick root that branches low enough to be within his reach. Diablo holds on to it and raises himself up; it isn't easy but there is strength in his youth.

Cumbersome is the climb, and it takes many a careful step in the dark before he can pull himself up and get a peek of the main deck. Astonishing and bright is the sight; his grip loosens and he slips. Despair... and in an impulse he wills a root to wrap and hold fast his hand.

A rope ladder is dropped from above, he sees it again, an uncertain glimpse of a human shape. A silhouette so white that the stranger's frame melts within.

A wet breeze carrying a scatter of dry leaves greets Diablo as he boards the galleon. He shivers and rubs his hands together. The ship is neither in light, nor in shadow. There is a crescent moon, which will have you strain your eyes, but thankfully for Diablo his host has cared to light lamps. They are somewhere up along the mast, concealed in the sail, within the canopies of Snow Queen Trees.

The flora here onboard is denser than he expected. In all his years at the Academy Diablo has never seen plants such as these: They are short and their soft green stems hold one extraordinarily large leaf each, together they obstruct Diablo's view completely. He can see little but greenery.

The ivy that covers the polished wooden floor of the main deck isn't half as comfortable to walk on as grass would have been. Diablo wades through the bush, leaves and thorns, moving deeper into the ship.

"Hello, is anybody home?"

It's hard work, walking through this mini-jungle, still he persists, traveling deeper into the ship, until he begins to doubt if he is welcome here.

He has traveled deep, he hadn't expected greetings, but without even an acknowledgment, it is not in Diablo to overstay his welcome.

"All right then, I shall be leaving."

Diablo turns around and tries to trace his way back out of the ship, but the path that had brought him here has disappeared. He is still among the shrubs and trees but they have moved and are all jumbled up. Nevertheless he makes a guess and starts walking back.

An hour or so goes by, he is still lost in the bushes, unable to fathom how it can take so long to reach the edge of the ship's deck; he is running out of patience.

There is an opening in the bushes. Through he goes, and finds a barrel overgrown with seaweed under a crooked street lamp that sways tardily with a creaking sound. Diablo gives up and sits down.

Why can't he find his way out? he wonders. Don't they wish him to leave? A moment or two pass by and silence descends; the lamp has stopped moving, and Diablo can hear himself breathing.

The hair at the back of his neck tells him he is being watched. He senses a presence, there is someone behind him. He must be calm; he wishes not to scare them. He keeps his head still, but slants his eyes, and there she is: White as a ghost. She might as well be one. She vanishes again, up a trunk, hopping over a branch and out of sight.

"Hello, hi? I saw you..."

Not a squeak in the floorboard, nor a whimper from the silence. She won't show, she won't tell.

"Where are you? I know you're there... Who are you? My name is... Hello?"

There are no answers for a while; he waits, and then sits back on the barrel, resting on the trunk of a tree.

"If you are not to tell me, at least let me go." Diablo still does not wish to break the decorum of polite society.

"I would tell you, if you were to make three promises."

Diablo turns around to face the voice, only to find more

greenery. He waits for her to speak first, then encourages her, "Go on then, what are your conditions."

"You will visit me every day, and in waking for a week."

"You won't speak of my room or of me when you leave."

"And as long as you are here, we won't talk in spoken words."

The Hive

A momentary sensation... in her imagination a billion ants have marched across every inch of her skin. It's unpleasant. She feels lighter, but is having trouble breathing, it's stuffy. Thankfully she remembers the old advice: she floats instead of stepping on the dusty ground, and keeps her hands closed, avoiding even a mistaken touch of the mossy walls.

It's called a cell, a narrow, short hexagonal tunnel, at one end of which is her Bubble of Perfect Existence, and at the other, the City. Designed to keep the noise of the outside at bay, letting Destiny have a chance to change her mind, turn back and return home. However, today is not the day for her hesitations.

Destiny feels small on entering the City. A tiny speck in the air, appearing from a window with eighty-three floors above and sixteen below. The sky is obstructed by an incomplete dome, sliced as a cake, one-fourth of it missing, letting the sun shine in.

Remote seem the people on the ground, but there is a buzz, a distinct sound associated with crowds alone. Slow and deliberate are her motions as she opens the glass door of her cell. Firmly she grabs onto the edges and launches herself out with all her might. Her descent goes unnoticed, and she joins the bazaar.

It's hot. Destiny must cover her eyes to see. The sun is in a cruel mood. It's called a plaza, and acts as the community ground for the residents of the 27th hive. "So few," she observes. Destiny wasn't expecting a party, but no more than a hundred Eutopians linger here today. That's around five percent of the residents of this hive.

She has heard tales from the older residents of a time when the plaza used to be a shade more alive. In its younger years, supposedly the entire neighborhood used to gather here to exhibit their work and discuss creativity. Its charm, they say, started to wane a year before Descartes and Destiny got here. The Incident of White she is told, is to blame.

Her generation braved and disregarded the terror of the incident. They did frequent the plaza a while, but now they too have wised up, and can't bother with the company of others. They are too close to perfecting their bubble, and are more likely to seek peace at home, in their companions than with those beyond.

She pities the state of things. In homage she decides to take a tour, if only to support the open-minded. She spots a familiar face, in truth, two. A pair of twins. She and Descartes have known the girls since their time in the Academy. Inseparable, the twins were much as herself and Descartes. She remembers well the fortnight the four of them had traveled together. One timid, the other loud, still they got along brilliantly.

They play with strings, the twins, their palms wrapped with threads, with every twitch of their finger a command communicates to a giant blue lizard of blocks with sharp corners. He bounces on one foot, then looks up to the sky and screams, and then bounces on the other. A dance choreographed by a pair of girls in real time.

Destiny runs towards them, calling out to them, "YOLA, ZOLA!" With brunette hair in ponytails, their eyes full of determination, they hear her not; the twins never take their work lightly.

Destiny stops a few paces away from the twins and their lizard. She pulls back her hair, and calls out again, "Yola and Zola! Remember me?" No response.

To catch their attention, without the intent of causing harm, but perhaps in slight mischief, Destiny decides to disrupt their little play. By a movement of her arm the beast was to freeze in midair, in ice. It was to grow stiff and hibernate, but her trickery fails. The lizard ignores her, and continues its funny dance. Her icy projectile misses the beast. A ton of it hangs above the ground for a while, as though it needs to realize it has missed its mark before allowing gravity to do what it does.

SMASH! Ice shatters and spreads across the plaza, and the twins awaken from their trance.

"Destiny what are you doing?" Yola shouts, stepping toward her.

"What's happening, are we taking a break?" Zola sounds delirious.

"It's Destiny."

"Yes it's me, at least one of you remembers; don't know which one of you though."

"Oh! Yes we remember you. I am Zola, that's Yola. Do you like the new block monster we came up with?"

"Sure, I do. What's its name?" Destiny lies.

"We call it Elizabeth, but for short, Liz, because it's a lizard," informs Yola, reminding Destiny how silly is the humor of the twins. "Would you want to see another one?" asks Zola, but before Destiny could refuse, another giant of a block creature appears.

It's a bear. It pulls itself to its full height, and bares its colorful blocky teeth. Its skin is covered with sharp conical, bright-hued thorns. It exhibits itself by a roar and falls back on its feet. Destiny considers slipping away while the twins are busy, but their persistence is quicker than Destiny's wit. The bear vanishes as quickly as it had appeared.

"Do you like it Destiny? Would you want one for your home?" they ask in unison.

Destiny isn't sure if she would allow such a beast free in her jungles. Would it be able to adapt to her bubble, and would the other creatures of her making fancy a bear in their midst. Yet, the easiest way to get on her way is to abide by the demands of the twins. "Sure, I would love to have one."

"Yay!" is the expression of delight from the twins. They reach inside their joint inventory, represented here in the form of a handbag, and extract a memento, a hand-sized figurine of the bear.

"Thanks!" says Destiny, accepting their present with pretended gratitude and with a twist of her hand the bear disappears, getting added into her inventory.

Destiny bids the twins goodbye and moves on. Next she encounters a skating ring, where kids who aren't yet old enough to be in the Academy play together. She hasn't had much experience with younglings in her adulthood, and though in no way does she dislike them, she does fear them. A fear rooted in mistrust of her own strength. They are too fragile and she might hurt them accidently.

Destiny stealthily walks by them, hoping they won't stop her and stay on their skateboards; thankfully, they do. Next she comes across a bunch of men sitting around a gaming table. "Don't you dare pour lava on my skirmishers!" The ridicule of that outburst attracts Destiny to the table.

She inches closer, they ignore her: the lanky gaming gentlemen in identical suits, white shirts and black shades. The table keeps a miniature detailed projection of a castle surrounded by armies on all sides. One of them leaps out from his seat in excitement, as a tower of the castle crumbles. His outstretched hand is about to hit Destiny in the face, when he realizes her presence. He pauses the game. "Hello, I am Cataphract. Would you fancy playing with us?"

"No, I was only passing by, but curiosity drew me here. What is it that you are playing?"

"It's a game, it's called the 'Age of Empires', a medieval war simulation found by my friend here." Cataphract points towards one of his peers, "Huksarl found it in the rubble his folks left him. It dates from the Earth of Old."

"May I watch?" She seeks their permission before pulling a chair. Cataphract takes the responsibility to introduce her to the game. "There are two teams, the reds and the blues. I lead the reds, and Huskarl here leads the blues. You see the castle in the middle? Whichever of the two teams is able to control it for fifteen minutes, wins."

Destiny nods.

"The pieces might be small, but it's a violent game, are you sure want to watch?"

"Yes, sure, I can handle gore; I have seen much of it in war cinemas that predate Eutopia." Cataphract looks impressed, "All right boys, let's fight." The game starts, but nothing happens for quite a while.

"You see, we have to build our bases first, and get an economy running before we attempt to take control of the castle."

"Ah, ha." Destiny can't see why they would bother with a tabletop game when they could easily have the happenings on the board be played out by life-sized humanoids, in a real field of battle. She is too polite to ask, they clearly seem to be having such a good time. On the board units build shelters, forage barriers, hunt deer, fish, build houses, and after a while troops start to pour out of the buildings.

"We have to collect resources before we start conscripting the town folk into our army." The war starts in a matter of minutes, and Destiny knows now why Cataphract warned her. It's bloody, the game shies not from showing limbs being torn, and people being decapitated by katanas.

Huksarl, who though losing, is the one to jump up in excitement. "I have an idea! How would you guys like to recreate the game in my Bubble of Perfect Existence? We can make it so much more real there!"

The two, Cataphract and Huksarl, exchange a look of thrill. "Yes, that's a swell idea buddy." says Cataphract. Destiny can't believe that the reason they weren't doing it already was that they hadn't yet considered it. "Let's," or something to that effect says everyone on the table, except Destiny.

"You are coming with us, right?" Cataphract asks Destiny.

"No I shall take a rain check. Though mayhap my partner would have an appetite for this game."

"They are more than invited to join us at Huksarl's, it's the fourth cell, on the hundred and forty-second floor."

"No," says Destiny with a distant look, "he isn't one to visit others. May I have a copy of the game, though; I am certain that shall cheer him up."

"Certainly." Destiny is handed over a miniature replica of the table and she bids the lads goodbye. She next encounters a banana merchant. A man of considerable girth, but with a high-pitched voice. In courtesy he gets up behind his counter and greets Destiny, "Hello there. I love fruits, don't you?"

It takes a moment for her to recover from the falsetto. "Yes, I crave them often enough."

"Mine are special," he says, waving his hands over his combs of bananas. Years of experiment has allowed me to come up with some very special designs, for instance, these." He picks up a bunch, "They have pomegranate seeds in their stem, for a surprise change of flavor with every bite." He keeps them back, and much like an adolescent asking a girl for a dance for the first time, he loses his voice.

"And the others?" Destiny eggs him on.

The merchant fumbles over his counter and then picks another. "These are flavored with bitter gourd." Destiny doesn't find that appetizing at all. "I will have the one with pomegranate for seeds." She takes a dozen dozens in generosity, before leaving his booth.

A line of taxis awaits her at the edge of the 27th Hive's Plaza. They are tiny and have space for no more than two passengers, their body light green, each with single doors placed at the front of the car. A slight turn of the metallic handle and the door pops open and a wooden stairway unwinds to welcome Destiny.

Waterfly

Static has the world been for days. Unchanging are the thousand islands that float between the sea and the domed sky. Some bear grasslands, some volcanoes, a few white snowclad peaks. The largest of them stretches a thousand miles across. The tiniest no more than a hectare. But now they are all quiet. The wind has halted. The animals are asleep with their heartbeats far and few. The birds are in their nests and the snakes in their pits and holes. The flying squirrels, his favorites, are all within the trees with shut eyes, unusually callous of their horde of nuts and peas.

Diablo the creator sits in meditation. His thoughts are far away from the worries of his dominion. Three suns and moons have passed since he has been frozen on the grass. He has traveled away in his memories, down into the past, nine years to be precise.

He remembers her well, the barefoot girl with her promises. He tries to regulate his dreams away from the week spent on the nursery galleon, he fails, and she slips back into his arms.

Diablo wakes alone in the sky on a grassland floating in the atmosphere. His realm wakes with him. His feet, though unused for a while, feel strong. He breaks in a run, with large quick strides. Diablo is tall, fast and agile. Along a stream, but before the wind, to the ledge, and with a leap he follows the waterfall down.

"Oooo-ooo-ooo-ooo!"

Diablo's Bubble of Perfect Existence features plates of surfaces that float not on molten lava, but in the sky. Thousands of islands float in the wind, often colliding into one another, producing debris.

He must glide with skill to avoid the deviant rocks. He never tires of diving.

His fist and knee break the crust as he has a perfect three-point landing; his biomechanical legs literally give off steam. Diablo isn't the same boy who had crossed the Olympus and walked into the city years ago. He has grown, not just the way people do over a decade, but the way one would if they lived in solitude. For better or worse Diablo is steadier with his thoughts, and definite to the verge of being stubborn. Today, however, he will take counsel from his only friend.

It's never easy to tell what is where in Diablo's Bubble of Perfect Existence. A sniff will tell him how far the sea is, he must take a full breath and tell of its density, then count the hills, and measure the sparkle of sunbeams on the far-off waterfalls to name the island.

This one is called Aurora. Here is where he will find Daedalus, in the cave in the shape of an eye, high up in the cliffs, though the hills are a good way off from Diablo's landing point.

He treks, first along a brook that winds down from the hills, passing by velvet flowers that line the waterside. He is in haste but his steps are careful. There is much to see for those who know where to look. The island is full of the subtleties of life, and Diablo must read them carefully to see how well his project is running.

He finds himself walking closer to the edge of the floating island. At the island's rim the ground is bare and dry, except for Elastic Palm Trees, which at first rise up like normal trees, but then form an arch to stoop down into the sky, off the island. Their heads often reach lower than their roots.

Closer to his destination, the babble of the stream is much louder. He climbs over rocks made flat by erosion over the years, which still keep narrow crevasses for crabs and snails to dwell in. Diablo pushes himself up to find a tiny plug pool. It's fed by a high waterfall appearing from the slit in the cliff face.

In this pool live ticklish fish called Waterflys. A few of them float above the surface of the pool. They are an airborne fish, choosing at will to return to the water. The secret of their flight is their capacity to filter the lightest gases in the air and collect them in special sacks under their cheeks.

Diablo never tires of playing with them. A light touch at the right spot, under their chin and above their air sacks and they laugh as loudly as giants, but as their collected gases deplete and their laughter turns into a high-pitched squeal, they are spent and sink back under water.

Diablo stays by the pool for a while. The cliff is much steeper from here on, and flying would have been the only way up, if not for the steps that are carved in the rock. Diablo must climb a thousand and thirty-two steps to make it to the cave.

Daedalus

A tiny creature rising a couple of feet from the ground, no taller than a four year old, but in truth only of about six months. In form it's part owl and part ape, but far smarter than either of the two. Its yellow eyes, that of his father's, are perfectly circular and far too large for its face. Its ears flap free, and its body is covered with feathers. As for limbs it has six, a pair of hands, legs and wings. Its tongue is human and is capable of speech.

Unsurely it stumbles, and then takes to the air with a timid leap.

"Come here, come to your father Icarus; no don't fly! You must learn to walk before you learn to fly."

The voice comes from the darkness, deeper in the cave. Diablo watches Icarus's struggle with his lesson before announcing his arrival.

"Good morning Daedalus."

"Diablo! It's been so long. How nice to see you. I have been trying to teach Icarus how to walk all morning, but he refuses to learn. Will either crawl or fly, but won't use his feet. Was I, too, this eager to spread my wings?" Daedalus steps into the light.

A larger version of the fledgling, Daedalus is set apart by the shade of his feathers. Where Icarus is entirely white, Daedalus wears a coat of brown with a golden band lining his neck. A deliberate creation of Diablo, his personality is intentionally talkative, yet logical and forthcoming.

"Well, when you were this small, even I had no idea how you would ever fly."

Daedalus smiles warmly; Diablo is far more than a friend to him, he hesitates to admit, in fear of being ridiculed, but he considers Diablo his older brother.

"What would you have Diablo? Should I catch a fish, put the kettle on? No wait, let's have one of those cigars you got for me from the City. I don't fancy smoking alone, your presence could be my excuse."

"Ha ha sure, and some water too, if you would be so kind my dear friend," agrees Diablo.

Daedalus bounces back into the darkness one foot at a time, and returns with a cigar and a heart-shaped leaf with a scooped up mouthful of water.

The two walk to the edge of the cliff and sit there with their legs dangling in the air. "I have some sad news Daedalus."

Daedalus lights up his cigar. "So, they are coming?"

"Oh! No, not yet, they aren't. It's not that bad, but they have summoned me... And they were sly enough to coincide their call with an invitation from Damon, to visit his dwelling in the City. I can't refuse them now."

"Phew!" Daedalus releases a smoke ring in relief. "I trust you will outwit the Elders Diablo."

Diablo turns towards the setting sun. "But you do know that they may come with me when I return. You must be prepared Daedalus, don't take this lightly."

"I know you won't let them hurt me or my family Diablo."

"No the Elders aren't cruel, but they do love their rules. They would limit my freedom in my own bubble."

"I won't break their rules, and we will be candid with them. You reckon they would leave us alone if we are honest, right Diablo?"

"Let's hope so Daedalus, let's sincerely hope so."

Oysters and Rosé

Destiny doesn't know why the journey is so bumpy and her ride so petite, loud and uncomfortable; thankfully it's short, and she soon crosses the hedge surrounding the Welcoming House of 27th Hive.

The hedge acts as the fence of the premises and the uneven mud road slips in through one of the four openings in it; cutting across the garden it leads to the doorstep of the house. The gardens on the two sides are identical to the curl of each petal, except the statues that line the road. They depict a fairytale from the first days of Eutopia.

There is no telling from afar where the garden ends and the house begins, for the green grass marches on climbing up the light blue walls. The verandas above are covered with freshly painted wooden shutters. Seven stories tall, the building has a magnificent red dome, which runs throughout its length. Destiny reckons it has a hundred rooms or more, and can't help but wonder how many old secrets the building must know. She steps on its front porch and pulls on the answering bell. The doors swing open and a pair of high-pitched but distinctly male voices herald her arrival. "Lady Destiny, my Elder."

Destiny has been here before, and knows where she will find her host, not in the drawing room she has entered, nor in the library to her right, but down the corridor in his study.

The sun coming through the window brightens up a square crossed spot covering the central round coffee table in the room.

It's surrounded by three chaise longue sofas made in eye-catching brown timber with red and minimally used golden fabric, much like those in a roman dining hall.

Behind the sofas is the large writing desk, where stands Machiavelli with both his hands on the table. "Mrs. Destiny, how nice to see you. I wasn't expecting you till sometime later this week." A receding hairline covered with a tidy red fringe, he wears his signature oversize blazer with many colors.

"I would rather have an unpleasant mystery solved, than let it lurk and cloud my thoughts," she replies coldly. She never took Machiavelli for a friend.

"You wound us deeply Destiny, you know the Elders will take every precaution not to disturb your happiness. Come now dine with me, and let us solve your troubles leisurely." He offers her his hand, intending to guide her to the sofas. She takes it, if only out of politeness.

The sofas in his own house are too large for Machiavelli; he appears shorter than he is as he sits down. He runs his bony fingers across his forehead, as if trying to recall something.

"Oysters and rosé. The Observatory tells me you would fancy them now, won't you?"

"Resistance is futile, isn't it? All right, oysters and wine it is." Her words sharp as icicle tips.

Machiavelli smiles as two goblets and a dish of baked oysters decorate the coffee table. He eases into the sofa saying, "Well, before we start, there's a little something I would like to tell you. Do please hear me out before you lose your cool. Someone else would be joining our discussion, but not to worry, it's no one from the government, he is not one of ours, but merely a gentleman who suffers similar woes as you do. Will that be fine?"

Taken aback by the sheer unconventionality of the suggestion Destiny retorts, "If you are truly asking, I do mind. Why would I share my troubles with strangers, for that matter why should he?"

"I know your instincts tell you to be suspicious of us. Why

should you trust the Elders when all we talk of are rules and things you are not permitted to do. However..."

Destiny cuts in before Machiavelli could finish, "Yeah, then you do know why I would prefer keeping our meeting short and straightforward."

"However..." Machiavelli continues, "on this account, I urge you deeply to trust us, and I promise you, meeting him would only ease your troubles, and help you keep the big bad Government out of your Eden."

"If it pleases you my Elder," she says with a sigh. "It might amount to naught anyway." She lounges on the sofa. It wasn't the authority in his voice that made her relent but the hint of desperation.

"It may, but it's worth a short!" Machiavelli looks up at the ceiling and requests the room, "Would you summon Diablo please."

White Pebble Room

His habit makes him rush to the 'safe place' every time his temper starts to get the better of him. A pause-less flight in which he looks at nothing in particular..., the ill-formed clouds bother him not as he rushes on, with no cares to spare he seeks his hideout.

Beyond his cottage and the webbed tree he flies, in search of a specific garden in the Lying-Man Mountains. The hills aren't easy to miss, true to their name; from afar the range appears like a man lying on his side with his arms folded below his head, kept as a make-do pillow. His legs are not stretched, but his knees are drawn close, as if he feels a chill, despite being covered by an evergreen blanket of pine and fir.

Between the woods are patchworks of groomed gardens. Descartes lands in a passway between the hills. In this bed are many illusions, intended to deceive the most vigilant of observers: those at home and also those who watch from afar. Destiny, too, knows not where Descartes finds solace when displeased with her. The knowledge that he would be fine, and that he is always back, keeps her from getting curious.

A sago palm tree takes the center stage of this plot, while a barren patch encircles the tree, which in turn is encircled by short but irregular grass. At the base of the palm is a miniature Flintstone house made of pebbles.

He shrinks. A beetle-sized Descartes pushes away the films of grass and crosses over to the empty dry patch. Here he stops to take a breath, and for the first time since his conversation with

Destiny do his nerves begin to calm. He is here, in his safe place. He looks up at a familiar sky: it's separated by a filter, a dozen times as high as Descartes is now, but it would have reached no higher than his knees when he was of normal height. The filter shares its paler brown tint with everything within it. Its surface appears much like one of a muddy pool would do from the inside.

Shadows of the sago leaves, pointed spikes loom on the dry floor. The wind here is softer, heavier and carries sounds majestically. He waits to spot his pet, until she appears from within the palm tree. A catfish with whiskers, bright eyes and all. Its temperament favors the feline family, rather than its native fish kind. It comes to Descartes with a rigid tail, shaking softly in excitement. Swimming in the air, its scales shimmer in the sun.

The fish revolves around him, rubbing against his feet in greeting. Descartes caresses her, petting her. Wet to touch, but not slimy. "Good Girl. Come let's go in Toro."

This house is one-roomed. There is no finesse to its flooring but that of mud. The walls are smooth and bare, with no painting, nor windows. To speak of furniture it has three: a bed and a lone unimpressive wooden desk with an adjacent fauteuil. Descartes sits on the chair, which albeit old is comfortable. On the desk lie many things: a book, an electric lighter hardwired to the wood, clean sheets of paper, an open pocket notebook that's been scribbled on, an inkpot, a fountain pen and a half-spent candle on a copper stand.

This book is made of digital paper, a relic technology more uncommon today than its predecessors. A creation of the post computerization age, its pages leap alive when Descartes runs his fingers on its spine. They flip open, disturbing the air as the pages turn to reach the point till which Descartes had filled them in.

It was invented in the mid-21st century for writers who preferred the pen over typing and screens. Its creators knew little of how big a role it was to play in saving the very art of writing by hand. Books such as these are the only reason Newmans of Eutopia still have handwritings.

It is possible to erase what is written here. One could even select words or paragraphs and ask the book for their meaning. It would then, in ink, make words and images on its pages in an attempt to give you the best possible explanation. If need be the book won't shy from making three-dimensional projections on top of itself. It is an excellent tool for storytellers and in this book Descartes is writing one.

It's a play. An enactment of a fictional tale of the Earth of Old, occurring in a city called Tokyo, one of the largest the humans had ever built. Today Descartes isn't here to write, but only to read and find comfort in the work he has already put on paper. His characters are perfect: Makoto the young adult professional living alone is made in the image of Destiny, only without Destiny's flaws. The other inspired by self-analyzation: Druse, Makoto's companion, who betters Descartes by always having the right words and tone.

He turns his chair around to face the empty room, and as he begins to read the description of the ancient city, from the mud floor rises a hologram of the Big Mikan. A place where people felt lucky to live in tiny houses on top of each other: in apartments. In a time when traveling by gas-guzzling polluting vehicles was considered a luxury, and riding in large coaches running on tracks being pulled by electric engines considered normal.

The projection has it all, the skyscrapers, the neon lights, the rainbow bridge, the palace ground and the autumn-hued icho trees, which are outnumbered by the cast iron lampposts. Here the concrete far outstrips bare earth in covering the landscape.

Except the two primary characters of his story, the others which man the sprawling city are mere skin deep simulations. Their limited actions are pre-programmed, letting them keep up the illusion of being real, until Descartes chooses to peek into their homes, but he never does. Coming across them only when they are out and about on the city streets, he pretends they have as many secrets as the people of the past who lived in the real Tokyo. Their code allows them to keep the act going as long as they are out in the open, pretending to engage in the mundane tasks of driving, being pedestrians, and walking out of stores with shopping bags.

Makoto and Druce too are programs, but they are far more complex. Their characters and attributes have been sketched out in such detail that they often dupe Descartes into believing that they have a free will, so much so that at times Descartes feels they aren't born of his imagination, and he is no more than a mouthpiece compelled to compile a record of their lives.

It started when Descartes was busy detailing an eventful day for Druce at work. It's the first time he came across the device called a shredder, and his task was to do away with a lot of secret company papers. Descartes writes Druce as being so very delighted with coffee in hand and using the high tech office equipment all day long. Durce comes back home with a hop, and a pair of peppy feet, not forgetting to buy a kaleidoscope of flowers for his girl from the nursery.

Descartes can see Druce enter his home in the projection; this is where Descartes' hand had written in cursive the story's conflict by its own device. Makoto is crouching barefoot on the kitchen floor. She is scared of visions privy only to her. Druce calms her down with a glass of water and gentle words. He carries her out to the sofa in the living room, and with light loving persuasion he convinces her to speak her fears.

She can see into the future. She sees Tokyo as it is in Descartes' today, outside Eutopia. The visions shake her deeply, and she retells them with horror. "It's all a ruin," she manages in a clean whisper. "We have all but abandoned the city. All fourteen million inhabitants of Tokyo have vanished. The forest has marched down the mountains, across the rice fields and is in the city. The parks have all broken their boundaries and creep up the rusting towers of metal. The subways are underground rivers, and all our streets and sidewalks have been taken by vegetation and grass."

Druce was able to calm her down by taking her into the sun, on the balcony, to remind her of their present. She feels safe to see the bustle on the rooftops below, and the sound of the traffic. Here in his own writing, in Druce, Descartes sees his mistakes, by the book he remembers who he should be, and is reassured of how easy it is to do good, and be a better, more supporting half of Destiny.

Caterpillar's Attitude

With her feet up she rests, unmindful of the approaching footsteps. She stares up in empty space, leaving her mind be a little while, until her thoughts land at an oddity of the ceiling. It appears to be much lower than it should be. There are only three galleries above them, she surely had seen six from the garden outside. Still the ceiling forms the concave of the building's dome.

An animated Machiavelli rises to greet his guest, "Diablo my child, please come, join us."

Machiavelli ushers the young gentleman towards the spare sofa. Destiny is slow at starting up again, but she rises to greet Diablo. Her customary smile nearly breaks into a titter when she lays eyes on Diablo.

Unconventional is the norm of Eutopia, yet surprises often outdo your expectations. His style peculiar, a fantasy of the past. In a double-breasted green vest, a tall top hat with a pair of metal-framed rubber-banded goggles resting on its bond, Diablo stands oddly tall. His leather boots are tight, with mysterious bronze clockwork dials and bearings rising from his soles creeping up underneath his trousers.

He lightly shakes her hand, but his face remains rigid, until Machiavelli introduces the two, "Destiny meet Diablo, a resident of the 173rd hive and a close friend. Diablo, Destiny lives here in the 27th hive, and is one of my flock."

"Nice to meet you, Lady Destiny," he greets her in a voice far too rough for his smile.

Under his belt hang several color coded pouches. He picks the purple one, the first to the right, and places it on the table, while his other hand reaches in his pocket to retrieve a silver cigarette case. Its front depicts trees and stems in mid breeze, and in the background, above the ground, floats a winged gray bearded being, clad in a purple cloth.

The pouch spreads on its own once on the table. A thin shiny copper tube protrudes from Diablo's sleeve for a flash, bearing a flame and lighting his cigarette. The purple fabric of the pouch reveals a tiny jazz band comprising entirely of caterpillars.

Pink and with electric blue dots are the two with the bull-fiddle and the Gibson guitar. Much larger, well-padded and green makes the lead, it taps the tiny silver steel grill of his microphone. The drummer, in contrast, is translucent, with a pair of droopy tentacles. It needs no drumsticks, for its first pair of hands is shaped perfectly for drumming, and his second pair is brushy enough for the snare drums. The unlikely star of the group wears his bad attitude on his sleeves, in a thorny fuzzy black coat; probably the most talented caterpillar in Eutopia, he plays the keys and starts the music with two notes of E.

Diablo's gestures have been too bizarre for Destiny to follow. It escapes her when they sat back again, and the deep playful tone of Jazz only sinks in her when she finds the three of them are all comfortably settled and chatting.

She has to make an effort to get back to the conversation of Diablo and Machiavelli.

"Any good news Diablo? Pray, tell me the mood of your bubble has improved," probes Machiavelli.

"If anything, it's getting worse my Elder. They are all equally heartbroken."

An awful silence befalls, barely hindered by Machiavelli's murmured, "Pity."

"Heartbroken? I hope you haven't used such a grievous word in vain," Destiny addresses Diablo.

"Mercy, we are not talking about Newmans here," Machiavelli answers instead of Diablo.

Destiny is unsure of what he implies, her expression, though, doesn't reveal her confusion. She waits for Machiavelli to continue.

Machiavelli hesitates, exchanges a glance with Diablo, who nods ever so slightly, permitting Machiavelli to tell more.

"Master Diablo here lives alone and remains uncoupled. In his solitude he sought the intelligent company of his imagination. He embodied his will in a few creatures of flight, and allowed them the human tongue."

"Wow, that sounds like quite a feat. How? But wait! First tell if I understand this correctly."

"Gladly," agrees Machiavelli, while Destiny continues, "He got up one day, felt he needed company, and willed instant creation of a being with human-like intelligence?"

"In a manner of speaking, yes."

Diablo isn't comfortable with the bragging. "It took me two years of trial and error before I could find the right combination and come close to creating a working prototype."

"Only two years! Isn't that known to require Elder-like experience?"

Machiavelli clears his throat. "It takes centuries to master such skills, but there have been known exceptions to the rule. Most Newmans unlock these capabilities only when they have lived for more than half a millennium. Diablo is still shy of thirty, quite remarkable isn't it?"

"It isn't, if you know the trick behind it," Diablo joins in, the cigarette in his right hand smoked only half but yet not ashed, forming a delicate tower.

"There is a trick?" together Machiavelli and Destiny ask him.

"Perhaps a little more than a trick. It's a theory, never written, or passed down, but learned by observation, and self-actualization."

Machiavelli laughs nervously, "I wouldn't know, I have never felt the need to seek intelligent company of any kind, but the Newman kind."

The caterpillars play softer, a gripping keyboard solo ensues and Destiny tunes away from the room, watching the ash tower give way and fall, but evaporate with a glow before hitting the floor.

"Tell me the secret," she asks, and then regards him once more, "Mr. Diablo."

"A secret, perhaps yes, is it one?" he repeats after her musingly. "The 'unsaid rule' I have named it."

"Do enlighten us Diablo, I shall be able to dispel superstition and misinformation only when you make me a pound wiser."

Diablo is taken aback; he turns away in displeasure, and reaches out for his wine. "All right then, but know I do so only because it's you who asks Elder Machiavelli. I hold my research in high regard, but today I shall relent."

"And for that Diablo I am duly grateful."

Instead of taking the glass to his lips, Diablo wills the wine within to float off its rim and hover over the table between the three of them.

First they are mere blobs, as they drift towards one another and form one single entity, which spreads to form a stage between Diablo and Machiavelli, facing Destiny. The stage spills from the edges forming two miniature animated replicas, one a four-legged beast, the other a human.

"May I have some more wine?" Diablo touches the temple of the two figures one after the other, and their red translucent rosé gleam is eclipsed by colors, completing their molding.

"Sure, sure." Machiavelli clicks his fingers and Diablo's glass gets refilled.

At first Destiny presumes the two creatures to be how they appear, but soon she begins to recognize the oddities. The human is limp, can barely stand, and is unable to support his own weight. He quickly falls in a heap of his own limbs, each part of his body unnaturally twisted.

On the other hand, the canine gracefully sits down, yawns and addresses Diablo, "What do we have here?"

"Bear with me Mufasa, I will tell you all about it once we are home." Diablo looks away from the golden retriever, and then addresses Destiny and Machiavelli in a serious tone. "The closer your intentional creation is to being physically human, the less would their intelligence be. Look." Diablo points at his wine graph, and a figure appears at the near left of the human. Its fish eyes are too large, its button sized mouth unsettling, and alien are the two holes it has instead of nostrils. A skinny malnourished creature, he growls instead of speaking and attempts to leap instead of walking.

"The more perfect their human form the dimmer their thinking, until they are inanimate, and don't breathe life, such as the immobile human here, at the end. Whereas the more unlikely their form, and distant from what we would consider human, the more intelligence we may attribute to the beast. Like my Mufasa here."

The dog lazily opens one eye, "Huh."

"Only a little longer Mufasa." Reassured, Diablo's friend goes back to sleep. Diablo smiles, stealthily catching Destiny's attention, and says, "Mufasa isn't the brightest of mine."

"How rude!" Not a shred of true criticism in her voice. "If that were true, each one of us would put forth an ancient creature such as a giant squid, and let it have the cerebrum of men."

"Yes Diablo, she is correct," Machiavelli agrees with Destiny, and then probes further. "It's well known that blowing forced intelligence into creatures has well defined limitations. They make no better company than talking pets."

Diablo smiles, "Yes, that's why my Musafa here, despite all his loyalty, isn't much into philosophy. The key is to bring into being a creature whose biological makeup is distinct from all those who had passed over to Eutopia from the Earth of Old. An organism of your mind's making alone. Only such unique breathers will be able to hold thought, capable of compelling us Newmans."

"Well perhaps my Dwar..." Destiny stops short of mentioning

the Dwarkoids; she is not ready yet to talk of them casually. "I do feel you might be right, or so my experience would have me believe." Steering them away from her near fumble, she continues, "It fits well and we were told we don't have the ability to make our own humans." She draws out her last words at Machiavelli accusingly.

"Don't look at me, I don't make the rules." Machiavelli turns to Diablo, "Your theory is one of logic Diablo, you might be right. I am impressed." He taps Diablo on the back.

"Thank you my Elder," says Diablo dryly.

"Might I ask what went wrong? Did you not mention occurrence of a tragedy in your Bubble of Perfect Existence?" Destiny asks, not sure if her concerns are welcomed.

"A tragedy it was, and hearts were broken, but in truth it is not my place to tell," admits Machiavelli, and then nudges Diablo, "You would do the deceased a better justice Diablo. Why don't you tell their tale."

"The house of Daedalus is my most prized creation. They are knowledge hungry, curious and wise. They might not be pleasant to look at but make great conversationalists. They are all that I do have for company in my lonely hours, and I am glad of them." Diablo pauses, and Destiny's only response is an encouraging nod.

"The trouble with embodiment of intelligence is that we, their creators, have no say in their personality types. You may look up the data book and choose a species with broad outlines of what you wish, but each creature is born with their own quirks and preferences, which by tuning or sheer will can never be determined. Furthermore, the kind of intelligence I seek can't be found in the data book, leaving me to experiment, hybridize and hope for the best. Here I will show you..."

The wine begins to gather up together and starts to form a translucent blob, close to where Mufasa is sleeping. A creature croaks to life, a lizard with three pairs of legs, with four on its hind, wings similar to a dragonfly's and the head of a frog. It croaks again, and begins to look around, more amused by its own anatomy than the room. Mufasa, though, is quick to be on his feet, and begins to growl and bark at the newcomer.

"I am sorry, I am sorry. I had forgotten how little you appreciate lizards. Hold on a second." Diablo picks up the golden retriever from the wine graph and places him in his top pocket.

"Vicious little scoundrel," Mufasa growls on.

"It's all right Mufasa. Isn't my pocket better?"

"Yeah well, sure." Mufasa tries to reach Diablo's beard and give it a lick, but it's out of his reach. He gives up soon enough, and cuddles down in the darkness of Diablo's pocket.

A touch of Diablo's index finger on its temple, and the new creature of his making gains the ability of speech: "What am I?" Diablo hastily gives the creature another tap, dissolving him into the pink rosé once more.

"I dare not chance it. It may ponder itself to despair, looking for the answers of life, universe and everything. Especially if I can't spare the time to give him some of the answers."

"That's kind of you," Destiny remarks.

They share a smile as the wine graph slips back into his glass, sounding "blop".

"That is how you make a creature of thought. True, I had already explored this combination before and had known it would work, but if you have the skills you can produce them infinitely."

Machiavelli clears his throat, giving Diablo a reason to pause. Diablo turns to Machiavelli, "I do not take it lightly my Elder, I am not responsible for the incident."

Destiny can feel the tension between the two men, and chooses not to speak.

"I didn't even say a word!" a wide eyed Machiavelli reacts, "I do know it was an accident."

"The House of Daedalus is wise, but curious to a fault. They must see and experience it all first hand. My telling them, or books alone won't do. They originally had three members, a perfect little nuclear family. Today there are only two. It could be argued that the passing of the mother was a product of my callousness. I didn't forewarn her of the abyss of plasma."

Diablo grows silent.

Destiny knows better than to ask what a plasma abyss is.

The passing of time is slow; everyone waits for Diablo to recover. He straightens up when he is ready and says, "Well then, where do we go from here?"

"Now you must know why the two of you are here," Machiavelli speaks authoritatively. "A creation that has such intelligence isn't a play thing. We the Elders will not permit inhuman mistreatment of such beings. Many Eutopians have had to forgo their Bubble of Perfect Existence when they fail to God over their own. Many have willingly turned their bubbles into an Eden for their creations, and returned to the City, forsaking all they once called home."

Silence.

"None of you foresaw such a fate, did you? All that you do has been done before, by those who came before you, and we the Elders have cared to learn from the mistake of others. We guide you, we maintain perfection."

"Surely we won't let the situation get so dire, that we have to move into the City!" Destiny protests, appalled by the notion.

"We will help you prevent things from falling apart, but the skills of Elders too have limitations. We can't dictate, you must be free to solve and choose your problems and options as you please. We will let you know when you do wrong, but we shall never tell you what to do; that you must learn yourself."

"He implies greater interference from the Observatory in our lives, and perhaps their physical presence," explains Diablo.

"Well there is a loophole that would minimize our direct involvement, but it requires the two of you to stir out of your comfort zones a little."

"Yet it would not eliminate your interference," Destiny says with a sigh. "Let us have it, what would you have us do?"

"Don't worry, not too much for now. First the two of you will learn from one another. Diablo will teach you how to create agents of influence who you can program more carefully and plant in your undersea civilization. Diablo will learn from you how to direct evolution and get desired results. Only then would you have the skills required to keep your liberty, by being benevolent to those you rule, in the same manner Eutopia is to you."

Destiny and Diablo exchange a glance and pause momentarily before bursting into protest.

"The only guest I have ever entertained is you Elder Machiavelli," Diablo nearly pleads.

"I am needed at home. I can't keep leaving my Bubble of Perfect Existence." Destiny doesn't sound kind.

"Ha ha, don't be hasty, why don't the two of you spend a day here, in the City, and tell me what you choose on the morrow."

Time Capsule

Bleak are the backyards of the welcoming house of the 27th Hive, static is the air, and dry are its gardens. The heat is harsh and mere moments in the sun would curl the skin. Their lips crack as they step out the door. Diablo and Destiny stand apart at the two corner pillars of the steps that lead down from the porch to the lifeless garden.

Their first hour alone begins in silence. Their years of isolation have diminished their communication skills. Besides, the heat is enough for thoughts of curtsies and polite remarks to all but disappear.

On the marble sill of the porch's white fence, Diablo finds a glass jar filled to the brim with lemonade and crushed ice. He pours a glass and then another. Destiny spots two black umbrellas resting on a pillar.

In a pair of two swift moves, as though choreographed before, they exchange an umbrella and a glass of lemonade and only after three hearty gulps do they speak.

Destiny is the one to start, "I wonder why Elder Machiavelli would allow his grounds to run this wild. And damned be the weather, why, oh why does it need to be so cruel?" She puts up her umbrella and walks down the steps.

"Machiavelli is a man of many colors with sleeves full of tricks, but all his doings are of reason." Diablo takes her lead and joins her walk. "He wishes everyone who comes here to scurry to the other side. He hopes the unpleasantness of this yard won't allow them to reconsider their visit to the City once they pass it. Whereas those who return from the City, but in their hearts no more take their 'Bubble of Perfect Existence' as home, are dissuaded from leaving by the nature of this garden. He wants to inspire us all to be more social."

Destiny regards him through the corner of her eye, "This would work the other way around too, right? Some might be discouraged to enter the City."

Diablo smiles, blows in his glass, carbonating his lemonade. "I had never considered that. Yes, I reckon he desires to deter the faint hearted from being injudicious."

With her smooth laugh she says, "Well then, we aren't faint hearted, and have no reason to suffer an Elder's lack of confidence." Destiny stops, and takes a giant breath of air, filling her lungs up to her cheeks. She looks up at the sky and blows, but instead of her breath, her lips release dark clouds of monsoons.

"This may take a bit," she pauses to tell Diablo and then continues to make clouds.

Diablo is amused, "Well, I don't know what you are doing, nevertheless I will help." He too joins her, his clouds being a quarter larger than hers with every breath.

It doesn't take long for them to fill up the backyard, the clouds soon start to block their sight, and one even thunders. "Send them high, as they must be," Destiny shouts over the rumble.

"On it." Diablo sends them all up at once, the process slower than it would have been in his own Bubble of Perfect Existence. An unforeseen hurdle occurs to him. "But my lady, they would scatter in the blue up there, how do you intend to keep them together?"

"Don't you worry." Destiny pulls out a single strand of her hair. She holds it with her right hand and then strokes it by placing it between her left index and ring fingers. As her hands extend so does the hair; the more she strokes, the more hair appears from thin air.

Her hair is of many colors, a yard in pink and then teal, followed by black, blonde, red, a little silver, amber and then it turns gold. Her hands move faster until its colors all flux in together to radiate a pulsating light. The hair loops at her feet, forming a lit bundle of rope.

She stops stroking and opens her right palm. The fallen end of the hair rises up to find her palm. She joins the two ends together forming a circle and then lets it go. Its loop turns rigid and floats up in the air; it hums loudly, an industrial sound, pausing and humming in sync with its shifting hue.

"I would tie the clouds in a knot," she says beamingly.

"Ahh, great idea."

The two together position the rope around the clouds, and thicken them where the light still manages to break through.

All done, Diablo reaches for his cigarette case once more.

Under the cloud cover she warns him with a sigh, "Now, we must hold our umbrellas tightly."

"Do you smoke? Would you like a puff?" He offers her the open box, speaking far more loudly than necessary.

She reaches out in an elegant play of her hand as it starts to drizzle. "Occasionally."

The rain begins to strengthen, but their umbrellas suffice. Diablo lights their cigarettes and takes a long drag.

"What's next?"

"We wait," she says, breathing out smoke. A still Diablo looks on at the rain, only half his mind spared for the words he speaks. "There is no wind, but it pours. Would our wait be long?"

"Not long, don't worry, I will speed things up. Though..." A noticeable hesitation in her voice.

The change in her mood isn't lost upon Diablo, and he is quick to ask, "Why, is there a problem?" He looks down at her, bites his lip and continues, "Alas, I won't be much help here, I am not much of a Time Tuner."

Destiny rolls her eyes, "I didn't think this through, nevertheless, now I must..."

"Sounds scary, what happened?"

She looks at him with resolve, and says, "It might seem forward of me Mr. Diablo, but I would have you know, it's empirical that I must hold your hand, or touch you in some way, for my plans to work."

"Oh! That's nothing to get perplexed about. Sure." He offers her his hand.

The moment they touch, the rain goes mad, and a curtain of water surrounds them. "I am not perplexed," she protests, cat eyeing him.

"My bad, you aren't, but I am confused, what's happening?" He looks away, and then back at her before she replies.

"We are in a Time Capsule, you and I. This backyard of the welcoming house is moving fast, ahead of us in time. It takes practice, and much learning, to know how to manipulate so many elements all at once; the water, the earth, the living. The veil will lift in a matter of minutes for you, but nearly a month would pass for the Garden."

"You are skilled. If I may ask, how far afield can you influence in the City?"

"The City resists, my will is restricted to the radius of a hectare," she admits meekly.

"Impressive, for it's true, the Elders limit us from changing their beloved City."

She leaves Diablo's hand with a jerk, and the last of the rain falls with one loud splash. The clouds begin to disappear. Diablo is filled with the light smell of petrichor distinct to gardens after a light summer shower.

Before either of the two could word their thoughts, the sky returns to reign supreme over the land, the way it was before the handiwork of Destiny. It's once more sunny, but milder and this time around, pleasant. The grass is green and fresh, the trees bear fruits, and Diablo can hear the tweets of birds but he yet can't see them.

They walk down the meandering path of the garden. It's been designed to look natural, deluding one to believe it has been trotted over by a thousand passersby. Of the two, Diablo visits the gardens more often, yet he can't say he has witnessed it in bloom.

They amble on, preoccupied more with their surrounding than each other. They sense oddities, both to the left and the right. Peculiarities of movements and form. There is much more at play here than meets the eye, a trickery not part of the transformation Diablo and Destiny brought to the garden, but one deep seeded from before. A work of Machiavelli.

Diablo voices his fear, "There is something sinister at foot here."

Perhaps in fear, perhaps dreamily, they walk together. Both alarmed and at guard, they watch for movements of the garden.

A speck flies in her eye, and is first taken for a grain of sand. It wasn't near her nose, but only appeared so, a glimmer at the bushes, half a dozen yards away from her feet. It brightens sharply, like looking at the sun, and then dims again. Destiny notices the liquid only then. Every leaf, twig and blade of grass, even the benches ooze out thick glass like liquid, covering all there is to see in the garden.

In a whisper, suspicious of the very air, Destiny asks, "What is that?"

"I have no idea, we better be careful. The joke seems to be on us." Diablo, too, is cautious.

A pair of wasps on both sides of the path takes flight at once, equidistant from the walkers, and of the same yellow shade and size, their loops identical in midair. Their landing, though, isn't perfect. In flight, the glass liquid takes over, covering them and jamming their wings. Crystallized and brittle, they shatter on hitting the ground.

A reminder to Diablo that the inert nature of Elder Machiavelli's grounds can't be overruled by him or Destiny.

"Do you see the symmetry between the two sides? Every stone, every breathing thing, whether plant, bug or bird has a replica on both left and right," he asks Destiny, unaware of Machiavelli's trickery festering in his blind spot.

"Oh, I did!" The pleasure in her voice feels more akin to a warning to Diablo. He looks on at her somberly and nods, encouraging her to tell him more.

"I decided to change it, bring in some chaos. Our rain melted a few things at random, breaking the untrue feel of the gardens."

Diablo opens his mouth as if to speak, but says nothing.

"Why? Don't you like this better?" Her eyes widen, "Oh! What have I done?"

Diablo hears a faint crack. He looks behind, and at the end of the steps of the Welcoming House, the crystallized grass splits and vanishes. The five blades surrounding it are next, and then in a domino effect with the sound of a house of mirrors falling apart does the entire garden begin to break, returning back to how it was before the rain. Under the shell of liquid glass is the original form of things.

"Quick, we must leave," says Diablo in all seriousness and takes Destiny by her waist, and before she can protest he adds, "Remember not to let your feet on the ground. We must run."

Destiny is convinced of the exigency. Diablo bolts. His legs breathe like the pistons of an engine, and steam rises behind him. They are pursued by the crystallization and shattering of the garden, managing to remain a step ahead of the blistering shards.

Destiny, still stunned, remembers to keep herself afloat; she can't help but hold on to the stranger. They reach the end; there are no gates or fences here to demark the boundary of the Gardens of the Welcoming House of 27th Hive, but only a cliff leading up to nothing.

Diablo leaps with no hesitation, and lets her go when there is no ground below her to worry about, shouting, "Now we fly."

The momentum has Destiny floating forward and tamping without exertion. She takes her time to turn around and ask in heavy breaths, "Was the rush necessary?"

Diablo has made himself comfortable in the air. He floats horizontally towards her, resting his head on his left palm. "Wasn't it? The Garden was transforming back into the image Machiavelli desired it to keep. Would you truly have suffered the dry arid air instead? Ha?"

"No I wouldn't," she pauses and then adds, "I pushed my luck with changing the Elder's garden, didn't I? I went too far."

"You tested his patience, that's for sure, yet I know Machiavelli, he is far too forgiving, he won't remember this incident."

A Siren's Lure

In the depths it matters little if it's night or day. Under the ocean in Destiny's abode, Descartes waits to see if his summons is answered.

"I will treat them well, I shall not be a brute."

Descartes waits patiently, parking himself on the dormant bust of a coral. He senses their approach but doesn't bother to look up. He busies himself with the only two things he has brought down from the surface, his old blunt claymore and a whetstone.

The phalanx halts a distance away from Descartes. He can tell of their arrival by the ripple caused by their crabwise march. The platoon keeps a brilliant silence, not daring to disturb him. Yet an impudent faint murmur buzzes in the background, growing steadily louder. Descartes isn't bothered by the hum of a thousand individuals speaking together. He keeps sharpening his blade.

It is easy to tell that the cacophony comes from Dwarkoidian lips by the high frequency of their voices. They are of a range far beyond what Newmans can commonly hear. Knowing this, Descartes had to make a special exception for this visit; he had to increase the upper limit of audible frequencies for his ears.

Satisfied with the edge of his double handed sword, Descartes looks up to find a welcoming party much larger than usual. The phalanx is accompanied by a crowd of commoners.

A soldier with an amethyst gem around his neck comes forward and kneels, blossoming its eight arms on the seabed. He takes off his helmet.

"Boomer my old friend, rise." Dwarkoids can only be told apart from one another by the tint of their eyes, and on looking into the centurion's, Descartes is disappointed to realize these are not of Boomer's.

"I don't imagine he could have anything better to do than receive me; where in my bubble is he?"

Instead of replying, the centurion offers Descartes a pill, a see-through one, identical to the one that Boomer had given him the first time he had visited the Dwarkoids.

"Ah no, I don't need it this time. Look at this."

He remembers well the anatomy of his body, the one he wore the last time he lived among the Dwarkoids. Changing skin isn't the sort of thing Descartes fancies, though at times it is practical, and he is a natural. The metamorphosis is quick and clean. The surface of his skin turns from teal to a muscular orange. Most of his bones dissolve and both his legs split into four tentacles each. The features of his face melt, his nose sinks into the skin, and his eyes change shape and color. They turn from oval to circular and the white in them starts boasting rivulets of brown, blue and yellow.

Descartes poses with two of his eight limbs outstretched, "Ta-da. Don't I make a fine Dwarkoid?"

The centurion can't help but giggle, "You do, Lord God Descartes, you do."

Descartes lightly punches the centurion on his shoulder.

"So tell me, where is my friend Boomer?"

The smile on the warrior's face vanishes, and he grows silent once more. His eyes travel onto the claymore, still firmly held by Descartes.

"What's your name boy? You need not fear me, speak up."

"I am Siren my lord. Boomer my grand uncle, perished in the unusually harsh winter of the year before."

"How could that be, I was here only yesterday." Descartes pauses, taking in the ill news. "Unless Destiny has made the times in these parts of her sea go faster," he wonders. "Yes, she must have, to hasten the progress of your society. Did she come to you again, after the time we had done together."

"No my lord, only the old and the bent among us treasure the living memory of your last visit. Your lore, though, is fresh in all our minds, a bedtime story for every child. We have longed long for your return."

"That explains the crowd." Descartes looks at the many faces that surround him while they continue to grow in numbers. They gather on top of each other, enveloping Descartes in a dome. An urge has him take center stage; he elevates above the seabed, visible to all those who have come to greet him.

"I believe you do remember who I am?"

"Yes we do!" is a daring shout from a lone young faceless voice.

"Good, good." Descartes takes a moment to pick his next words. "It feels as if only yesterday I was here with your grand sires. They taught me how to be a Dwarkoid. I learned your tongue, and the rhythm of this body." Descartes points at his torso with three of his arms. "I learned much of your ways, and your style of living. I visit you again for your kind still has secrets I haven't found, though this time I shall actively participate in your lives. I am here not to only imbibe knowledge but to impart it too. I shall not be a silent spectator who slips into your minds at will and sees their inner workings. Rather, I shall be present in flesh and blood to guide the river of your civilization."

The soft rumble of the crowd changes to elated cheers. Many thump their chest, and the phalanx beat their pilum on the ground in a rhythmic beat. "Olé!" is their chant of jubilation. Their God has come down from the heavens to guide them. Their savior is here, there is not enough dancing, or hats to toss that can adequately express the waves of ecstasy that reverberate from Dwarkoidian hearts.

Descartes, too, is overwhelmed by their response; he is humbled by their dedication, and wishes they would stop making such a big deal of him. A spiral twirl of two of his limbs indicates to the crowd to quiet down. His signal goes unheeded by most, except the soldiers. They are quick to move, changing their formation from that of a turtle to a protective sphere around Descartes. In unison they each reach for their gladius and with its hilt slam their shields, causing a thunderous boom, drowning the voice of the onlookers.

The punitive implementation of silence seems a notch too harsh to Descartes. *"This isn't going to get easier Destiny."*

It's Siren, who has been entrusted as the mouthpiece of the Dwarkoids, "Almighty God Descartes, on behalf of the realms of the sea, ruled by three kings, a countess and a chancellor, we invite you to take your rightful place in the halls we have built in the glory of mother Destiny and you."

The centurion rises, turns around and announces, "Make way for the King of Kings, our lord Descartes." The mob retreats towards the city, parting to make a path for Descartes and the phalanx. They still pile on one another, but leave the top open so he may have a good view of the nearing City.

Their settlements have grown much since Descartes' last visit. They used to build only perpendicularly on the walls of the crater, and had covered one fourth of its total surface. Now not an inch of undeveloped space remains, and to expand they build within the cracks and caverns of the cliff's face. The familiar bioluminescent lamps bring fond memories and a smile to Descartes. The new include the choice of the beast of labor; giant turtles replace giant slugs, they appear carrying tons of rubble away from the wall.

"Weren't the slugs better at holding onto their burden?" Descartes asks Siren, the only one of the Dwarkoids walking beside him.

"They were, but the turtles can carry far more and are much swifter. In my personal opinion it was very unkind of us to use slugs, they would often be squashed by the weight. The turtles don't seem to mind it at all," the centurion explains hesitantly, not sure if it's his place to speak.

Descartes is pleased. "I am impressed by your reasoning lad. Quite human."

Siren wiggles with elation, one doesn't receive praise from a God every day. "Here we are my lord! I present you the halls of Newmans."

Descartes has trouble seeing anything noteworthy. The procession has stopped with them, and the crowd has grown silent. They wait to see how he reacts to their wonder. Descartes feels the pressure of expectation, as he struggles to find magnificence in seaweed that floats up from the windows of limestone constructions.

"Consider the monument in its entirety my lord," the centurion whispers to Descartes.

Descartes looks at the shape the buildings form, as a collective, and only then does he spot it. They have been carved in the rock as a pair of humanoids. It's him and Destiny. Her figure stands taller than his, though both the statues scarcely resemble their muses. Descartes would have laughed off their 'wonder' if he had not seen merit in the manner that they were being used.

The eyes are doors and Dwarkoids swim through them carrying out bricks, sand, crystals and other building materials. In their chest families have built their dwellings. Their apartments are made accessible by equidistant glass panels running from the collarbone of the statues to their waists. In their bellies are city squares for play and lazy evenings.

"Splendid. I am glad you thought of putting these edifices to good use, instead of letting them be hollow monuments wasted as tributes to those who rarely, if ever, visit."

The Dwarkoids receive his compliment well and once more burst into cheers.

"Come God Descartes let us show you your throne room," Siren speaks for everyone.

"*For crying out loud Destiny, every time I think our children make a reasonable folk they reveal something over the top like a 'throne room'. There is much correction needed in their interpretation of dharma.*"

Through the ocular holes in the statute they enter the said throne room. Siren leads the way, holding a torch in an otherwise dark hall. Descartes and the rest of the phalanx follow.

It is hard to estimate the size and the shape of the room in the limited lamplight, though Descartes takes it to be oval and elongated in the likeness of his face. He glimpses a hand mirror abandoned in marine snow and sheets of papyrus floating free in the hall.

The phalanx spreads out around the chamber, disappearing in its darkness, but remains visible by the glimmer of their armor. One after the other they are seen floating close to the ceiling; there they pour bioluminescence into glass cups and jars, which hang by ropes made in spider's silk.

Their work unveils a colosseum of a room with verandas a plenty at different levels. Descartes had not expected decorations of curtains made in purple cloth; they carry his family crest: a black beetle hanging by a branch-let of a lily.

Dwarkoids in fancy attire swim down, filling the halls as they enter through the ear doors of the statue lining the corridors above and packing the balconies. "My lord if you may please take your divine seat." Siren points to an apparatus in the center of the room. One look and Descartes recalls how it is used.

Made of metal, it firmly holds the torso of Descartes' fragile Dwarkoidian body. His eight arms find their designated holes, which stretch them apart independently, relaxing them. At the other end they each find adjacent levers. He remembers how to work them too.

He swirls his throne around, and to a courtroom in full attendance he says, "Fine! I will rule."

Baths and Tea

In the dark cylindrical tube of night, dim colored balls of light pass by Diablo and Destiny as they rush deeper into the City. Destiny has seldom ever visited the City, barely staying even during her Coupling Season. Once they agreed to be together Descartes had wasted no time in getting an empty Bubble of Perfect Existence allocated to them.

She didn't have much reason to contest the suggested destination by Diablo. He is having them visit a close by neighborhood, where he mentions he has a City Dweller friend, but they have been traveling for a while at much speed, and the end is nowhere in sight.

Destiny slows down purposely, yet flying so fast that she only gets a peek of the landscape below. There is much in the City that Destiny would like to pause and observe, but her manners won't let her request a stop.

She manages to keep pace until a glimpse takes off her speed, grinding her to a halt in a place where the ocean curls up like the insides of a rolled up scroll, where the water is not below her alone, but above her too.

To her north, a little over a couple of miles away, she can see the ocean rise and pour onto the sky, filling it up with equal consistency. Much nearer are the stilts of steel rising from the water, the carcass of dead skyscrapers covered in seaweed, they bridge the two waters together.

Diablo overshoots her, but Destiny is too overwhelmed by

the scenery to spare him a thought. He notices her absence immediately, but is in the mood for speed, and would rather form a massive misty circle to return to her than lose velocity.

"Why have we stopped?" he asks, finding her perched on a rusted steel column.

"To admire the City of course; isn't it beautiful here?"

"Well, here is admirable, I concede, but this isn't a real city."

"How do you mean, not a City? We are in the domain of the Elders, and isn't that the only Newman City?"

"Its scenery can't be this sparse, where is the chaos, the lights, the music and the most vital ingredient: people."

"Why? Do only those things make a city?" She isn't convinced, but is curious.

"Well, technically yes, we are in the City, but to me a place which you or I or for that matter any Newman could replicate in their Bubble of Perfect Existence isn't the true City. There are little pockets here, far and few, where the Elders and the Dwellers pretend they are still on the Earth of Old. Where I implore you, we must go."

Destiny's eyes brighten at the mention of Earth. "Let us go then," and they jet off away on their journey.

At dusk they reach the foot of the Red hills.

"We shouldn't fly into this neighborhood," Diablo tells her.

"Why, who makes the rules?"

"Those who live in this hood, you do want them to be welcoming, don't you?"

"You are asking of me to climb up this hill by foot? I reckon I will be able to, but seriously? What if I don't fly, but just leap to the top?"

Diablo sniggers, "You don't wish to, not here, you don't. End up losing out on all the fun, you would. You would only experience the charm of the forthcoming lands by hiking up with me, all the way to the canyon on the other side. Just imagine you are visiting a stranger's bubble, the etiquette is nearly the same, if anything, it's more lenient."

With a sigh, Destiny accepts Diablo's argument, "Fine, but this better not be a letdown."

"I dare not be presumptuous, but I have a feeling you would fancy it here."

Destiny raises her eyebrows in doubt.

They hike up the hill, a thousand steps and a thousand more, crossing brooks, thorny bushes and littered mangoes. Stepping firm on the sludge of nearly dried up streams, they walk up until the grass ends and they reach a steep stone wall, which rises into the clouds.

"Where do we go from here?" Destiny asks, hoping the answer would be 'fly'.

Instead, Diablo begins to feel the rock with the tip of his fingers, as if trying to pick a particle of dust. It takes him a quarter of an hour to find the switch. While Destiny waits, on the brink of losing her patience in the moist cold air of the cloud.

A flight of railing-less stone steps emerges out of the wall on the pushing of the switch. Diablo starts first, "Be careful, we can only walk in a single file; mind your steps, for wet stones are treacherous."

"Ha ha! A true taste of the Earth of Old? 'The fear of tumbling down', aren't we overreaching a wee bit in our game of imitation?"

"We would never be able to perfectly imitate Earth, we are too privileged a species for strain and manual labor, but here we Eutopians have built a society close to the style of the old. Pray, don't make me spoil the surprise Destiny, if you do slip, you **better** fly, but enjoy the climb."

One flight of black stairs and then another. Destiny tires, but there is satisfaction in the strain, in work, in the unfamiliarity of the landscape, in not knowing when their journey will end.

Looking down, all she can see is the mist; there is no way to tell how far up they have come. Slowly as their altitude rises the cloud thins and their sight improves. The steps end at an arched gate lit by a pair of flaming torchlights. Beyond are the ruins of a castle barely visible in the fog.

Walking through the gate they find fallen stones and boulders scattered on the thin grass that covers the hilltop. Soon they reach the edge, where the green land gives way to the sky filled with clouds up to its brim. Turning around Destiny sees the old castle in decay, above the cloud line, the entirety of it visible.

Overgrown and sprawling in the rock and above it, the castle is a mystery to Destiny. Only one of its six visible towers shows any sign of life, where the rising spiraling stairway windows emit a shy green light. The rest of the castle is in such ruin, that many a flight rises to nowhere, the arches bear no ceilings and the walls fail to enclose rooms.

She points and asks, "What's there, up in the tower?"

"I know not, I have always descended down the valley without investigating the fort. I reckon it's nothing more than a set of dusty rooms, if anything at all. They say the first Newman brought the memory of such places from the Earth of Old, but it means little when compared to where we are off to."

Destiny looks at him sternly before declaring, "We shall explore the tower with the green candles, and if we fancy it, we shall have a rest there." She takes a step toward the castle and stops, turns around and asks, "Do you know how to get inside?"

Diablo smiles, letting her dictate terms, but he knows not the way. "I have never been there either, perhaps we can find a way in together."

They walk up to the base of the tower. They revolve around it once, feeling the black stone bricks in search of a lever, but their first circle reveals nothing.

"There is no way in," says Diablo, looking up at the windows.

"Let us try once more. This time we walk in opposite directions... be on the lookout for the switch."

"There won't be a way in, yet I would do so diligently if it satisfies your curiosity." Diablo doesn't move for a while, until Destiny shoos him away, waving her hands, "Go, go."

"Oh! Yeah, was waiting for you to start." A moment of

awkwardness and Diablo turns around and is on his way.

He inspects the rock closely and tries to look for an anomaly, yet he finds his thoughts flying back to where he had left Destiny, as glimpses of her flash across his imagination. There is a strange satisfaction in knowing she is right here, only a dozen steps away.

"I found it!" he hears her call.

"Awesome!" says Diablo. He is surprised by his own delight at the shortening of his wait to see her, but he lets the thought pass him by. Destiny is still right where he had left her, only now the stone bricks of the tower in front of her swirl back, parting to reveal a door.

Diablo looks at her and then at the opening in the wall, and then looks at her again. "Hmm, you willed the door, didn't you?" he asks her suspiciously.

She smiles, and claps her fist. "Ah! Ha ha, I was wishing you wouldn't be able to tell."

"Well," Diablo takes a deep breath, "it's all right."

"You are displeased?" Not only a note of regret, but displeasure too in her voice.

"I reckon you must know how we must conduct ourselves in these parts of the City. Don't shoot the messenger, I don't make the rules."

"Fill me in."

"The inhabitants here highly regard the continuity of things. There are so many Newman here that it's very hard to maintain balance and keep order. It only takes one to project their will to disrupt the carefully recreated mimicry of the days gone by."

Destiny's expression remains unchanged; she isn't moved by his words.

"If even in the slightest we were to resemble the Old Earth, we must act as creatures of Earth. The Newman kind was only born when we moved on from the Earth of Old, and that is why we can never return, but we may replicate the past world by forfeiting tuning, and pretending to be the ancient humans."

Destiny speaks up in protest, "That's primitive, how could they live that way? How do they manage?"

"Well, tuning isn't banned outright here, they only use it in the little ways, like igniting a kindle with a tuned in flame, or killing the swamp bug that bites."

"What about when you really need to, say an accident is about to happen, if a rock is to crush your best friend dead?" Destiny chuckles at the choice of her own words.

"Ha ha, yeah, they use it then too." Diablo must hold his stomach for this laugh. "Not so very funny considering we are to soon meet my friend. Anyhow, let's go explore your tower."

Destiny nods in agreement and walks in and up the spiral stairs of the tower.

The lights turn on, cued to do so when visitors enter the room. Here the walls are stone but the roof is held up by wooden trusses, where hangs a glass chandelier with candles. It's warm and well-lit for there is also a fireplace burning.

The room seems to have anticipated its guest's fatigue and need for refreshments; it is all stocked up with piles of fruit, a loaf of bread and a jug of lemonade placed on a corner table between two armchairs. In an open casket filled with hay, hides an assortment of rum and brandy bottles. The most peculiar of the room's qualities is the presence of a ceramic bathtub, very much in the center, on the carpet.

"Homely isn't it?"

"Wow! I had no idea this was here. I have never noticed the lights of this tower, when traveling alone. It seems as if the Dwellers know we are coming, and have intentionally made these arrangements for us."

Destiny titters, "And somehow they leave a bathtub here? I think not." She walks up to it, and turns on the tap. Water gushes out; it's warm to the touch and starts to steam.

"Nevertheless we are here. Would you like some tea?" Diablo asks, noticing a jar of tea leaves and a kettle on the shelf.

"I would very much like to bathe." Destiny holds the door of a closet open, checking for towels and bathing sundries.

Meanwhile, Diablo fixes the kettle in the fireplace over the flame. He turns around to find Destiny naked, with her white dress lying on the floor. She ignores him, but he hesitates in taking his eyes off her.

Surprise isn't the emotion Diablo expects to encounter in such matters. It is true though, that it's been long since Diablo has been with a woman, but nudity alone cannot unsettle him. Wearing only one's own skin is favored by many in Eutopia, and everyone is inherently comfortable with it.

Yet, he finds himself in awe of her thin legs as she steps into the tub, her frame slender with not a blemish on her fey skin. She notices his eyes only when she turns around, still he won't look away.

Diablo is puzzled for he hasn't felt the urge to visit the 'Halls of Bliss' in quite a while, where many men and women have besieged him with their kindness. Yet he knows now he would never forget the sight of Destiny's tiny breasts slipping in under the water and out of sight.

Destiny wonders what he wants; it still hasn't occurred to her that he might desire her. Diablo regains his composure, "The water boils already." He turns around toward the fireplace. He takes the kettle off the flames with a pair of tongs and carefully places it on a wooden stool. He adds the tea leaves and leaves the solution to brew. Destiny hasn't said anything since she got into the water, but she isn't particularly looking at him anymore; instead she revels in the little pleasure of a bath after a long hike.

The silence that lingers over the few minutes it takes for the tea to brew properly leaves a bad taste in Diablo's mouth. He fears if left uninterrupted for too long the silence would betray his thoughts. His mind blanks as he tries to salvage the situation, until he utters, "So what are they like, the intelligent race of your creation?"

"In love with water as much as I. Would you pass me the soap?"
He does as he is told.

"Besides, you promised you would first take me to the neighborhood you speak so highly of, before we part," her voice is meeker and unsure.

"Did I? I made a suggestion, at the most. I didn't give my word," Diablo smirks.

"Yes you did." Destiny sinks in, submerging her lips in an attempt to hide her white lie, but her tiny nose can still be seen.

"All right."

She can tell he doesn't believe her. "I would rather show you, than tell you, anyway. Why not we enjoy our baths and tea while we are here, and discuss the hard parts later."

"Tea! Absolutely." He reaches for the shelf and fetches two cups, and blows them clean.

"Ahem." Destiny clears her throat, catching Diablo's attention as he pours her a cup.

"Yeah?" asks Diablo without looking up, being careful with the kettle.

"You would have to take one too."

He looks up at her, "What, a bath?"

A permanent impression forms in his memory of the stream dripping off her elbow as she gets out.

"Yes you too, you got to clean off all the dirt from our little trek."

Diablo passes her the china once she has draped herself in the towel, regretting telling her that tuning isn't permitted in these parts. Showers aren't his favorite. Eutopians have quicker ways of staying clean.

The Puppeteer

Hearing the definite thud of the doors closing behind Diablo and Destiny, Machiavelli leaps out of his sofa and rushes to the far corner of the room, onto a specific tile under the galleries. The square moves up, disjointing from the ground, taking him to the floor above. Machiavelli looks out the window to make sure they have left the premises; he has no time to waste, but he can't be spotted leaving.

He conjures a pair of binoculars to watch them more closely. He is glad to see them take to the ice breakers he had placed in the veranda: the lemonade and the umbrellas. Never mind the distance, their stance speaks of the spark between them.

Machiavelli inserts a golden Beethoven's hearing aid into his ear when he notices them mouth words. He is relieved to hear Diablo trying to persuade Destiny to move quickly out of his backyard.

"What is she doing now?" Machiavelli wonders when Destiny starts blowing a black mist.

He overhears her, "This may take a bit."

Machiavelli rolls his eyes, and with a sigh says, "It better not."

But all his hopes of an early exit fade when it starts to rain outside. It pours, making it harder for Machiavelli to eavesdrop. He paces at the window, getting restless; his patience cannot be tested for long.

"Kids these days, so awkward, and queer. What in Eutopia are they doing?" Risking detection, Machiavelli bursts the window open. He intended to leap out, turn invisible and in stealth creep up behind Diablo and Destiny to learn what they are up to, and if he could find a way to shoo them off his backyard. Instead, he is greeted by a downpour so grand it feels as if a giant heavenly tub is being unloaded. The water splashes inside, threatening to spoil his shoes. "Sheesh! I can't be bothered by rain." He stamps his foot in frustration.

Sure, if he chooses to, he can ignore the rain and still venture outside, but he won't. It's not the Newman way to be subjected to the will of others. Instead, he waits. Thankfully, Destiny has speeded up time in the backyard, and her sphere of influence does not include the building.

Machiavelli's jaw drops when the veil of the rain lifts. His arid garden of rock, moss, dry grass, and stiffened crooked trees has received a facelift by the hands of Destiny. She has ruined his precious delicate balance of life and death. In his yard all that lived had to push hard to keep breathing. The very act of survival was a miracle, and the poetic struggle of life in his lawn could nearly be touched. Here Machiavelli has spent many idle days observing and admiring the resolve of life to go on against all odds.

Destiny, in arrogance or perhaps ignorance, Machiavelli isn't sure which, has replaced his backyard with a typical garden of Eden, where trees bear fruit and flowers, where bees have a blast, and the music of birds is never out of earshot. Machiavelli finds such styles a drag. He needs to get them off his yard.

He leaps out of his window, invisible and quiet. The two have started off again, but stroll all the more slowly to admire their works and the changes they have made to Machiavelli's garden.

To avoid discovery Machiavelli stays a distance away from the two, remaining at the foot of the steps of his house. He rubs his hands together and starts, casting first a blanket of his tuning over the garden, designed to revert the garden back to its original form.

Destiny stops, and Machiavelli is quick to bring his hearing aid back in position. "What is that?" Machiavelli catches Destiny's faint voice, and is impressed by her keen observation; he'd better be careful now. She notices his works, his casted blanket, barely visible as a faint film of silver liquid over everything in the garden.

He waits for them to start walking away again, and then in jest, to spook them, he takes out the creatures of the air. All that the amblers see is the crash landing of a wasp or two, nothing more. Machiavelli smiles. "This is fun," he whispers.

The two now know something is up, and are huddling together to take council. Machiavelli is enjoying himself, and the time is right for the last push, but before he commands the mold of his blanket to crack and reveal the original form of his garden he mistakenly steps onto the grass, breaking the brittle crystals that keep the green under his sole. Diablo notices the sharp sound, and he turns to stare straight at Machiavelli.

Machiavelli fumbles under Diablo's stare. He forgets he is invisible and in fear commences the quick turning of the backyard. It starts from the foot of the building, and moves fast towards Diablo and Destiny, and as expected, puts them on a run.

Standing on the first step of the house, fist raised, Machiavelli cheers in victory, watching Destiny and Diablo flee. Excitement overwhelms him when the two leap out of his grounds and into the skyway of the City. He too jumps with delight and laughter, "Ha ha, kids..."

His celebrations are short lived for he remembers his exigency. Machiavelli floats up to the top of the Welcoming House, right above from where he had exited the building. He opens up another white wooden window and goes inside.

The third floor is very different from the ones below; a hangar for a zeppelin is tucked away here. Half its balloon protrudes out of the building, colored a rustic brick red, a decoy for onlookers, so they may mistake it for the dome that runs along the entire length of the building.

Here the gallery and its railing are made of steel, not stone. They are narrower, sticking close to the wall. The floor is padded with grippy aluminum sheets, which squeak on every step Machiavelli takes toward the zeppelin. An indoor bridge connects the gallery to the gondola of the zeppelin.

A carpeted room with many tables, capable of entertaining three dozen guests, a relic from a time the Newman were more numerous, and it took an entire building of Elders to administer a single Hive. Today, however, Machiavelli is the only Newman traveler and Warden of 27th Hive. The seats aren't vacant though, half of them are occupied by inanimate gentlemen and ladies of teak.

Refreshments and leisure can wait, the airship must get going first. He walks straight to the control room, swings open the door, but doesn't step in. The cockpit is made of glass, walls, ceiling floor and all. Inside, a wooden man stands by the controls. It takes many clicks and a couple of precious minutes for the doll of a man in a bright blue sailor's uniform to leave the gears and turn to greet Machiavelli.

"Where to, my Elder?"

"To the Observatory captain, with Godspeed, not a zeppelin crawl."

Machiavelli retreats back to the passenger segment of the gondola and takes his favorite seat near the exit, by a window. He begins to roll his fingers on the table, and with his beat all the wooden mannequins in the room come to life.

There is chatter, laughter, the clatter of cutlery and the crackle of glasses being poured. In elaborate military uniforms the redcoats with their Victoria crosses are accompanied by their adversaries in green, of the imperial guard, and their shared ladies.

A stewardess comes up to his table and asks Machiavelli, "What would you like to have sir?"

"Will you get me the menu?"

Nike

The two are back down from the tower, and stand at the edge of the cliff. They are well rested, clean, and ready for the journey ahead. Below all they see are the clouds of yesterday, which still fill the valley, obscuring their view.

"Would you clear them up Diablo, so we may see where we are going? Shift them a little so I get a peek of the valley." Destiny knows Diablo would do no such thing. She guesses he would only get more uncomfortable with tuning Gaia and the world around them, as they get closer to their destination. Still she tests him, for amusement alone.

To her surprise a strong wind begins to disrupt the clouds at the end of her words.

"You listened?" Destiny breaks into a smile.

"I am not doing a thing? It's you? Isn't it?" Diablo's asks her.

The wet wind wails as it forces the clouds to scatter, revealing the far-off plains below. Destiny eyes him with suspicion.

"Don't know who, but someone did hear you," Diablo remarks. "Can you guess how far up we are?"

Looking below, Destiny's eyes lock on the vastness. A river meanders at the bottom of the valley, streaming toward the horizon. The peaks of the hills on the two sides are covered with snow, but the forest starts soon enough. The woods march down to the banks of the river, covering the scenery with a tropical dense forest.

A little detail catches her eye. Kissing the banks of the river, parallel on each side are strings of lights. They don't seem to be there to demarcate the borders for the water flow alone, but often they move deeper into the forest, appearing as a network of brighter points. It's hard to be certain from this far, but Destiny thinks they might occasionally be climbing trees and webbing up their canopies in yellow.

"Maybe six thousand feet," Destiny whispers, barely bothering with Diablo's attempts to make small talk.

"Ha ha, no now that would be too many. I reckon about three thousand five hundred feet. Do you know, the altitude makes our horizon appear twice as far off as it would have been if we were on the plains? No creature of the savannas gets a chance to see that far..."

Destiny isn't listening. "What's that?" She points at a small figure flying below them. A pair of brown wings, with streaks of white, but the body isn't visible. "A kite?"

Diablo spots what she is pointing at. It's too far for him to tell if it is mechanical or biological. He makes an educated guess, "It might be someone from the neighborhood's watch, there are four of them. Which one, I can't tell, not without switching to the sight of an eagle; and that is a modification that will break the charm of the neighborhood."

She reaches within her mind to her inventory and calls upon her spyglass. It forms in her hand, a glowing outline at first, which fills in. Metallic with Celtic engravings, bright gold on the rims, but solid black in body.

She looks up at Diablo to check his reaction, "I hope we are allowed to reach in our personal inventories, or is that tuning too much?"

"Sure, you can," answers Diablo. "Haven't I been doing so all this while?" He fears crossing her now.

Pressing it onto her eye she sees and says, "It's a girl who wears a metal helmet, two sets of feathers protrude from it on each side. She wears running shoes and an open jacket that is much too large for her. She has a sling bag on her back, and a pair of wings. They too are far too big for her tiny body."

"Oh! Is she a brunette or a blonde?"

"How is that relevant?" Destiny resents his question.

"It isn't, if you don't want me to recognize her for you."

Destiny bends forward and leans off the edge to get a better look. "I think she is black of hair, but it's hard to tell from this far, for her helmet conceals her head," says Destiny. While they talk, in flight, the subject of their conversation begins to turn away from them.

"NIKE!" calls out Diablo, his voice loud and followed by an echo. "Let us call out to her Destiny."

"What, really? But I don't know her."

"Never mind that, she is coupled to my best friend."

"Well, okay."

"Nike!" they shout out together.

Nike flaps her wings once, and it takes no time for her to reach them. She does a three spot landing and then looks up at them. She has a fringe, her cheeks are red, and voice high-pitched. "Diablo? The Mayor never mentioned you were coming, I suppose it slipped her mind. Welcome."

"How do you do, Nike? The fault lies in me, I come unannounced, but not without invitation. Didn't Damon mention I was coming?"

"Well, he isn't the one to remember such things," Nike smiles. "You are our friend Diablo, you are always welcome in the Leaf Neighborhood."

"The Leaf Neighborhood." Destiny repeats her words, she knows she has heard of it before, a long time ago, before she crossed over from the Academy, before Descartes had suggested avoiding the coupling season and choosing each other for love.

Nike stares at the girl who has interrupted her conversation.

An awkward moment, and Diablo realizes the two have not been introduced to each other. "Destiny, this is Nike, she and three others who are winged keep watch over the Neighborhood."

"Hello," says Destiny, nodding her head in a greeting. Nike does not respond. Destiny notices that she is chewing gum.

"Nike, this is Destiny, a recent..." Diablo stammers, looking for the right word, but Destiny is quick to quench his uneasiness.

"A recently made friend," she fills in.

"A new friend, yes, a new friend." Diablo smiles and looks up at Nike.

"That's the magic word, and it would do. A friend is always welcome in the Leaf Neighborhood. You may enter." Nike reaches in her messenger bag and extracts two smaller packs from it. She flings one each at Diablo and Destiny.

"Open it, and come down the mountain whenever you are ready."

She turns around and walks to the edge. She spread her wings, and is about to fly, when Destiny calls out, "Wait a minute. All one has to do is claim to be a friend of the Leaf Neighborhood and they may enter your settlement. Why, what if I had lied?"

Nike looks back at Destiny, "It would matter none, if not a friend, what would you be? An enemy?" Nike chuckles, "This is Eutopia." She adjusts her hat and is off in the air again.

In flight she remembers, and shouts out to Diablo, "I shall let Damon know of your arrival Diablo."

Destiny waits for her to flap away before speaking, "I have a feeling I haven't made a good first impression."

"Sure you did. You aren't expected to know all the rules of a house before you visit it. Let's go down?"

"With these?" Destiny asks, unzipping the small package given to her by Nike.

"Well, you are in luck, you happen to be with an expert. All I do is glide, and these birdmen suits make it as easy as drinking water. Remember to spread your arms and legs, like this..." Diablo demonstrates. "And keep them that way, until you land." He unzips his package, and puts his on over his clothes. The skintight suit fits him so well that it seems he isn't wearing anything underneath at all.

"You are no good at teaching, Diablo."

"You do have an Absolute Defense, don't you?" he asks, adjusting his collar.

"Yes I do, but I am no daredevil."

"Nor am I," mumbles Diablo, and then steers the conversation away. "Let me help you get those on." He unpacks her suit too and while helping her get her legs in he inquires, "How does yours work? Mine is that of air, it gets dense and forms an invisible wall on the impact side, cushioning me whenever I could get hurt."

"It's that of water," says Destiny. "If Eutopia calculates that I am to have an accident, it will place me in an impenetrable bubble of water. But I don't wish to fall off a cliff Diablo. It won't be fun," she pleads.

"Trust your instincts, don't tune. Glide. Aim for the river. Land softly," are his last words before he leaps off the cliff.

Destiny hesitates, her thoughts go back to Descartes. He would never put her in such a position, his priority is always to make sure she is comfortable and safe. She watches Diablo glide; he looks back at her, and perhaps he beckons her, but he is too far for her to be certain.

She isn't convinced. The plunge would undo the bath she had in the tower; she trusts not the suit's design. She nearly gives up on thinking of home. She wonders what Descartes would say; in all probability, he would have disapproved of her taking such a risk. "A leap without tuning isn't right" he would have insisted.

Then again, he isn't here, and she need not consult him. "What the hell," she says out loud. "What's the worst that could happen? A spoilt dress? That too is unlikely." Under her breath, she gives herself a count down, "1, 2, 3," and she takes the plunge.

The wind is loud, the fall steep at first, and unnerving. She knows her Absolute Defense will kick in if she gets in trouble, yet adrenalin clouds her thoughts. In a while she spreads her arms and legs, and decelerates.

Rock face with patches of snow give way to a blur of treetops.

She doubts if she is gliding, or it's the earth that is zipping by her. She will tune if necessary, but like a real daredevil she will play with death.

The hills don't form a gradual slope but are steep and then they rise up again. She knows she is falling but the knowledge that death in moments isn't an impossibility fills her with thrill. Reaching closer to the center of the valley, her attention is focused on gliding; she notices not the trees, the lights, and those that live in them. "Aim for the river, land softly," Diablo's words echo in her.

She panics on reaching the river, and is tempted to tune and fly. For the life of her, she can't tell what he could have meant by 'landing softly'. It matters not now, she has no time. It's all too fast.

Instinctively she aligns herself parallel to the river, the best that she can. Habituated to regulated flight, the freefall touchdown occurs far too quickly for her. It isn't smooth; instead of a firm landing, the water pushes her back in the air. She bounces like a skipping stone. Fear grips her, and on her third contact water gets in her lungs.

"Swim to the shore Destiny," she can hear Diablo call, when her head reemerges. "You landed gracefully Destiny. Full marks for bravery." Destiny lets a water fountain out of her lips. Speaking not a word, she starts swimming to the shore.

Her legs feel fatigued, though she can't consider free falling as much work. Reaching the shore, she takes a few steps on the narrow beach and falls on her back, flat, panting.

Destiny can see three figures towering above her, Nike, Diablo and a stranger. The stranger speaks first, "Are you okay?"

Diablo speaks second, "How did you like it? Gliding."

She tries to reply, but coughs out water instead. Seeing Destiny in distress Diablo extracts the water trapped within her; trickling up her mouth it forms a free floating mass above her chest. He then commands the water that drenches her to leave her body and join the spherical mass, and by a flick of his fingers this ball of water finds its way into the river.

Nike and Diablo help Destiny get on her feet. They don't let her stand on her own until she is steady and utters, "Let's do it again." They both crack up and Destiny too joins them, though she is careful not to cough again.

Machiavelli's Mannequins

The ransacked room is bright with large windows that let the sun in. Shards of glass, turned tables, and wine stained clothing litter the floor. The desolation of the gondola being complete, Machiavelli dines in relative quiet. He occupies the only unspoiled table, whose riches include a bloody steak, an unused napkin, and a bottle of rosé spared from being turned into a brawler's knife.

He slices into the steak, lazily eyeing a wooden ripped off arm crawling on the carpet. He tosses the knife back on the table and looks at his writings on the table cloth. There are two columns of digits written in ink.

"How could I forget the City coordinates for the Observatory?" he mumbles, and then a little louder, "Any luck spotting the right island Captain?"

A hollow musical voice from the chart room responds, "No my Elder, there are far too many of them, and these maps aren't precise. Many of the islands aren't where they are supposed to be."

A whoosh and a clang of metal on metal persuades Machiavelli to look back up from the table. "Ah, there is still fight left in you. Good." A pair of mannequins cross swords. The one in green has the upper hand, cornering the other, forcing it to cower.

"You have might on your side Green, hack him down, target the Red's feet. This will be so much more entertaining with music." Grilled speakers set in the walls and the ceiling loudly play a composition of majestic proportions. 'O Fortuna'. The mannequin follows its master's command, puts down its defenses and attempts an attack on the opponent's legs. Bad advice.

It goes ill for the Green; twice the Red's blade makes contact with its torso, slicing through the uniform, chipping away on its wooden frame. "Fool of a puppet. That wasn't an order, I was rooting for you. Use your own judgment. Oh wait, you can't. You don't have a brain."

The mannequins aren't able to understand Machiavelli's commands. Confounded, they step away from one another.

"No, no, no. Fight, and let your fate decide who lives." Machiavelli gets up from his chair, takes off his coat, folds it, and places it on the table. He takes his time to roll up his sleeves, paying little heed to the dueling puppets or the broken ones.

The Green gains his footing again, pushing the Red through a glass cabinet door, breaking shelves and china. Machiavelli closes his eyes, and starts dancing, wording parts of the song along. "Status Malus, Vana Salus." He leaps on his toes, never touching the rubble of the room.

The Red's comeback is hurling Green headfirst into an airliner sized window. The battle's end is timed perfectly for Machiavelli: the crescendo of the medieval poem recited, he may revel unhindered in its climax.

He reaches the mannequins before his favorite couplet of the song passes. Red stands a distance away from Green, resting his hands on a long sword, the tip of which touches the ground between its feet. A style typical of mannequins. Green may struggle all he might, he can't retrieve his neck back from the window.

Machiavelli flicks Red's blade away and severs Green's head in one smooth gesture. "Quod per sortem, sternit fortem." His body crashed to the floor in a heap. Machiavelli hands back the sword to Red and remarks, "The trouble with listening to classical opera is you can't hear anything after, and the trouble with breaking all your toys is you don't have anything left to play with."

The music stops. Machiavelli strolls back to the table and takes a deep gulp from the bottle of wine. "Are we there yet Captain?" He wipes his lips with the napkin.

"No my lord, but I might have found the right cluster of islands."

"Good, good." He wears his coat again, and enters the control room. Made in its entirety with glass, it's lit better than the insides of a prism. The sky is clear with no hint of clouds. Below his feet through the glass Machiavelli finds the blue: an ocean teeming with tiny islands. Scudding over them, in search of the hidden institute of the Observatory, Machiavelli knows locating the institute by chance is unlikely.

The captain of the vessel, a puppet with a cylindrical head and a round mouth reports, "We are close my Elder, it's here somewhere, underneath us, on one of the fifty islands we can see from up here." His pronunciation is riddled with whistles; he wears a sailor's blue uniform, with large black pointy collars.

They come in all sizes. The smallest ones enclose lagoons, and are covered in heather, ferns and palm trees. Machiavelli knows the Observatory is an establishment too large for such tiny islands to conceal.

The middle sized ones are flat, with inviting virgin beaches, and thick tropical flora. The Observatory could not be hidden among these either, their tree lines are too short to keep the tower out of sight.

The bigger islands are most suited for a structure as large as the Observatory; their hills cast shadows large enough to hide the white complex in their shade. Thankfully there are no more than a dozen such islands, and all Machiavelli needs to do is fly over them one after the other.

"Let us check them out in descending order shall we? Take me to the one with the highest volcano."

"Aye sir." The puppet holds the metallic wheel controlling the rudder with his wooden palms and turns it clockwise. The ship shudders as it turns, the floor shakes, and Machiavelli leans on the wall to keep his balance.

The captain keeps at it, and the control wheel spins many full turns, but Machiavelli sees no change in the scenery outside. "Spin it harder, the Zeppelin isn't turning." The mannequin does as he is told, causing a near earthquake within the airship. Still there is no change. Their vessel appears stuck.

"Stop. Let me think captain, something very strange is afoot here."

The puppet releases the control wheel. The motion of the airship slows down to a halt.

"The rudder is working, we surely are turning, otherwise the vibrations would not have been significant enough to cause such a ruckus."

"Aye sire. We are turning," the Captain echoes him.

"I got it!" Machiavelli is back up on his feet. "The Zeppelin isn't at fault, it's the islands. They are in motion."

Indeed, once the Zeppelin stops turning, the islands appear to be sailing. In irregular shapes they move in unison, taking a circular path clockwise. "Look at them Captain, they have only but started. Soon they shall gather speed, and rearrange themselves in a manner so that all your charts and maps are rendered useless. How will you find me the Observatory then Captain?"

Machiavelli's toy has no reply, it merely moves on its two legs at the spot where it stands, bobbing its head.

"You won't have to though, for I have lost the element of surprise. The white tower has spotted us." Machiavelli is about to ask his captain to leap off the gondola as punishment for his failings when the translucent rotary phone begins to ring.

"Machiavelli what are you doing in my skies?"

"Cassandra darling, it's been so long since I have seen you."

"I am no one's darling Machiavelli, and spare me the smooth talk, you know you are wasting it on me. Why are you here, and why didn't you ring in before and say you were coming?"

"All right, all right, you got me, this isn't a casual visit. I am here on a mission assigned by the Beloved of Eutopia, and I am already running late, so would you please tell me where I can park my ship?"

The line remains silent a while. "Hello, Cassandra don't leave me hanging on the telephone."

"Go to the window on your left."

"Yes."

"Do you see a cliff with a waterfall on an island?"

"Wait a minute, hmm. Yup I spotted it."

"You may park your vessel there Machiavelli."

Vague Vincent

"Destiny, meet Daphne, the current Mayor of the Leaf village."

Destiny regards the stranger, her face is pale and childlike. Her hair hay, and her skin the light green of a young plant's shoot. "Hello," she greets Destiny and then addresses Diablo, "It was good of you to tune and will the water out of her. Her distress necessitated it. Though it's my duty to remind you to avoid using the bestowed powers of Eutopia in this neighborhood as much as you can."

"Sure Mayor Daphne."

"Let us go then, it's quite a walk. Damon is waiting for us at the Market, on the other side of the neighborhood, at a Ramen bar."

Destiny skips the conversation the others are having by hanging back and letting them amble on ahead. She is taken by all that's new. It's not Daphne's vogue, nor is it the hundred meter tall trees. It isn't the intricate woodwork which makes the verandas around their trunks and the bridges joining one tree to another, but the hustle of the busy ways and streets that stands out the most.

"Destiny is everything all right?" Diablo waits for her, letting the others move on.

"Oh! Yes, I am fine."

"Aren't you coming along?"

"Sure I am."

The two dwellers of the Leaf Neighborhood lead the way, walking a few paces ahead; Destiny and Diablo follow behind them. They walk under the giant trees and bridges of bluish translucent glass, which play so neatly with the light seeping through the high canopies.

Several easy wooden steps take them up into the neighborhood among the leaves. Each tree is surrounded by verandas around their trunk; they act as pathways, all six feet wide. Enough for a pair of merchant carts to move in opposite directions without blocking each other. The carts that do tour the streets aren't pulled by man, machine or beast but they move themselves. Each of them piled with one colorful item or another. The first one to pass them by is full of grapes.

"May I have some?" asks Destiny.

"Sure. Everything is shared here, there isn't much sense of possession in this neighborhood." He picks up a bunch of grapes from the cart and hands it to Destiny.

"I don't believe it. We do share at our hive, too, but only the lesser products of our imagination. Everything? For real? Won't they get jealous of one another?" Destiny blabs on, munching on yum grapes, finding the idea quite unearthly.

"Well, I don't understand it quite well. Let us run up to Daphne and ask her." He rushes ahead, and Destiny is left with no choice but to chase after. They catch up with Nike and Daphne together, Destiny to the right of Daphne, and Diablo to the left of Nike.

"How does this place work?" Destiny asks, being closer to Daphne.

Diablo is embarrassed with Destiny's choice of blunt words, but to his surprise the Mayor replies with utmost seriousness. "It's a novel idea, and still a limited subculture among Newman, but here one does not compete with others, there are no duels, no show of strengths, will of tuning, or comparison of style or art. Here we are all simple. Everyone must choose a handful of things they make best, whether food, tools or something bigger. We make them in sufficient quantity that all in this Neighborhood have plenty. We store them in the Eutopian Library too: the recipe for them is available to one and all."

"Ever heard of an open source economy?" Nike sweeps in the conversation.

"Yes, I think I have seen it mentioned in an old paperback book."

"That's it then." In the same breath Nike continues, "Mayor Daphne if you don't mind, I will do another flyby patrol of our borders, and then join you all for super."

"Sure." Daphne has an uncanny habit of responding far too hastily, at times before the other has finished talking.

Nike takes to the air again; the spread of her wings appears much larger now in the context of these streets and glass bridges. "Sayōnara." She waves at them, and disappears within a couple of flaps of her wings.

Daphne continues as if she was never interrupted. "The creations here are partially tuned into existence, and part result of the skill of our hands. We know we don't have palaces as grand as you may have in your bubble, nor match the billion year knowledge of the Elders, but those things we do produce, such as the grapes you are having, are worth being sought after."

"They sure are delicious, I can't stop having them."

Daphne smiles with care. "Nice! It is only here in the Leaf Neighborhood that our ranks didn't shrink after the incident of White. Some dwellers did desert us, but they too couldn't keep away for long. The simplistic charm of our community proved irresistible," she boasts. "We are nearly there. I shall tell you more once we get to the Ramen restaurant."

The avenues here aren't as crowded as the Boulevard Amsterdam, and the streets are quieter. They are not deserted either; in between the carts do parties of two or more, at times five, walk together. They speak in whispers, not to keep secrets but to keep the sounds of the forest. Destiny has been trying to catch their faces, but all she manages to see are their eyes and their hair. Many wear scarves or hats, a few even fashion themselves with head to toe robes, and for those who aren't making an effort to hide their features, it so happens that they look away every time Destiny tries to see them.

A gradual turn along a tree reveals another set of stairs leading to the heart of the Leaf Neighborhood. A banyan tree, which makes everyone feel like ants. Dotted with neon signs, the twin stairway avenues that spiral around the tree reach far up to the canopy. They have many apartments and joints along them, some carved within the trunk, others weaved as nests hanging by the branches.

"I wish Descartes was here. He would have loved this tree."

"Who's that?" asks Diablo.

"The other half of me. He is my companion, together we make a couple."

"Oh! All right." Diablo hesitates a little before continuing, "I am quite fond of the Leaf's marketplace too."

The setting sun all but disappears as they climb another long set of narrow crowded wooden planks to the first level of the market.

"We have to go up, and it might be strenuous, but the effort is worth the food and the decor of the restaurant."

"Restaurant. That is so old school," Destiny giggles.

"Didn't I tell you we have been trying to recreate the Earth of Old here. I don't mind the hike Mayor, do you Destiny?"

Destiny is still all smiles, she shakes her head to convey she is fine with the climb.

Unlike the galleries of the trees before, the pathways here weren't a later addition, but the tree's mold incorporated them. From its trunk protrude grooves that serve as the streets of the market. On their left, within the tree, is a line of spacious shops, cafés, and bars, lit by inviting candles, lamps, and chandeliers. To their right, from the pathways above hang stores in nests, a gap away from the street.

The alleys are crowded here, and the chatter of the neighborly folk is more noticeable. Destiny is too preoccupied with admiring the market for conversations, and so is Diablo, even though he has been here before. They let the walk and the place sink in, until Daphne suggests, "Let us rest at the next diner, it's called The Vague Vincent, and has the most appetizing calamari."

"Sure," Destiny agrees.

"I don't think I will be able to stomach any food until I see Damon, though I would love to give you company."

"Well then you might have to wait for a while," Daphne tells Diablo with an air of knowing something he doesn't.

The moment they take iron chairs under the pergola of the Vague Vincent, it starts to rain: An instant downpour that catches the pedestrians off guard, scattering them, forcing them to run for cover.

Daphne reaches down under the table to her waist, and brings up a pocket watch. She checks the hour, and declares, "As the Mayor of the Neighborhood I have the authority to set the rain times. I have asked it not to stay for more than twenty minutes."

Diablo is the one to probe further, "If you do decide when it rains, why don't you warn everyone? Only so none suffer any inconvenience."

"The Leaf Neighborhood wishes to experience the rains as it used to be on the Earth of Old. They wish to be surprised. My instructions are clear: make it rain for a total of sixty minutes every day. Those who find themselves outside consider themselves lucky."

"Magnificent." His attention is then taken away by a group of four dwellers who run across the street by the Vague Vincent, laughing, shouting at one another, carefree of the rain. They are followed by heartfelt music coming from across the alley. Diablo's thoughts now rest on its source. A nested stall filled with old records, but with no shopkeeper. A jazz tune escapes it, in which a lady seems to be struggling to find the bitter sweetness of a gloomy Sunday.

Destiny, on the other hand, peeps into the diner. There seem to be two guests inside, a pleasant looking girl in red and a gentleman in a proper coat and tie with a trilby hat on. They both sip whiskey, not talking to one another. She wonders who they are, how old they must be, and how often they leave their own Bubbles of Perfect Existence.

Daphne, the only one truly present there, picks up the only two things on the table, a stack of sticky notes and a pencil. She takes a page and writes, "Salted calamari with garlic." The note flies off with the wind, but Destiny stretches out and catches it.

"Let it go," instructs Daphne.

Off Destiny's hand it flies inside the diner, makes a swirl and lands, pasting itself on the docket counter. "I apologize, I didn't realize its flight was intentional, and not the work of the free willed wind."

"No harm done. It's okay, it's all good," Daphne reassures Destiny, when they hear footsteps from within, with the hum of a rain song coming close toward them.

A man in a chef's hat, beach shorts and nothing else approaches their table. "Greetings Mayor, the thought of rain had just crossed my mind, and you dropped in, along with the clouds. Such a pleasant coincidence. Here are your favorite appetizers; would you stay for supper?"

"Good Evening Vincent," Daphne greets the host. "No not a coincidence, I was thinking of the rain, of you and your calamari too, so here I am. Regrettably my stay can't be long, I have already promised a visit to a few friends up-tree." Her disappointment is genuine.

"Well, perhaps some other time. Enjoy your meal." Vincent turns around and retreats back inside the dinner.

Daphne picks up a ringlet and announces, "Dig in everyone."

Diablo wasn't too attentive of the conversation between Vincent and Daphne, yet he found it odd. "Why didn't we ask him to join us? This is his café, isn't it?"

Destiny, who is done picking her grapes and is about to reach for the squid, withdraws her hand. "He is right, where are our manners; should I fetch him."

"Ha ha, you two are a considerate bunch. It's good, but there is no need, he won't join us. It's a part of his act, we are his 'customers'. Vague Vincent won't feel authentic if he dines with everyone who visits his 'joint'." Daphne gestures her apostrophes. "And besides, he takes a long time to warm up to new people."

"Oh!" says Destiny. "I do feel awkward though, not sharing."

"It's fine. I shall have his share." Diablo takes a bite.

"That doesn't count, you weren't eating anyway."

"Sure it does." Diablo beams at her, and has a huge chunk of the servings.

"Oh! Yeah, I can play too." Destiny has a go as well, and now half of the serving is gone. An alarmed Daphne takes away the dish from them. "Wait a minute, it was I who ordered. Slow down now would you guys?"

Diablo's eyes bulge as the juices fill his palate, "It's amazing, I want more."

"All right then take the sticky note and order some more, but you must get done with them soon, the rain is about to stop and we have a long way to go."

Oracle Cassandra

The Captain is accompanied by the last functional mannequin on the passenger side: the victorious redcoat officer. They pull hard together on a heavy chained anchor, attempting to wrap it around an immovable rock.

"Secure the anchor, I don't want my zeppelin straying away with the wind."

Machiavelli's command appears to have a paradoxical effect. The weaker built captain loses his grip and the chain skids out of his hand, and the red court warrior isn't able to keep the anchor steady either. His unwavering devotion to his master doesn't allow him to release his grip, and he boomerangs into the sky in the elastic rebound of the anchor and its chain.

"Oh fate, why must I have to do everything on my own."

Machiavelli calls the anchor back to the ground and its inanimate soul obliges. A light circular motion of his index fingers is enough to bound the Zeppelin to the island. "I suppose I should have been more forgiving to our other passengers Captain. More hands could have saved the Red. Never mind now, I shall renew the crew before we set sail again."

The puppet does not voice his opinion. He has none.

The Observatories' island is made peculiar by the absence of regular trees; instead, it's graced by a swaying forest of bamboo grass. They are tall, thin and shrill as the zephyr in them. There is an abundance of rock pools spread out between the bamboos, with the people in charge peering in them. Uniformed in white and silver livery they take notes and ramble around with a hastiness only the very important people have. One such masked Observer, who happens to be passing by the visitors on his pressing exigency stops to deliver them a message, "The Oracle awaits you in the tower Machiavelli."

"Thank you. I shall be with her presently."

The Observer speaks into his mask, "Elder Machiavelli has landed and parked his Zeppelin with little complications, wrecking a puppet, who is stuck in the higher reaches of the grass. We are sending him upstairs."

A moment's pause in which his eyes betray him, and reveal he is receiving a reply, "Go on sir, I have been asked to remind you not to disturb the tranquility of the island."

"Not to worry, I shall be doubly careful young fellow." Machiavelli gets going, brushing by the Observer, murmuring to himself, "The new lot these days have no appetite for the nuances of the spindle and the wheel of fortune. 'An Elder will I become, serve Eutopia I will.'" He mocks them. "What do you say captain, should they not learn first to humor time? They do have years innumerable on them, would they not do better by lighting up the air they carry around themselves?"

The wooden pilot stays on Machiavelli's heel but does not partake in the conversation. "Don't bother, I know your argument already. Were you not about to say that I must understand they have only recently been inducted into the Order of Elders? That they are expected to be enthusiastic, how else will they keep a watch... yadi-yari-yara."

They reach a gorge at the foot of the volcano. From its plunge pool rises the White Tower of the Observatory, which scrapes the sky higher than the adjacent mountain. "Wait here," Machiavelli commands the Captain, and then flies up along the tower, entering its highest chamber through an open tinted cathedral styled window...

'By waiting for him' Machiavelli had not imagined that the

Observer meant she would be in the veranda standing in front of drawn curtains, blocking his entry.

"Welcome Machiavelli, what mischief brings you here?" Cassandra stands in the center in a black dress, wearing her hair in an extravagant long living blond ponytail, which moves by its own device. With cheeks in blush, crisp lips, teeth white as snow, and a body which isn't meek or loud, Cassandra, though rarely ever spotted in the House of Pleasure, is quite a celebrity there.

Machiavelli reaches her hand and kisses it in a formal manner. "Oracle." He continues, "I am here at the bidding of the High Mentor Ananta himself. Do you remember the failures of the coupling season a decade ago? The pair that refused to part ways, choosing to be coupled together, citing the excuse of self-discovered love? And the unfortunate man for whom we could never find a suitable companion?"

"Yes, yes, I have been keeping a close watch on them at the behest of the High Mentor. What of them? They flirt with evolution and artificial intelligence, but haven't yet broken any rules. Wait a minute." Cassandra loses some color. "Don't you say the decision to realign them has already been taken. Only a week ago I petitioned the council to give Destiny and Descartes more time."

Machiavelli splutters, faces away, and informs her, "It's unfortunate that I must disappoint you, but the scheme has been approved and is already in motion. Under my supervision Diablo and Destiny have met, and are presumably frolicking in the gardens of the City."

"How dare you? Are you here to poke fun at me? Add insult to injury?" Cassandra isn't pleased and her sharp tone reflects this, but the motion of her hair is clearer at spelling out her displeasure. She takes a quick jab at Machiavelli, and her hair shoots at him with a loud whipping crack.

His reflexive Absolute Defense of rocks attempts to prevent Cassandra's strike. Machiavelli had not ruled out such a reaction, and so he was quick to get on his knees, reducing the size of her target. A stone shield wall is brought into existence between the two Elders. "You got my arm Cassandra, I am bleeding."

"A pity, you will soil my floor." Her rage embodies itself in the darkening of her chamber. "Are you unaware of your own foolhardiness. Has the entire Eutopia gone mad!" She stretches, growing taller, and her expression grows grim. "I have seen into the future Machiavelli. I have studied the data, and have watched these children their entire life." Machiavelli can't see her forbidding form, but he can feel her thin bony fingers grip his stonewall defense. "We should let them be," Cassandra's voice cracks. "Ananta's scheme won't work this time." Yet a note of defeat rings clear in her tone.

"Don't shoot the messenger Cassandra, I don't wish to duel with you. I have merely been following orders. The decision has been taken, I am here to make sure it's executed in a manner such that no one is harmed."

Cassandra mulls it over – she is out of options. "All right, you may come out. I won't harm you."

The stone wall crumbles adding unwanted rubble onto the white marble floor; Cassandra returns to her deity form.

Diablo conducts himself around the heap with care, so the many colors of his blazer aren't stained by dust.

"I must observe how the courtship of Destiny and Diablo is going, and keep an eye on Descartes so he doesn't do anything rash." Machiavelli appears unscratched. "Why wear such a cruel frown Cassandra? Yes I lied, you didn't touch me, I was fast enough. And don't worry about the floor, the rubble will fade away on its own soon enough."

"Your well-or-ill-being isn't a concern of mine. I just don't understand, it was Ananta who appointed me as the Oracle three centuries ago. Why bestow me with such a lofty title, if he deems me incapable."

"Fate works in mysterious ways Oracle Cassandra."

Ramen Bar

Further up-tree in the canopy, the market spreads away from the trunk onto the branches, creating a network of tiny alleyways. The street Daphne leads them to is wrapped in a green creeper encircling the wood. Each of the creeper's spirals that hug the banyan's branch shoots out an independent set of dangling leaves.

The first of these leaves don't hang low, but are looking up, rigid and cup shaped. They resemble the hues of a dark green shrub: the little hobber. It is accompanied by two horizontal cylindrical spikes, the curved surfaces of which act as seats for the patrons of the Ramen Bar. The leaf itself works as a bowl for the Ramen. Under the green bowl, hanging by a chain, a polished copper plate nests a fire to keep the broth at an optimum temperature. Further below dangle petals in the purple of wisteria.

A vertical neon sign at the start of the street reads, "Ramen Bar. The food of Gods, not magically turning you into Pigs!"

"Damon happens to be on the table number 404," Daphne announces.

"Let us hurry, have we not made him wait for quite a while already," Diablo is growing impatient.

"He very much fancies spending his evenings here, so I don't think the wait would have bothered him much; nevertheless, let's get moving. Mind your step, jump over the creeper's stem, they are hard and aren't moved easily, don't let them trip you."

They don't have to walk far, skipping thrice over the tube-like stems of the creeper, they find Damon sitting with Nike. A tiny limb that has them walking in a single file connects the spikes for seats and the leaf for a table, with the rest of the tree.

Damon reaches out to Diablo, holds his hand, and helps him onto the bench. They hug each other as old friends do. Damon is the first to speak, "It's been too long."

"Far too long," confirms Diablo.

The two lads then help Destiny and Daphne onto the benches too. The three dwellers of the Neighborhood take one side, Diablo and Destiny take the other.

"Hi again," Nike greets Destiny.

"Hi."

"Destiny meet my old partner in crime, from the days at the Academy: Damon. Destiny is my new found friend, and mayhap a colleague in the near future." Diablo hesitates with the introductions, not yet confident about how to explain her presence.

"Any friend of yours is a friend of mine. Welcome, Destiny, to the Ramen Bar, the only known Ramen restaurant in Eutopia. The night is young and we haven't even started. I need to know everything about you, and more, while we get drunk out of our wits."

Before Destiny could respond, he turns around and tugs on the tendril, causing his seat to shiver, and a tiny panel in its green stem to open up. He sticks his head inside and screams "Whiskey!" He then shuts the panel and explains, "It works on air pressure, you see, our bottle will be here within a minute."

"That's remarkable," observes Diablo.

A popping sound notifies the table that their order has arrived. On opening the panel Damon retrieves a bottle which only spells its age: twelve. The bottle isn't alone though; it's accompanied by a slab of clear ice, crystal glasses, and knives.

"The finer things will always have you wait on them, so give me a moment to fix your drinks." In a flash Damon draws out the ice slab onto the table, and hacks it in five equal pieces. Then using the knife he begins to carve them rhythmically. "Tick, Tick,

Tick," sounds the beat. Neither Destiny nor Diablo know the purpose of Damon's handiwork, though they do find his manual precision soothing. Mesmerized, they watch him until Daphne chooses to lead the conversation once more, "Are you comfortable here, Destiny?"

"Yes, I guess, though I would admit sitting on a spike without a backrest feels risky. I wonder, what if one of us slips and falls?"

"That's my favorite part, you glutton here to your heart's delight and once satisfied, you kick back, relax, lean back and fall... only for a leaf of autumn to find you on your way down, catch you and cradle you to a spot of comfort and sleep," Nike spurts out with glee.

Destiny giggles and says, "That's sick." She looks at the back of a leaf, which seems to float free over the slow cooking ramen within the table. Bubbles from its depths sporadically disturb the surface, altering the direction in which the covering leaves have been floating.

'Tick, Tick, Tick," Damon hacks on.

She looks up to find both Daphne and Nike stare at her crossly, "Oh no, I wasn't criticizing, I mean the good sick. I apologize, I better be more careful, you aren't used to me. I have a habit of calling things I like 'sick'. It's a silly habit, I know, but I am stuck with it."

Damon is unaware of the mood, but still butts into their conversation. "What's a good sick? A small or a large?"

"Large," replies Destiny.

"It used to be a common style of speech, to appreciate things you fancy with words that traditionally have a negative connotation. Though the fad fell out of use a few generations ago," Daphne informs the table, being the only Elder present there.

"That's interesting," remarks Destiny. "I think I picked it up from my mother."

"Well that explains it," Daphne grins.

"The first timer will be served first." Damon hands Destiny

her drink. The ice is a perfect sphere, touching the crystal at five points: One at the bottom end of the glass, and the other four on each side. The whiskey fills the convex negative spaces left by the ice, covering the frozen ball in its amber filter.

"It does look beautiful," Destiny observes.

Damon winks at her, "All right then," and continues, "Before we probe you further Destiny, it would be impolite of us not to tell you a little about ourselves. Diablo and I used to be best mates at the Academy and formed a Duo; for years we traveled and trained hard together under many Mentors. We parted ways on leaving the Academy. Diablo had a prolonged, fun filled, but alas, a fruitless coupling season. I, on the other hand, was unaware of Nike, who had been in waiting for me in Boulevard Amsterdam for years. She sensed my arrival and was drawn to me. On first sight it felt right, and soon enough a letter from Elder Pax confirmed our suspicion: we were to be coupled together." Damon takes a long breath at the end of his monolog. "And now it's your turn Destiny."

"Wait a minute, this doesn't add up. If you are as old as Diablo, and Diablo has four years on me, then why would you choose to live in a Neighborhood of the city, instead of your personal Bubble of Perfect Existence? And how can a coupling season be fruitless?"

"I am glad you asked," Nike starts off loquaciously. "It was my idea, and a brilliant one at that, to correct the wrongs done to us by circumstances, and the result is right in front of you. Isn't it wonderful?"

"Tell them already Nike." Knowing how poor a storyteller Nike can be, Damon edges her on, as he continues carving another ice ball.

"All right, all right, so I had about two score of years on Damon when we met, and the one aspect of us that resisted aligning was maturity. The Elders told us it would take us thirteen years for the age gap to turn irrelevant."

"You are kidding me, I did not know this," Diablo exclaims.

"No I am not. What is more, the Elders suggested we don't take a Bubble of Perfect Existence but wait here in the City, until we were ready."

Both Destiny and Diablo gasp, "You have been living here for nine years?" Destiny asks in horror.

Damon passes Daphne her glass. "Don't be ridiculous, spending a year here is hard enough as it is, nine would have been the death of me."

"So then what did you do?"

"We refused," Damon tells them with a shrug.

"The debate lasted for days," Nike continues. "The Elders would again and again bid us to stay in the City, they would warn us of the un-pleasantries and conflicts that lay in store for us in our bubble. We rebuked them, saying they underestimated us. We reminded them of their own promises, on how a perfect companion could never let one down. We argued that our lives in our very own Bubble of Perfect Existence would be a breeze compared to a life in the City."

"Oh! Don't get me started, I am well versed with the arguments of the Elders, Descartes and I were subjected to them too." Destiny rolls her eyes.

"Well we were lucky for that's when my Nike had an epiphany." Damon places two more glasses in front of Nike and Diablo.

"Don't you steal my thunder Damon, let me tell the story."

"Sure love, the stage is yours." He gets back to the ice slab, crafting the last ball for himself.

"My suggestion was simple: we would spend every alternate year in the City, freezing our bubble. But to keep our bubble in sync with the rest of Eutopia, we speeded up time within it, making every day of the years in there twice as long."

Nike stops and looks at them, expecting applause. "Don't you get it?"

"No, I fear, you would have to elaborate." Destiny isn't sure where the genius lies in all this.

"Duh, we only ended up shrinking the era of awkwardness between us from thirteen, to a mere nine years."

"Ah!" exclaims Diablo. "Now I see. Destiny..." Diablo affirms he has her attention. "They speeded up time, just the way you had in the backyard of Elder Machiavelli's Welcoming House, only they did so for their entire bubble. They set it to run at a speed twice that of the General Eutopian Time, quickening the pace at which they got used to each other. They would spend one year in the City at the bidding of the Elders, and the other in their bubble, with the year inside being twice as long."

"That's not only an ingenious idea, it also calls for constant effort and deliberation. Didn't it tire you, always keeping in mind that your bubble's clock mustn't slow down?" Destiny inquires, more for the sake of learning.

"One gets used it, besides it's a small price to pay for perfection, don't you think."

"I wouldn't know." Destiny voices her thought so softly that it doesn't reach the others.

Diablo can tell the slight dip in Destiny's spirit, and judges he should distract her by pushing the conversation on. "If my calculations are correct, you are soon to complete the tenure suggested by the Elders. Though I wonder if they will see it that way; won't the Elders call your speeding up time foul play?"

"Yes, there is always a chance, and that is why we shall be visiting the Omniscient tonight."

"That too, pretending to be a bickering couple," Nike adds with mischief.

"We shall ask the Omniscient once more how compatible we are. I believe the results would be more favorable to us than the Elders expect. Armed with the new report we shall approach the Council of Elders, and demand they rid us of the mandatory stay in the City every alternate year."

Daphne, who has stayed quiet, yawns, "I do realize friends

reunited often get carried away, but let us not ignore the food. Pick up your glasses now."

"Apologies Mayor, our chatter must feel quite naive and dry to you. Besides, I am famished, let us dine." Nike is respectful.

Everyone on the table picks up their glasses, not to have a sip, but to make way for Daphne to remove the leaf that has been substituting as the desktop all this while. Peeling off the covers releases the warm aroma of pork and spices. Its surface doesn't boil, but the liquid sizzles every few minutes, with bubbles rising from its depths.

"There is a lot happening in there," Diablo ponders aloud, spying some spring onions floating inside.

"Yup, that ramen is alive. Here, take your chopsticks." Damon tosses a pair of chopsticks to everyone on the table. "Dive in everybody."

The noodle seems to have a will of its own, moving free, at times dogging the diners' attempts to gulp them down, but often relenting and wrapping themselves around their sticks. Pieces of mushroom will entangle in the noodles for every alternating bite.

"This is so much fun," Destiny chuckles, going for one of the dozen sliced eggs floating on the surface. The eggs tread carefully so as to not sink and remain available for the scooping. The meat is sliced pork, and they, too, do their best to remain close to the surface, sailing the violent broth in a steady formation, individual pieces of them partially covering one another, but letting each member breathe. The spinach leaves lump together, occasionally drawing close to the chopsticks, but usually staying clear until they read a definite movement that seeks them.

The food is engrossing, and the reward of every bite and scoop relishing enough to grind the talk over supper down to grunts of pleasure and munching.

Master of Mind

The table holds far more ramen than our party of five can devour. The broth still brings them heart filling warmth, yet they can no longer eat with the same ferocity as when they had started. Their chopsticks take longer each time in making the trip to their lips and back into the bowl. Each morsel is a challenge; they doubt if they can stomach another bite, or as Nike had warned, would gluttony indeed get the better of them.

"That was delightful, wasn't it?" Damon comments.

"Hear, hear," manages Diablo.

"I have nothing to follow that with, but yeah, it was a great meal."

Daphne, the lightest eater among them, unhinges the cast aside pair of leaves from the branch where they hung in waiting, and covers the cup shaped bowl with them, hiding the residue ramen, and giving them a tabletop once more. "Make me another drink Damon, we still have to hear the tale of Destiny and Diablo."

"Yes, my Mayor."

He spreads his hand, reaching out to the panel, attempting to fetch more ice. He does so with all the lethargy he can muster, expending no real energy at all. "Would blocks of ice do? Carving them in globes is far too much work for now."

"Sure," Daphne accepts, and Destiny adds, "Yeah, that would do."

"Come on mystery girl, tell us your story." Nike keeps her feet up, with her heavy boots on the table, and balances her back on Damon's side.

"Where do I start?"

"From the beginning."

"Beginning of what, life has been too long to be capsuled in a conversation."

Daphne chuckles, "Imagine how I feel, I who counts her age in decades instead of years. Give it a try Destiny, tell us those things that matter, the things that makes you: you. Share the things you are comfortable with, but don't forget: one is always entitled to secrets."

Once again Destiny stares at the table. "What's important?" she ponders aloud. She knows all eyes are fixed on her. "I never had a chance at perfection." The words echo in her mind, and she can feel the truth in them. "A few more days, and you Nike and Damon shall share a bubble world better than Eden. You worked for it, you knew its value." Destiny grows quiet. "I am sorry, I did not wish to criticize you guys." She knows her guilt is born of envy and not of ill manners.

"Oh darling, don't be hard on yourself, let it all out." Daphne caresses Destiny's bobbed hair.

In a moment of weakness Destiny admits, "We were but kids. We rushed in. Descartes and I weren't paired by the Elders, nor did the Omniscient confirm us. We weren't apt for one another." She stops, and revisits those fateful days when she and Descartes had held strong against the Elders, how passionate they were, and how uncurbable was their will. Destiny laughs, she will not be patronized by strangers. "We made a choice. In hindsight it might not have been the wisest one, but it wasn't wrong. We knew what we were signing up for, it's only that at times I forget the bargain we made, and the things we so readily gave up. You must think I am silly, defying a social practice older than Eutopia, whose wisdom is undoubtable. Yet I am not the only one, many have done so before me, and they have been fine."

"No one here thinks lesser of you for choosing a different path. Eutopia is a celebration of individuality, and free will is sacred.

The path you choose shapes your personality, and makes you a unique wonderful creator."

"Thanks Daphne, I hope you aren't saying this to only make me feel better. Anyway, let us move on, for someone has been awfully quiet for a while. How about you Diablo? I still know very little about you."

Diablo knew his turn would come, though he wasn't expecting to be addressed so very soon, and so brusquely. He shifts in his seat, and can't help but flush. "What can I say? My problems are small, because I have kept the keys to my happiness with me. Damon has already revealed that my coupling season was fruitless. Yes, it is true. I was told there was no one suited for me, and I was to soldier through life alone." He raises both his hands together, and then claps them on his thigh.

"That's impossible," exclaims Destiny. "Never before have I heard of such misfortune."

Diablo can't lock eyes; he looks away and says, "It isn't. They say it's rare, perhaps one in a million. A matter of chance, but not impossible." He looks back at her, "I never let it be a real bother. I have friends." He gives a slight nod to Damon and Nike. "One's other needs can be fulfilled by visiting the House of Pleasure. Though I am tied to no one. Happiness is a state of mind and I am the master of mine."

Destiny wishes to offer him her condolences, but she hesitates, for Diablo's bruises burn too defiantly for him to accept sympathy. A prolonged awkward silence descends. The conversation has grown a notch too sour, and no one on the table dares to nudge it on.

After a while of nothingness in which Damon, without breaching the silence, serves everyone their drinks, Daphne rises from her seat. She balances herself on the spike and announces, "I am afraid my responsibilities need me down-tree, and I must leave. Have a nice night, all of you." She regards them one after the other, and collects waves and nods before she turns around and leaps off onto another branch below.

Her sudden departure does nothing to make them all less ill at ease. Diablo makes up his mind not to be grumpy any more, and is about to speak when colors leak from Nike's lips. Cool visible circular waves of music. Red, orange, blue: her voice causes each heart on the table to shudder; a flowing swipe of her notes splashes clean all conflicts and self-doubt from their thoughts.

Diablo is astonished by his own ability to grasp the essence of her song. He can tell the tongue Nike chooses is one well suited for poetry. It's Persian, a language that dropped out of use ages ago, a vestige of the Earth of Old.

She tells them a story of travelers, of a gypsy couple who were bound to the road. They used to hike through continents year in and year out, and on a fateful night they rested under the cold sky of a desert village. The man was unwell, and his breath grew weak. His wife sang to his breaths, begging them not to leave, all the while boasting how well her man had kept his body: A body built in the image of a palace, a garden, a bowl full of flowers. She calls upon them: his breaths, to consider how unkind it would be of them to desert him tonight, and besides, there were so many new lands to see, wouldn't they like to hitch a ride?

Nike still rests on Damon's side. Damon shuts his eyes hard, speechless, bewitched by her voice with no care of the world.

She is a learned artist, it's plain to see. "How do I understand you? I haven't yet had the years to learn Persian. Your voice, sharp as icicles, it cuts me so deep. How do I know the semantics of the syllables you recite?" Diablo asks; he is mighty impressed by her.

The heel of her shoe rests on the table, the other dangles loosely, about to fall at any moment and be lost to the depths below. She smiles. "A secret of the Temple of Mentor Rumi, you might have to revisit the Academy to learn it."

Diablo laughs out a reply, "Maybe when I am a hundred and two."

Damon opens his eyes wider than he has all evening. "Well then my love has managed to uplift your spirits again." He begins to get up, and so does Nike. "Sadly it's time for us to part. The two of us must be prompt for our appointment with the Omniscient. You may stay here in the leaf neighborhood for as long as you wish." Nike begins to open her wings as Damon puts his hands around her waist. "We should be back perhaps tomorrow afternoon."

"It was lovely meeting you." Destiny means it.

Nike regards Destiny and says, "I would very much like to see you again. We should do this again sometime, the four of us, we should find the time." She looks at her companion, "Hold me tight now Damon," and then looks back to Destiny: "Remember, if you seek rest all you need to do is fall back down. If you two wish to be together hold hands when you fall, so you are carried by a single leaf of autumn." She stands as a ballerina and leaps backward and down. "Sayōnara." Both Diablo and Destiny turn around on their seats, as Nike flips below and then shoots away with a single flap of her wings.

The Hall of Spies

The curtains are lifted, revealing a hall far larger than it appeared possible to fit in the tower from down below. It favors a dim blue tint and is held up by archless columns in five rows, each row being twenty columns deep. The black marble floor is covered an inch deep in water.

"Come on in," Cassandra invites Machiavelli. He follows her. They walk on water, careful not to cause ripples on its surface. It's no harder for Eutopians than learning to swim. It's tricky at first, but everyone's a natural, and soon one can stand on a liquid surface without conscious effort. Most Newman learn how to when with their parents, before they join the Academy.

Machiavelli hasn't been permitted in the hall of spies for centuries. Not since he himself was an Observer, in the early days of his Elderhood. Long though it may have been, he easily slips back into his formal role. Skidding along the livery clad and masked professionals of the Observatory, across the water, keeping a watch over Eutopia.

Ever moving, they patrol the waters, always looking at the shadows and images emitted by the floor. The surface of the hall is squared off into seventy-six windows by its hundred pillars, each of them an opening to spy on a critical part of Eutopia: Half of them dedicated to the public City, and the other to peer into the lives of private individuals living in their Bubbles of Perfect Existence.

Fast swimming Denison barb fish outspeed Cassandra and

Machiavelli as they move amidst the columns. In the floor their red streak scales are visible more clearly when passing by windows that aren't being used and the background is black.

Cassandra leads Machiavelli to the center of the hall. "Here I shall dedicate two of the windows to watch over Descartes, and two more for Destiny and Diablo."

Machiavelli catches his tongue before answering. Only the Oracle may speak in a human voice in the Hall of Spies.

In a wave of her hands a water stream rises from the floor; looping around it displays the digit zero written four times in a cursive style, before returning back to the fish. "What are their numbers?" Cassandra asks Machiavelli, turning around.

Machiavelli shows her the digits by the count of his fingers and thumb. A one, a six, three twos, and a seven. By Cassandra's will the stream starts to spell the numbers identified by Machiavelli. Once set, they pour back onto the floor with a glob. On touching the surface, the floor lights up, displaying Descartes in a Dwarkoidian form seated on his throne.

Cassandra takes a moment to make sense of what she is seeing. "Impressive skin changing. I didn't expect him to take up the role of kinging over her children. See, he is not that bad for her."

Machiavelli uses the common sign to show her his lips are sealed.

"I am amused, didn't think you still had enough cares to respect the rules of the Observatory." Her hair shoots left, to the closest pillar, touching it at a specific spot with no recognizable markings. A switch. And behind Machiavelli the silent surface of the water breaks and with a noticeable loud trickle emerges a divan on which lies a pair of masks. Machiavelli puts one on with the haste of a delinquent mind kept away from its wits. He flings the other to Cassandra.

"I follow the rules not for the Oracle or her Observatory but for the sake of the rules themselves. We are made civilized by them rules, and I hold them dear."

"Don't you dare speak of rules Machiavelli. They were in the right, by your rules, to choose one another over a suggestion of an algorithm. How is us manipulating the lives of fellow Newmans by the rules?"

"Where is your mind Cassandra! You the Oracle, of all among us know well the work we do. The Elders maintain perfection, not mediocrity. The kids are known to make mistakes, that's why they are kids, but is it not our duty to mend their folly for them, or are we to let them wallow in their mistakes?"

"Yes, but were we not to resist the temptation of intervening, is it not policy to do so as a last resort? When the alternative is known to be letting our subjects harm themselves or one another."

"If Ananta thinks it necessary, who are we to doubt him?"

All this talk and not an echo in the hall. There words are muffled and stay in the masks they wear, and are whispered into the ears of the other. Telepathy, though quicker – and would have well served the purpose of keeping a library's silence in the hall – is considered to be a process too disarming for conversations between those who aren't intimate.

Machiavelli props himself up on the free floating divan. "Come join me Cassandra, let us take stock of what Descartes has been up to."

"I am fine here on my feet, thank you. Besides, one of us needs to operate the window."

"As it suits you." Machiavelli doesn't ask again, instead he makes himself comfortable lounging on the daybed. "So what do we have here? I am up to date with the reports the Observatory has been mailing me. Destiny has created a near human intelligent oceanic species. Descartes didn't take much to the idea at first but he changed his mind on meeting these vile creatures. What happened next? Other than Destiny leaving for the City."

Cassandra finds it hard not to comment on Machiavelli's unfair criticism of the Dwarkoids. In a crisp tone she replies, "Destiny had accelerated time in those parts of the ocean where her children inhabit before leaving her bubble. I reckon she wishes them to nurture fast, and hopes they would take a form more pleasant and peaceful by the time she is back."

"I wonder why she bothers," Machiavelli remarks with a grimace. "What of Descartes, I bet he flipped, going proper cuckoo on her departure."

"For all that's good! Would it kill you to speak of them in a kinder manner?" Cassandra has had enough.

"Didn't you tell me to leave my charms at the door? These are my actual opinions."

With a sigh Cassandra yields, "Forgive me Machiavelli, truth be told, I would rather bear your pretense than suffer your true thoughts. Would you put on your grace again. Please." Sarcasm oozes out of her.

"As it pleases you, my Oracle."

"Good." Cassandra continues, "The last I had looked they were spooked about us entering their bubble, but they were happy. I am certain Descartes took it fine. I am asking the Observatory to generate a report."

A crystal corked vial formulates in Cassandra's hand, it holds a white fluid. She unscrews it and discharges it on the floor. The liquid makes a milk cloud bloom in the water window. Machiavelli can't read the meanings that are in the shape of the clouds, but the Oracle can.

"They had an argument before she left." Her eyes grow wide as she dwells further in the past. "Over your letter." Cassandra strains her eyes, "Oh! Their parting was not pleasant at all. Tempers flared, Descartes tried to rescue the peace by offering to accompany Destiny to the City. She refused him. I assume she wasn't amenable to any of his notions." Reading events that have already occurred is hard, even for Cassandra. She speaks in bits, pausing after every few words. "He didn't insist, and chose instead to leave."

"Well, that explains the foul mood she was in when she came over."

"I am pretty sure it was meeting you that dampened her spirits," Cassandra takes a jab at Machiavelli.

He gives her a look, but doesn't respond in kind. "Where did Descartes go from the beach?" he asks.

"He went into hiding, cupping all that anger inside him."

"Hiding? He hid from you, the eye of the Observatory?"

"Yes, he left for older regions of his bubble, which are all but dormant. There is too little tuning there for our windows to register any readings. We would have been able to tell his whereabouts if we were watching his activities live, but this is all I can tell by peering into the past."

"Does he have a safe place? Do you know where he goes when feeling the blues?"

"Descartes is quite the wanderer, rarely sleeping under the same roof for two nights in a row. He has built many spots that are dear to him; at times he would make it snow and bundle in heavy *razais* by a fireplace in a rich cottage. On other occasions he would call for torrential rain, and brave it out in a tree house. His favorite, though, would be the solars of medieval castles, often overlooking quaint landlocked lakes. These are the places he fancies the most and where he could be found on a good day. Blacksmithing or raising new walls in the image of forts and keeps of the Earth of Old."

"No, no, I ask where he seeks refuge when recouping from an unpleasant incident, for instance, after an argument with Destiny." Machiavelli is not happy at the need of explaining himself twice.

"They don't clash often, I haven't noticed a pattern. But..."

"But?"

"There were times when I felt he took special care to hide his tracks, as if he knew he was being watched. To lose the gaze of the Observatory he would busy himself in mundane acts of recreation, which we recognized as his routine. He would wait for a long while before setting to work on his secret project."

Machiavelli is now at the edge of his seat. "What is his secret project?"

"I discovered it by chance, when I spotted him in the act when I was initiating a window to watch their bubble over. He is writing a book."

"Writing a book?" Machiavelli breathes a sigh of relief. It isn't the trait High Mentor Ananta had warned him about. "Writing a book?" he repeats and bursts into a laugh. "You mean by hand, in words?" he asks between insuppressible cackles. "In a time when one can physically walk inside a story. When anything he can imagine can be enacted in front of him and more, he struggles with a medium as old as books? Now that is funny."

"I think not, the best thoughts are formed when penned down on paper. Many do write to compose their ideas, and then later they may adapt it for another medium, be it music, or immersive plays. There are many who still welcome the old art of writing."

"I guess I see your argument." Machiavelli regains his composure and asks, "You tell me he has taken his place among the so called Dwarkoids, and has decided to rule over them in Destiny's absence. How is that turning out for him?"

In another wave of her hand the image of Descartes in the oceanic sea throne appears again. "Let me read."

Machiavelli knows better than to disturb her, he amuses himself with peeping in the window. He can't hear the happenings in the court of Descartes, but he can see them. His first theory is that they are performing a ritual in their God's glory, but for all he knows, it may well be a party that has every attendee dancing. They are moving with an agility peculiar to those with eight limbs. Machiavelli may not approve of the Dwarkoids but he can't deny their artistry.

There is a sudden burst of activity beyond the window. Descartes leaves his seat and withdraws to the forehead balcony of the face-shaped hall. "What's happening now?"

"Shush!" Cassandra silences him.

Many of the Dwarkoids make a dash for the exit, but are soon restrained by Descartes' will. Machiavelli enjoys watching them struggle. They each seemed glued to the ground, as if trapped by invisible webs.

"Splendid! Glorious I would say." Cassandra breaks the silence with bright eyes.

"Yes, I am certain the fell creatures deserved it."

"No, I am not talking about the present, but Descartes' rule so far."

"I don't understand Cassandra."

"His trapping them is probably an act of kindness. He rules them with a light hand, yet he has changed them significantly. He is nurturing them Machiavelli."

"Care to elaborate?" Machiavelli would rather have a disagreeable bit of news quick and be done with it.

"He reformed them, breaking down the traditional power centers of their society, those which restricted the individual creativity of the Dwarkoids. He is attempting to instill the idea of liberty in their collective consciousness, and the commendable part is he is doing so without eradicating their culture.

He has brought peace to the bickering regions of their city, diminishing the strength of those who profit from dividing the society. He has shown tact in using his Godhood to justify the abolishment of the divine right to rule of the royalties, turning the titles of the King, the Count and the Chancellor into mere ceremonial positions. Their arms of war now make props for fashion and souvenirs, unsheathed only for sports such as jousting."

Cassandra's appreciation of Descartes' reign isn't pleasing to Machiavelli. He watches over the Dwarkoids, some of who leave the courtroom, while others return.

"Hmm that's quite curious. I don't claim to know him as well as you do Lady Cassandra, but aren't those the qualities the Dwarkoids had taken from him? Why does he water down his own influence on their kind?"

"Descartes understands that some notions that humor him are best left as thoughts and daydreams, and should not be allowed to have a physical manifestation. See here, do you notice the pump over there." Cassandra points at the chin of the hall.

"You give him too much credit. Yes."

"It's a gift of invention he made to the Dwarkoids. A lava pump. It extracts lava from the mantle caves, and uses it to for home heating."

Machiavelli was practicing his selective hearing on Cassandra. Still transfixed by the happenings beyond the window, he interrupts her, "Where is he off to now?"

Cassandra in her eagerness to defend Descartes was so busy reading the improvements brought by him, that she didn't notice when he and his mates left the balcony of the courtroom through a pipe of the plumbing highways of Dwarka. "I don't know. There is little down there, under the surface, other than private houses. Mayhap he seeks a place of rest and some privacy to break bread with his friends in leisure."

"He lives in a mine?" asks Machiavelli, genuinely perplexed.

Cassandra grows pale. "That isn't a mine."

The Elders watch Descartes and his friends silently as they dive into a crack in the rock filled with unknown nectar.

"Are they doing what I think they are doing?"

"Yes," Cassandra admits, turning the window dark with a wave of her hand. "Is that even possible?"

"All our discouragement failed to prevent this boy from having the forbidden fruit. No law of Eutopia is beyond breaking, if the perpetrator is skilled and possesses the will. You see Cassandra, we have not been poking around in the business of others needlessly. Do you appreciate the solemnity of the situation now?"

"Yes, but what are we to do? What if Descartes makes a habit of it, we can't lose him to the Dwarkoids."

"Ananta would know, only he has the knowledge and the experience to solve such a riddle. Watch over Descartes, and let me know if he engages again in this indecorous act." Machiavelli steers his levitating divan onto the now shut window through which, moments earlier, they were spying on Descartes. "Reveal to me the whereabouts of Diablo and Destiny, Cassandra."

"Wait, don't you think we should write to Ananta immediately?"

"Do you doubt Ananta? He had predicted the failings of Descartes' character and had asked me to be on the lookout for the signs on his behalf. His instructions included keeping an eye on Destiny and Diablo too. Their happiness is as much at stake here as Descartes'."

"All right." Cassandra reaches in her inventory to seek another vial; instead of milky white the contents of this one are sandy, and include the occasional glimmer of quartz. On her pouring of the vial over the floor, it spreads as gradually as honey would have. It reveals the City. They get a top down view of a circular flat disk – similar to how the world was imagined by the ancients. Its surface area is equal to that of five Earths of Old.

On this interactive live map there are many regions over which hang opaque clouds; these are the regions kept private by other Elders, and not even the all seeing eye of the Observatory may know them. Most places are lit up by the slanting light of a nonexistent sun.

Cassandra mumbles a command, "Search: Destiny. Diablo." The window begins to zoom in, quicker than the drop of an eagle. A valley. A mountain, and cliff on which stand an ant-sized Diablo and Destiny. Off the cliff, in the air glides a winged Nike of seldom flaps. "They are at the edge of the leaf neighborhood."

"Good, I had planted the thought in Diablo's mind, telling him how much Damon misses him."

"It's a fine place, the leaf, I do fancy visiting it once in a while." The trivia shared by Cassandra seems innocuous enough to allow Machiavelli to presume she has softened up to his cause.

Their voices are muted to Machiavelli, but are not to Cassandra. He mimes the conversation in his thoughts as one of Diablo introducing Nike and Destiny to one another. Unexpectedly though, Nike flies away, leaving Destiny and Diablo to linger on the hilltop, worrying Machiavelli.

"What are they saying Cassandra, why don't they go down to the neighborhood?"

"Oh, they intend to! Diablo is teaching Destiny how to glide," Cassandra tells him with an affectionate smile, one not aimed at Machiavelli, but at Destiny and Diablo.

Diablo puts his suit on and helps Destiny in, before leaping off the cliff. Machiavelli isn't pleased by Destiny's hesitations, but the kindly awe in Cassandra's face reassures him that all is well between Diablo and Destiny. A couple of skipping bounces on the river's surface, a short swim and Destiny is received by the Neighborhood's welcoming party. Machiavelli breathes a sigh of relief. "She is there."

"Why, did you expect her to have trouble landing? Wait, she is coughing too much." It's Cassandra who worries now. "Water fills her lungs."

Diablo extracts the liquid from her. "It's Daphne whose presence I am thankful for," says Machiavelli.

"I find that odd. How are Diablo or Destiny important enough for the Mayor of the Leaf to receive them personally?"

"Oh, Daphne would not have bothered, if left to her own devices. It is I who asked her to be present. To make sure the conversations between Destiny and Diablo don't grow sour, and to keep them from any accidents that may make them part ways prematurely. All they have to do is stick together a while, to learn the undeniable truth."

Cassandra protests, "Why do you need to choreograph everything? Is it not good enough that you have manipulated Destiny into meeting Diablo without her leave?"

"You are much too kind Cassandra, but at times leniency leads to mishaps. Instead, we have to be insensitive, and do what needs to be done. To protect those whose happiness we are entrusted with." Cassandra appears unconvinced. "It's no crime to force their hand for their own good." Machiavelli waits for another argument from her but none comes. She hasn't changed her opinion, but has accepted defeat, and so is now amenable to his instructions. "I must get home, and be ready to welcome Destiny and Diablo. Will you please keep an eye on them all, and write to me if you notice anything of alarm. Especially if Descartes shows greater affiliation to the Dwarkoids."

"Should we not notify Mentor Ananta?"

"Yes, I will update him on my way back to the Welcoming House of the 27th hive."

In the Undergrowth

Falling... They had expected to be scooped up instantly when leaving the Ramen Bar. Instead, hands outstretched but still entwined, four seconds in, perpendicular to the ground, they are losing altitude fast. Unaware of the leaf which has unplucked itself up-tree, and is moving toward them with god speed. The looming ground seems increasingly unpleasant, until it reaches them from their blind spot. To their relief, the leaf catches Diablo and Destiny in mid fall.

Beating the wind, it glides back up again, spooking the riders, making them hold firm the edge of the leaf. No more are they holding hands; Diablo uses his stronger left to keep a grip on the leaf, never noticing when he slipped his right one around Destiny's waist. Their shared but unspoken fear – not the hurt of a fall, but of separation – in case instead of one, two floral vessels had carried them apart. Her legs dangling free, hair in face, Destiny considers it not as gentle as Nike had suggested; nevertheless, to her it's mighty fun.

Their ride starts to float steadily once it escapes the tree-line, though it's not high enough to threaten the supremacy of the clouds. Languidly, they fly by the dwellings of the leaf neighborhood and soon the sky clears. It is lit up by stars whose positions mimic how they appeared in the northern hemisphere in the teen years of the twenty-first century. None of these wonders, though, charm Diablo.

Never before has he held someone who felt like the real thing. In him, Destiny could see her worries melting away. Her thoughts seep through, lost from her consciousness, leaving her with nothing to do but regard his bearded face.

The eclipse of time goes unnoticed as they drift on the wind. They are carried to a meadow rolling down from a hill; here the autumn leaf finds the grass. They don't rush into action, but wait under the purple gulmohar on the hill, disturbed by none but the calm rustle of the tree.

Still they take a while to move, until Diablo well-nigh can't resist pulling her close; instead he rises. He wasn't sure if it would be proper. Getting on his knees he says, "Look!" Destiny raises her torso on her right hand, and turns to find a meadow sprawling down to the horizon. In it are thousands of warm lamps placed on waist high pebble podiums, all equidistant from one another, illuminating the field.

There are but a few flowers; instead the grass is tall and the breeze whispers through them. In the gush swirl the fireflies, who line themselves by rank and file, they fight back the wind, and are not ready to desert the nectar of night blooming moonflowers.

"Fancy a race Diablo?"

Diablo laughs her dare away, "A race? No, no, not a race."

"Why not?"

"You can't be serious."

"Rea-ady!" Destiny is in a bolting stance.

"What, right away?" Diablo fumbles to get up.

"Ready?"

Diablo isn't. "Yeah," he conforms out of his habitual chivalry.

He is slow to leap after her. When he rises up, Mufasa, who until now was asleep in Diablo's pocket, chooses to leap out and join the excitement. A few barks, but the helter skelter of the run is too thrilling for him to pose any questions.

Diablo follows after her with Mufasa running along, while Destiny gains a decent lead. The barks catch her attention; she is tempted to look back, but the race is too important for her to give away.

Downhill they go, and she grows more confident of her victory as Diablo's footsteps sound fainter. She is quicker than him; she looks back to take stock of how squarely she is to defeat him. Though she had noticed the barks, she had not expected to see a life size Mufasa sprinting alongside them. It takes her a moment longer than necessary to register the golden retriever's presence and dismiss it. Enough for a now barefooted Diablo to make a serious effort to catch up with Destiny.

She starts again, but Diablo is about to cross her with a smile and a taunting wave, when he stumbles against a misplaced stone and trips. She tries to catch him, but instead he takes her down too, rolling them up in a bundle once again.

They laugh but don't ponder why, perhaps at the licks and sniffs of Mufasa, who finds them both. They lie under the first podium lamp they had spotted from their starting point. The warm yellow light travels through the curtain of her hair, lighting up Diablo's face. He can tell of her smirk in the shimmer of her eyes. She kisses him. It lasts not long at all.

"You get along with your Newman work. I notice lizards!" Mufasa leaps away from them in a dash. Destiny parts from Diablo, and falls on her back, lying alongside him. A winter quietness of being in a vast landscape keeps them very aware of one another and the uncomfortable cold.

The sheet of stars above them seem pressed hard on the artificial sky, not appearing all that far from them. Words are not exchanged; they both keep from looking at one another until Diablo, from the corner of his eye, notices a band of rainbow colors spreading out from a gesture of her two fingers. It hangs in the air between them, and before Diablo could ask, Destiny tells him why, "Let us see if we can help each other save those who are dear to us."

Diablo's silence is a yes.

Destiny draws outlines in the space above them. Diablo considers them as connections between the stars beyond, marking the constellations, but the very third point she chooses doesn't mark a star. He is at a loss while she fleshes out a three-dimensional model. His second guess is that it's an impression of a landscape, but he learns its nature only when she begins to brush in the colors.

Shown in color and high definition, it occupies no more than a cubic meter of space above them. It's the depiction of an under oceanic vent, in a deep trench that spills black fumes of chemicals. It is imagery, a mere representation, and it isn't real to the meadows that they are in.

The chemicals bloom and rise to the surface, and spread and enrich the entirety of the ocean. She lets the water brew for a while, and then introduces simple strings of DNA, micro-organisms that feed on the energy being released from these vents.

"They will multiply fast."

Diablo, who knows the lessons of evolution in theory, had considered it too troublesome to tinker with. His reasoning: why should one bother with single cell beings when you could have complex mammals to do your bidding on a whim. Seeing evolution in action for the first time, and witnessing Destiny work it with such ease, he keeps mum. He watches as photosynthesis lets algae and plants leave the blue and march onto the land, the first to colonize the surface.

Similar to watching a time-lapse recording, with quick brushes of her fingers, life starts to spread. Diablo is at a loss as to why she keeps modifying the rock structure of the seabed, until he notices varying species of polyps being attracted and claiming their home in the rocks designated by Destiny. A little touch of change in the topography, a slight increase in the water temperature, and she stops.

"Ready?" Destiny asks him. "Are you ready for it?"

"Sure, let us have your revelation." He isn't about to let her know how impressed he is by her.

Destiny speeds up time and in the blink of an eye millions of years pass by, and a vast chaotic reef grows to cover every stone. Polyps grow in blooms and pillars in search of the sun, using their dead as a foundation to reach closer to the surface. In this reef are brought forth many creatures familiar to Diablo, a collection that Destiny fancies among those listed in Gaea's databook. They weren't uncommon on the Earth of Old.

A cavalry of seahorses hides in staghorn corals of bright hues, charging in teams on passing clouds of plankton, ravaging them to extinction. Sea Stars who wipe the floor readily sacrifice a limb or two for the cruel king crabs who descend on them from above.

Invertebrates such as shrimps, snails and jellyfish populate her sea, as expected of any respectable reef. The manner in which Destiny's creatures stand out is by their sheer size: the giant squids and octopi are the Kraken of her sea and fear no one but the Blue Water Dragon.

Diablo watches wide eyed as the Dragon bites a giant snail's shell with its teeth, in an attempt to seek the soft juicy fluff on the inside. In one clear motion Diablo reaches out to the cube and pauses the simulation.

The playback stops. The snail's shell has developed deep cracks. A tiny triangular piece of it has broken free, and is moving toward Destiny. She asks, perturbed, "What? Don't you like it?"

"It is all very gorgeous Destiny. I am honestly overwhelmed with enthusiasm here, I wish to partake, I can't resist but add a few things into your vision. May I?"

"Oh!" Destiny had expected criticism, not a plea for participation. It dawns upon her that Diablo is unaware of the true nature of the simulation. He hasn't been able to guess that the cubicle acts as a window to Destiny's Bubble of Perfect Existence. If he knew, he would not have presumed he would be granted the liberty to join in. "Well okay, don't alter it beyond recognition. It's still my simulation."

"Don't you worry." He rewinds the simulation, the snail's shell is renewed, and the dragon jaws unhinge from its prey. Diablo goes back to the moment when the predator had spotted its intended before pausing. He picks on the Dragon's brain, switches a few neuron cells, adds a cluster and tucks it back in with little difficulty. "Made it a pinch wiser, and..." Diablo pushes 'Play'. The dragon approaches the snail once more, but instead of deploying his teeth, the beast wraps itself around the shell as would a python around a deer, and with brute strength breaks the snail's armor to smithereens.

"A shorter struggle for the dragon and a quicker end for the snail. Not bad," Destiny concedes, taking back the reins of creation once more.

She takes them onto land. There is little there but a white beach, shored horse crab shells and discharged seaweeds to welcome them. An entire continent lays bare, covered in grass, moss and algae. Diablo is yet again tempted by the empty canvas to join in. A bale of baby turtles hatch, break sand and make their way toward the sea.

"I was just about to do that... it's eerie, can you read my thoughts?"

"I felt we needed them," Diablo explains. "I did it all wrong though, we should wait for evolution to do its business right."

"The trick is to tame evolution Diablo, not let it run amok. Let us have fun with it, and have a nice time, isn't that the important bit?"

"Yes." Encouraged by Destiny he makes up his mind not to hold himself back with the simulation.

Destiny intends to school Diablo, she wants to dazzle him with her creativity. She would set the record straight once and for all; her forest would outwit him and prove her the better Newman between them.

Under her will comes a teeming undergrowth. Many of those who were well suited for sandy ocean floor shift shop to land. They find novel ways of breathing and staying hydrated, those who do it better spread deeper in the early forests.

Destiny is well trained and is certain in her skill. She brings creation with the precision of a master music composer, and moves real fast. Her confidence keeps her from recognizing the subtle but constant diversions from her will the simulation is taking. The discrepancy grows as she moves on, further embellishing this small world of grass and mud.

The ants, which herd tinier insects for their honeydew, have learned how to farm fungi too. They make tighter shelters to keep their cattle dry, meanwhile digging canals to keep the fungi moist. Destiny's favorite plants: those who prey on the six-legged are made more vicious with a larger arsenal of weapons. New additions include poison tipped thorns and Venus flytraps that respond to the buzzing of wings, positioning themselves with stealth to better receive their food.

The more striking of changes that make Diablo the chief suspect are in the color tones; they are more vivid, yet subdued; to Destiny it feels as though she sees the simulation through a lens with a soothing filter.

"It is you! Are you fiddling with my simulation again?" She doesn't sound amused.

"Am I ruining it? I have been tracing your hand, trying to add and upgrade the things you draw. Should I stop?"

"No, I can't say I dislike your workmanship. It's just that I am not used to collaborating with someone new." Destiny pauses, realizing she has lied; the bone of contention isn't Diablo being a stranger. The trouble is hers, Destiny isn't used to collaborating at all – she has never been successful at doing so with anyone.

"All right then, let us do it the proper way. Let us collaborate." Destiny offers Diablo her hand. He slips his over hers, she holds an invisible pen, and Diablo covers her grip. It's Diablo's first time, he understands the basic principle of Collaborative Tuning, but he has never before put it in practice.

He opens up his telepathic channels and finds himself in complete darkness. There is no sky, no floor and, mayhap, no space. The sense of Destiny's hand weakens and comes back to him again and again. Diablo tries to hold on to her, and he can tell she is making an effort too by the faint translucent image of her, which he may or may not have glimpsed in the blackness.

He fears his fumbling would reveal his inexperience at Collaborative Tuning. They struggle together a while. Diablo can't measure it, but Destiny's image is increasingly getting sharper. She isn't in her customary white, but wears a skirt made of royal blue and a gilded bodice of stiff platinum. He knows not when, but he finds himself standing awfully close to her, pouring himself into her eyes.

In this realm time is rendered useless once the bridge between their consciousness is built. Here they lack the freedom of motion and are bounded to gaze at one another unblinkingly.

Her lips don't move, but he can hear Destiny. "Are you ready?" she giggles.

They might not be able to move here in the dimension of their thoughts, but their physical selves, which lie in a field together, are still subjected to their commands. As agreed, Destiny is to lead the way in the simulation.

Her thoughts are his. A novice, Diablo is astonished to find himself able to read the workings of her mind as it churns. He can grasp her ideas at their point of inception, much before those ideas compel her hand to move and draw the simulation further. Effortlessly, he patches and modifies her will, so when their hands do move, they do so with the combined intent of Destiny and Diablo.

Destiny has never before witnessed perfection. Her hands move with a new grace. She can tell the style in which they tune remains distinguishably hers, but the colors that leak onto the three-dimensional cubicle are far richer and daring. Her brushes have grown bolder and thicker, yet they never blot or take away from the elegance of her art. In the simulation she can envision a world of ecstasy, where a regular walk every morning would chase away all possible misgivings. A place where words such as gloom, sorrow and disappointment are neither uttered, nor hold meaning.

Here in a castle in the sky within Diablo she finds herself sated, without the longing for things she has never seen.

Destiny is at two places at once, in the meadow lying next to Diablo and in the telepathic black standing in front of him. In admiration, by its own device, causing an upheaval in the turns of the skirt's flair, her limber arm reaches out for Diablo's face. He is still locked, unmoving, until she caresses his cheek. At her touch, the bridge of telepathy falls apart, the simulation pauses, and all parts of them are returned to their physical bodies in the green.

The intellect of Diablo, which was deep in the process of tuning and running the simulation, is joined by his vulnerable half, whose limbs had been kept immobile against their will. They move the moment they are set free, reaching out to Destiny before the rational half of him could take charge.

He takes her by surprise, pulling her on top of himself. He stops. Destiny finds herself looking down at him once more, this time straddled on top of his waist, with both her knees touching the ground.

She need not be articulate: "We must seek the Omniscient after," she whispers in his ears.

Crusher Claws

Years have passed, and Descartes has worked through all of them. Each day in eagerness he has taken his throne and has dispatched justice and advice to the Dwarkoids. "This is not a command only a suggestion," are the words he finds himself saying most often. His subjects, though, tend to strive and achieve his every utterance with absolute dedication.

Today is the fifth anniversary of Descartes' descent and in his honor a banquet is being held. Their calendar is a metric one, with each month a set of ten days, and a year of a hundred. Descartes eases on his throne with the languor peculiar to Kings. The festivities, which once amused him, bore him. His 'suggestions', though, have made them more sightly.

They dye the thick locks of rubbery flesh that stems from their head instead of hair. Purple, black, pink, and blue are the shades popular in his court. Descartes has been generous with the stories of land. Captivating and hard to envision are the mammals that roam the savannahs above; so are the rosewood trees, and the season of fall, yet the Dwarkoids have done their artistic best to drape his hall in detailed murals inspired by tales of places they have never seen.

The mood has been slow through most of the day, and Descartes is painfully aware of the wearing off of his fascination with the Dwarkoids. He licks a frog's back for intoxication. It isn't as displeasing to his Dwarkoidian tastes as it sounds. He waits for the hour of rumble, when the real party will begin, while allowing an old geezer a retelling of the time when he had been blessed enough to catch a sight of Destiny.

By the saga chronicled in their legends, Destiny used to live in their midst when they were waking. The records of the early mornings are hazy; some claim it was she who taught them how to communicate with the world around them and with each other, teaching them the words to identify every creature and element of the sea. Other myths will have you believe that she merely encouraged them to name all that they see. They say she swam alongside them in their infancy, often playing with them, but urging them to make the rules of the game themselves. Where all the sources do agree is that her visits dwindled as the Dwarkoids started coming into their own. Their will got stronger, and as they did more of what they pleased, Destiny grew distant.

They do still keep a watch though, over the plains above the crater, in the hope of spotting her elegance. It isn't much too uncommon to see her shaping the sea bed, or willing a cave into existence. The Dwarkoids, in respect and fear, would not rush out to her immediately, but would often find much needed boons near about where she was spotted.

Once, when a sickness had begun to cripple their children – with a disease whose sorrows spread quicker than the currents, bringing them wails and pessimism so strong that the very will to strive seemed would fail – then a sighting of Destiny had lead them to a garden of medicinal mushrooms.

The raconteur speaks with breathy clicks from the voice box organ within him, his sounds slowed with age: "In my adolescence I was a bit of a vagabond. The street lads, my older brother and I had found an unused, unguarded passage leading out of Dwarka. We were wicked enough to dare into the open, breaking the city rules." Descartes turns to this dignified looking Dwarkoid; his stare ruffles him up, stealing his speech.

"Go on, I do find your story entertaining." He doesn't truly.

"We were drawn toward the open sceneries of the ocean's

greens, the forests of seaweed, which dance with the waves, and are easy to get lost in. The brightness of shallow waters often called us closer to the shore. Laying there hiding, we would wait to spot the seagulls that fly in that blue."

Descartes' eyes meet a friend's in a balcony on the far side of the hall. Echo, too, was stormed with sharing pleasantries. He beams at him.

"On one such day, on our way back, we spotted her. Children in their innocence often prove to be more courageous than adults. We dared approach her... luckily, we were mindful enough to be cautious, and did so in stealth. My elder brother, who had lead us so far out in the open, away from Dwarka, then tried the unimaginable."

He pauses. Descartes waves to Siren, who too is swamped in conversations. The old Dwarkoid isn't about to risk pressing Descartes' attention back onto his story; instead, he rambles on, "He decided to capture Mother Destiny. I protested to his casting of the net, but he was beyond reason my lord. He took it on himself to bring her back to the city, and I failed to deter him. He being stronger than I, neither could I restrain him."

Descartes laughs and laughs, taking a long while to catch his breath, and then he laughs some more. "Your brother tried to capture Destiny? With a throw-net?"

"I apologize my lord, we were but children. We imagined we would be heroes, that our return with Mother Destiny would be lauded and canonized. Forgive us for our irreverence."

"What happened then?" Descartes asks.

"Nothing at first. She was busy choreographing a dance of lobsters. We waited with our hearts in our mouths, until a yawn and a stretch made her realize the constraints we had put her in."

"And?"

"The threads of the rope that made the throw-net dissolved. She turned around, and the rock that we were hiding behind crumbled, revealing us to her."

"Boy, oh boy, you were in trouble. What did she do next?"

"She set the risk of lobsters at us, all eight thousand feet charged. A pair of snaps of their crusher claws managed to reach me, nearly getting me captured, but I escaped. My brother, though, wasn't as lucky."

A Dwarkoid-at-Arms who stood by his throne leans down and whispers, "It's nearly time my lord." Descartes nods, conveying that he understands.

"You survived, because she let you. What of your brother, did you ever see him again?"

"Yes my lord, he returned a day later. Sore all over, he could barely swim. He said the lobsters were very thorough with their business."

"It was Destiny's benevolence that kept the lobsters from making him their dinner."

"I guess you would not have spared them if you had taken offence to their foolery. I would not have been as kind. Anyways, I shall not undo your decision."

Descartes' chair hisses, releasing jets of air in the deep. Its clasps and locks unhinge, releasing his limbs. He is much larger than an average Dwarkoid. He pulls himself to his full height. His rising is enough to kill the hall's murmur.

"The rumble begins in five," Descartes announces. A frenzy to reach the exit is won by the Dwarkoid Descartes had so patiently been entertaining. He calls out after him, "Wait, you didn't tell me your name?" Half of those present rush the door, and the old geezer loses himself in the crowd. A stampede seems imminent.

Music starts to fill the hall, drowning Descartes' calls for order. He turns to his Dwarkoid-at-Arms, whose duty demands him to wait at Descartes' throne, only to find him missing too.

The 'Rumble' is Descartes' idea. It's an evening when the concept of social order is to be forgotten. He hopes that with a pinch of anarchy everyone will have a blast, once they are free from standing on ceremony.

Descartes turns around to let the chaos in his panorama sink in. The footmen who were to man the Rumble have deserted too. *"It was a hard sell Destiny. But now it seems they have taken up the idea much too literally."*

Siren and Echo, his two friends, swim to the center of the hall and join Descartes. "Didn't I warn you, they would lose their minds?" Siren greets him. "Thankfully someone remembered to drop the banners and the flags."

Descartes notices cloth art; imprinted with abstract shapes in perfect symmetry, they celebrate not nature but the brilliance of numbers and geometry. They favor the darker shades, such as purple and tropical greens. "Mayhap you were right Siren, someone might seriously injure themselves." Descartes looks again at the exit.

Echo answers before Siren, "So now, you, Descartes, will do as we had agreed?"

"Break out of Dwarkoidan character?"

"It's not like we can let them walk over each other dead," Echo argues.

"You are not thinking of letting them be trampled, right?" Siren doubts Descartes' sincerity.

"No, what do you make of me Siren? Let us go up to our private balcony, it would be much easier to direct them from up there." The three of them swim up, away from the exit to the largest balcony of the hall.

"One can never tell with you, you may very well argue that they won't learn if not allowed a free hand."

Descartes turns around to face the ruckus, "Not when it's a matter of life and death, lessons can wait." He begins to sway a pair of his limbs in a dancy fashion. The actions of those in the hall slow down. Against their will, their limbs resist motion, stopping them in their tracks. Echo watches Descartes' motions carefully. It could have been a play of the light, but in between the two limbs that swirl so gracefully, controlling every element that makes the world, he thinks he could see an outline of Descartes' true hand, held out with an open palm.

"Did you see it?" Echo asks Siren.

"What?"

"Never mind."

Those who clog the neck are repulsed, as if flung by a blast; glowing lines appear between them all, measuring the distance of each body from one another. They move apart until all of them have a precise gap of one meter from one another. Losing voluntary control of their own limbs is first greeted with silence by the crowd, but they soon break into an uproar of cacophonic clicks. A screech, which Descartes catches, pleads, "Let me out of here!"

"There is no need to panic," Descartes booms from the balcony. "Quiet down, I am still in charge." Siren and Echo follow Descartes' cue, and add their voices to his, "Calm down." They shout down to the crowd, and after much struggle silence is achieved.

"The doors won't close until morning and you may come and leave as you may please. There is no need to scramble, for beyond the doors all of Dwarka remains the same. Here in my hall the laws are lax, but they don't vanish. Plundering or causing physical harm will still be punishable, but the boundaries of wealth and stature don't matter. You may speak freely, approach anyone you fancy, and dine and lick frogs together. Are you following me?"

"Yes!" is the loudest word to reach Descartes.

"You shall exit in an orderly fashion, and I will return your bodies to you one row after the other."

Descartes turns around to his friends and says, "That's that."

Rumble in the Deep

"It was magnificent." Echo has been showering praises on Descartes throughout dinner. "How could you miss his hand Siren, it was so strange. Nearly delicate looking and weak, if you don't mind my saying so Descartes. Yet it emitted such power."

"That's no great shake, I have witnessed Descartes in the entirety of his Newman form." They quarrel, while Descartes floats free at the edge of the balcony, looking down, surveying the 'Rumble'.

Descartes might as well declare it a failure. The hall is divided in cliques, in an assortment similar to the pre-existent divisions of Dwarkoidian society. Those affluent are closer to his balcony. The noblemen on the right and the traders on the left. The commoners are in the back, closer to the exit: the soldiers and the peasants. They stay edgy, and are made hesitant by the vogue of the rich.

"Alas, they don't mix." Descartes accepts defeat with a sigh, and then turns around and clears his voice box, catching the attention of his two friends. "There is something I have to tell you two."

"Here it comes." Siren leans back in resignation.

"Yes, go on tell us how we bore you, that you tire of Dwarka, and would be leaving for the surface," Echo taunts him.

"No! Not at all, you are the dearest friends I have ever had. Yet, I have other responsibilities; I do have to go back to the surface." Descartes won't admit it, but they were spot on. The surprise here is how a lesser being was able to read his mind.

Behind Descartes, mumbled disjointed rhymes catch rhythm

and start growing louder. Siren gets up and joins him in the balcony. "Look," Siren points down to the throne room.

Under them the rumblers sing of milking venom from the gardens of Portuguese man o' war, of getting drunk and falling apart. It was the younger ones on both sides who initiated the mingling of clicks together. They took the floor, at the bridge between the eyes of the hall. The tune is a song of labor, sung at work by those who extract the nectar from poisonous creatures tamed and herded by the Dwarkoids.

Music knows not the limitation of class. Composed in the purple shades underneath the Portuguese armada, it was brought back to Dwarka by the toilers on their return home on a hard day's night. It spread quickly across the city, in humming hearsay from one Dwarkoid to another, moving up the social ladder until now, when it fills Descartes' court.

"See Descartes, they do get along. Dwarka isn't all bad." Under Descartes' gaze a new dance form begins to emerge, they tap their feet and jump high, singing while they sink back down again to the floor. A few of them blow deep horns recreating the music of the whales.

"You are changing us for the better Descartes. It might be slow, but your efforts are not in vain."

"True," Descartes agrees with Siren. "If I may dare speak my mind, I have, by now, learned nearly all there is about Dwarka and your people. You must not forget, I have been here before, when your parents were but children."

"True as that might be, you have nevertheless ignored the finest pleasure of our kind," Echo argues.

"And pray tell me, what may that be?"

"Copulation."

A silence falls between the three friends, filled by the hums and laughs rising from those below. "Do you forget to whom you speak Echo?" Siren grinds his words in disdain.

Descartes laughs, "It won't work, even if I was willing." He doesn't consider Echo's audacity a crime. It is he who with deliberation has tutored them to speak freely to him.

"Why won't it. You are physically able aren't you? You have your ninth limb down there somewhere."

"How is he not crossing a line there Descartes? You are still a God among mortals, why stand for such blasphemy?" Descartes looks at one and then the other. It isn't possible for him to grant Echo what he asks; deep within Descartes remains a Newman, and the laws of Eutopia do not permit Newmans to mate with anyone other than their own kind. It will not come to pass, he knows not how, but an attempt will simply fail. Eutopia will not allow it.

"Fine, we shall try it once, but irrespective of if we are successful or not, you will not urge me to remain in Dwarka later."

Echo jumps up in delight, "Let us go then, you won't regret this Descartes, and Siren you too shall be joining us, right?"

"Go where?" asks Descartes.

"Sure," Siren agrees, but his tone isn't void of bitterness.

It's Echo's turn to burst into splits, "I thought so, no one is foolish enough to pass up an opportunity to mate with Descartes. We go to the jelly juice crack beds of course. The viscosity of water is too low. It's no fun anywhere else."

Siren turns away from Echo, "In the rock are many shallow cracks, which we fill with an amber colored pulp, extracted from the coral. Regrettably he is right, sex won't be half as fun without them."

"Why don't I know anything about this? No one has ever mentioned a jelly juice bed to me before."

"You never asked." Echo expresses a smile by a swift change of color in his eyes. "Most of us are scared to death by you, though I am certain you are the heartthrob of the entire city." He can't help but be cheeky.

"I didn't think much of it. I know the science behind it that you are a hermaphroditic species, but that's about it. In all seriousness, I doubt this would work. There are rules that even I am not capable of breaking. If we succeed in the act, and that's a huge if, it will not lead to any offspring." Descartes takes a pause and then continues with distaste, "There is no way, I am not laying any eggs."

"Laying eggs is a breeze Descartes, they flow away with the current and the plankton. If they survive to their adolescence they return to Dwarka and find you. Of millions that we unleash, only a handful makes it to adulthood."

"No if I am to try this, there shall be no consequences. I shall sterilize this Dwarkoidan body of mine."

"Our endeavor isn't of procreation, it's about you having a fuller experience as one of us, as a Dwarkoid." Echo moves to the back of the balcony, he pushes aside the stone lid covering the exit tunnel. He works then with the multitude of his arms to free himself from the constraints of his armor. His body slips out smoothly from the chain of mail, leaving on the floor a bundle of belts and metal. Without a word his agile body pours itself inside a pipe in the floor, which, if he was any bonier than having a single beak, he could not have gone through and vanished.

"Are we to follow him?" Siren asks Descartes. "He does expect us to." Descartes too undresses and leaps after Echo, shortly pursued by Siren.

Only a fourth of Dwarka is visible on the surface of the crater, the rest of it is underground. Most public establishments of the City are exposed, and the private quarters of the citizenry are within the rock. Except the Night Bazaar; it's the only market kept under the surface, and that is where Echo leads them.

Swift is their passage through the plumbing highways of Dwarka, they ride the pressured water using their limbs only at turns. They are ejected in a sea cave, where the roof emits an aurora of bioluminescence.

Echo and Siren have visited the Night Bazaar before, so they know they must swim the moment they leave the tunnel. An unaware Descartes makes no such efforts. He fails to break his momentum and overshoots his friends, drifting off the cliff, reaching the center of the market.

On the sea bed and in the walls, he spots cracks a plenty. They all emit light and bleed colors. Amber is common, but a few emit a toxic radiating green.

"Are they safe, won't they burn? Where do you find the pulp?" he says to no one in particular, unaware that he has left the others behind. Siren catches up with him, slips one of his arms around two of Descartes' limbs and ushers him down toward the jelly juice crack beds. "Oh it's perfectly harmless, the recipe has been kept safe by the Drude bed keepers of the Night Bazaar; it is mostly not made of poison. They say it holds sea salp pulp, dragon eggs, glass squid ink and extractions of certain corals." They stop at a crimson looking crack with streaks of gold. "Shall I go in first?"

Siren extends an arm in front of the jelly juice crack bed, and at its approach the surface splits, letting the tip of his arm skid in. One after the other as the surface ruptures, Siren fits in more limbs, eventually entering the slime entirely.

He beckons Descartes from the inside, but Descartes hesitates. Echo, who stands behind, reaches and makes another opening in the bed, saying, "Oh dive in already!" He pushes Descartes in and leaps in shortly after.

Suspended, weightless, the jelly juice crack bed stops feeling slimy once all of Descartes' body is inside. It feels comforting, the way a massage does. Every inch of him shifts to a state of limpness, supported by the buoyancy of the bed.

Echo with his eyes asks Descartes to imitate him. Siren wasn't expecting them to gang up on him. Following Echo's lead Descartes begins to wrap himself around Siren in a manner only a Dwarkoid can. Each of their muscular tentacles follows the other's, spiraling around to form tight knots. The sensitive cup shaped suckers on their arms attach to their intended's rubbery skin to enhance the sensation.

Soon Descartes isn't able to tell where he ends and Siren or Echo begin. He falls in a pool of ecstasy. It is fun. It is novel. His last meager thoughts before he dispenses with his mind altogether are, *"Oh Destiny how pleasant would your surprise be when you see how I have bettered your Dwarkoids, and how deeply I have learned them."*

Nile's Toad

The infinity cool sky assumes the hues of Destiny's skirt. It's light and nearly touches her feet, bouncing with her every stride. The sky's above them and below, there is not a trace of a cloud to blemish its clearness.

Trapped in a globe of blue, they approach an upside down feline face, which hangs free at the core of the sphere. A road sign in green and Helvetica white spells out a mirror image instruction: "Be barefoot on the glass."

"Ah! The trickery at play here is strong. The reflection of the heavens is too pure for the mirror to be seen." Diablo reaches above his head and grips the not so thick glass, and pulls himself up and around. His action is smooth, as it should be in zero gravity. His hat, though, stays firmly on his crown.

Destiny mimics him with equal effortlessness. "The sky is now up, and the ground is beneath our feet, strange how we didn't know we were upside down." She unties her shoes and surveys the glass, trying to find where they may keep them securely.

"You could command them to float here, resist the wind, and not leave the spot," suggests Diablo.

"I do carry an extra pair in my inventory, still I am certain the Omniscient must have made some provision for his guests," replies Destiny. "Here it is!" She points at a hole in the glass, made visible by the refraction in the rim within the hole's circle. "Pass me your boots." She bends down to the hole and ties the laces of her shoes around it. Destiny looks up at Diablo, but he protests, "I? No, no, I would rather not take them off."

"They are only shoes Diablo," she says. "And I have already been privy to your naked feet." He hesitates, bites his lip and then relents. Reaching down, he undoes his buckles, setting in motion a chain of mechanical actions. The vamps of his boots release jets of air and then unhook, revealing his feet. They dismantle on their own. A network of gears that reinforce his calf muscles unscrew and organize themselves in the sole of his footwear. Without them Diablo feels exposed, and much weaker.

An unsympathetic Destiny takes his shoes and moors his along with hers. "Here." The two watch their shoes flutter in the wind, rising up by their laces as though filled with helium.

Their steps on the glass leave pressed stains of the grooves on their toes. The high wind whistles in their ear, but the air doesn't impede their gait. On their approach, the beast's face opens up to reveal a pair of transparent icicle canine teeth and a red tongue that rolls out, imitating a carpet.

Diablo happens to step on the tongue first; he shrieks and skips back instantly. Destiny lets out a laugh. "What happened?"

"It's much too rough. It's slimy. It's rubbery."

Destiny giggles and speaks, "How can it be all those three things at the same time? I am sure it's not that unusual." She jumps onto the carpet with both her feet together. "It does feel odd." She wipes her upper lip with her tongue. "It's fine. Weird, but not particularly unpleasant."

Diablo steps onto the carpet again, staring at his feet mired in the saliva of this inexplicable floating head. "I don't like it at all." He grimaces. "I reckon we have lost our way."

"We haven't Diablo, Daphne did say that the house of the Omniscient is never the same twice. It's random and new every day, and pleasant to only half of those who visit. Perhaps I am the better half today," she taunts him.

"Fine. You win," Diablo starts, waves of displeasure sweeping over his features with each step he takes. Destiny enjoys his plight immensely; she sizzles, on the verge of wounding him with a disheartening cackle.

Soon the slimy flooring ends and they are inside the cat's head. Their feet don't carry the stickiness of the tongue onto the tatami mat made of straw. They are greeted by darkness, and it takes a moment for their eyes to adjust and see the outlines of the room. A large gurgling figure snores at the far end of the house. Much closer is a low long table inviting them to settle down, with a pair of plain bamboo vases.

They abide by the suggestion the room seems to be making and take their place at the table kneeling, folding their legs underneath their thighs, while resting on their heels. The Omniscient seems deep in repose. "Would it be rude of us to wake him up?" Destiny asks.

Diablo starts his paean, following the instructions of Daphne, "O'Omniscient wake up! We are here, Destiny and I, to ask you how well we are suited for one another."

Destiny adds to his plea, "O'Omniscient wake up! And let me know if Diablo is the one I should have favored in the Couponing Season."

"If you would have recommended us to be coupled together," Diablo asks with a hint of despair. They wait on their host, but there is no change in the breathing of the Omniscient. Diablo turns to Destiny then, "I had my doubts with the mantra. Daphne as much as accepted she had never been to the Omniscient, and that her knowledge is limited. "

"Let us not lose heart Diablo. The legend of the Omniscient is shrouded in mystery. Nothing is known of its origin, except its purpose. Nobody said this would be easy."

"True, but what are we to do now, lounge here?" Diablo keeps her gaze for longer than necessary, expecting a flash of brilliance from her, but she is equally out of ideas. He looks around, to notice the rectangular nature of the chamber, and the canvas art on its walls. "Well, why not?" He beams, reclining away from Destiny. He reaches for the contents of the vase kept on the table, "It's filled with ice and it's melting fast."

Destiny is quick to seek one cube out and place it in her mouth. "Yum, I needed this."

"Is it flavored?" Diablo asks. "No one **needs** plain ice."

"It's an ice cube, cold and crunchy as it should be." Destiny bites into it with sound, causing disarray in the rhythmic snores of their host. "It's pleasant," she adds. A faint fluorescent green glow shines down from the ceiling, lasting as long as the Omniscient grunts, and turning off when he settles down in his slumber.

"I will eat ice," Diablo declares, scooping out a cube. He too munches on it loudly, further disrupting the Omniscient's sleep. The green rays are stronger this time, the matted floor turns variegated, but not for long. All the illuminants dim again once he swallows the ice.

The Omniscient mumbles in his dreams, "Welcome... Is it... not... Dest... and Diablo... Wel...co...," but much like a windup toy, its voice runs out of air.

Realizing what they must do, they fish out more ice cubes and rings. Diablo attempts to crack on three at once, but they are much too cold for him. He is stuck.

It would be too embarrassing to expel them on the table. "Ah!" is his soft cry for help. Destiny looks at Diablo struggle: mouth open, he faces up, attempting to swallow quickly. "No, no that won't work. How many do you have in there?" she asks, riddled in giggles.

Diablo shows her three fingers. "Not too bad. It's manageable. Try keeping two of them between your teeth, on the sides, and one between them on your tongue. Yes, that's right. Crunch them down now." Diablo does as he is told. "Now swirl them around." It's taking the last cube off his tongue, and switching it with shards of ice, the relief Diablo had been seeking. "Better?" She asks watching his apple chirp up and down.

"Much. I will be cautious with the next round."

They eat ice, constantly keeping their mouth full. Their grinding rouses up the room. The lights begin to steady. The matted floor keeps in it a figure of a lady in red peering in a bucket, eyeing her pet fish playing in circles. The walls are adorned with fine brushed painting of flowering trees in the foreground, and an ocean in the back, where fishermen of old battle the waves to keep their raft afloat.

The Omniscient is a toad. A well fed toad at that, its eyes are jazzy with green where white is expected. Its pupil, an imperfect cylinder with corners on each side, attempts to imitate a rhombus shape, but fails. It blinks at them with his translucent eyelids, as is the fashion with toads. "Welcome," it croaks, "Destiny and Diablo, long have I waited for you."

Its guests are too zapped to respond instantly, they are taken by its vivid wet skin, its patterned texture, and by the towel it keeps to cool its brow. Destiny is first to address the elephant in the room, "Are you a skin-changer Omniscient, or truly a toad?"

"Neither little girl, I am the Omniscient of many forms. I remember not who I was yesterday, nor can I predict who I would be on the morrow. If I would be anything at all, for I won't be here if no one chooses to pay me a visit. Though I do know it's hot in here, and I still would fancy some tea."

"I could fix that. I do have some tea leaves at hand."

Destiny stares at Diablo severely. "What?" he asks her. She says nothing. "You never know when cravings for tea strike you, so I carry some." He reaches for one of the many pouches attached to his belt. A green one. He unties it, and sniffs hard at its contents.

Diablo offers the pouch to the Omniscient, who with much effort bends toward his hand. Inhaling loudly it proclaims, "That's some good tea." Diablo then offers the pouch to Destiny, who contemplates taking a whiff, but decides against it.

"All right then," Diablo says with pretend hurt, knowing well she won't be able to resist the aroma of the brew once it gets going.

Destiny had not noticed the presence of a ceramic kettle kept near the table, in a wooden frame. Diablo behaves as if it being there is the most natural of things. He checks it for water, and is delighted to find it full.

He bends down beneath the kettle and wills out a fiery blow from his lips. He commands the flames to stay there and get the water boiling. Meanwhile Destiny attempts a conversation with the Omniscient, "So who are you today the great Omniscient?"

"Let's see," it replies. "I can feel my name somewhere here." He croaks again. "Today's name tastes earthy. It's Hekit." His laugh fills the room. "My hunch was all wrong, usually I am good at such things. I am not a male but a mother. A kind mother, yes, fierce, but kind."

"A mother you say? Where then are your children?"

"Hmm. I don't recall any tadpoles." The toad looks at the ceiling, thinking. "You are my children. You Newman." Diablo removes the kettle's cover, releasing a tiny mist cloud over their table. He sprinkles the tea leaves in, and then covers it again.

"You say it as though you aren't a Newman, Elder." Diablo smirks, ridiculing his own thought. The Omniscient does not mirror his sentiment, staying pensive. "You are, right?" Diablo asks.

"I am Hekit of the Nile, and a mother."

Destiny whispers in Diablo's ear, covering her words with her cupped hands, "I reckon he isn't a skin-changer."

"Didn't I already admit to that my child? I am an anomaly. I am unique. My thoughts are deep, and in my amphibian brain I keep the collective memory of your entire species." A thoughtful pause before the Omniscient observes, "I have always liked the tick-tock way amphibians think."

"No one in their right mind can deny how mighty unique you are Hekit the Omniscient of the Nile," says Destiny.

"Here." Diablo offers a cup to Hekit, who accepts it by the saucer, and pours it boiling and all at once, down his throat. "You can't help me solve the mystery of my birth, but I might be able to help you with my infinite wisdom. May I have some more?" he asks Descartes.

"There's only enough for three, you may have Destiny's share, I presume she won't be having any, would you Destiny?" Diablo asks.

Destiny takes a bit, but then replies with pressed lips, "Why won't I?"

Diablo knows the correct thing to do would be to refuse her, in favor of keeping Hekit in a pleasant mood. Yet he finds himself saying, "You are out of luck O'Omniscient." He pours a cup for Destiny.

"A pity," remarks Hekit with a knowing smile. "Let us address your dilemmas then, but first, tell me if I am not misremembering. You Destiny chose a certain Eutopian who goes by the name of Descartes. You and he made a fine duo back in the Academy, and believed would make a good couple together. That, in all fairness as I see now, wasn't a bad choice." Hekit waits for her response.

Destiny takes a slow sip of her tea, "Yes," she confirms.

"And you Diablo might be the unluckiest man in Eutopia. You waited to no end, as you watched your peers be gone with their ideal partners. The Elders didn't introduce you to anyone, and though you had a merry good time over the Coupling Season, you were let down."

Diablo laughs it off, "It's not as bad as you make it to be Hekit. I was glad to have a Bubble of Perfect Existence of my own, and it took me years to even notice my loneliness."

"Yes, I am not unfamiliar with your experience Diablo. Few the unlucky ones may be, but many among them are filled with pools of unexpressed creativity. It takes a while for it to wear off, and for them to see where they really are."

Diablo says nothing.

"If I didn't mishear you in my sleep, you are here to see how well suited you are for one another?"

"Yes," admits Destiny.

"The answer you seek is within you. I may know all there is

to know about everyone in Eutopia, arguably I might be second to only you at knowing you. Yet you won't believe my plain word, for it won't sound like the truth, but play like a weak opinion. Instead I would have you see it: you shall pry into each other's memories so you may learn each other as well I do you."

"Why is it that you claim to know us so well Hekit? We, I reckon, have never met you before. Isn't your duty limited to reminding quarrelsome couples why they are together. The way you must have done yesterday for our friends Damon and Nike." Diablo winks at Destiny, who nods confirming Diablo's concerns and the need to probe the toad.

"Didn't I say I keep the memories of all Newmans in myself. I can look back to the first time you saw snow Diablo, and the last time you kissed a dame... all I must do is go back in my thoughts and fetch your memories as though they are my own.

"Your friends? I would not know who visited me yesterday, for it was yesterday and I was someone else then. I could reach back into their memories too, though sharing it with you without their consent would be improper and beyond my jurisdiction."

"Spying on the memories of my friends. That's preposterous. I would never do that," cries Diablo. "It should not be possible, and if it is, it should immediately be outlawed, and treated as the most severe of crimes. One's memories are personal, they are sacramental, are they not? They are not to be bartered by you, as you may please. " He is outraged.

"There, there, my son, the troubles you imagine don't exist, for I am unbreakable, and no one has the will that can bend me. They weren't careless when they bestowed me with such power, they took the necessary precautions. I am the best keeper of secrets.

"You better be," Diablo sighs, reassured by Hekit.

"Who are they?" asks Destiny. "Who weren't careless?" Destiny has been keenly hearing the explanations of the Omniscient. "Who else, but the first Elders of Eutopia," replies Hekit as though Destiny's queries were the most common of knowledge.

"How do you remember them, if you don't remember who you were yesterday?"

"The same way I remember I had been waiting for you. My memory doesn't work the way yours does Destiny. I seem to remember the matters of my profession better than those of my identity."

Destiny cracked it. She leans in and whispers in Diablo's ear once more, "She is not a Newman, but a creation of the first Elders. Her personality is an illusion." This time Hekit does not barge into their private conversation, pretending she can't hear them. "Her intelligence isn't genuine. She is a tool, and unlikely to have any motive of her own."

Diablo nods, "O'Omniscient you said you would show us how well suited we are for one another. How would you do that?" He then whispers to Destiny, "That explains why Daphne recommended asking it direct commanding questions."

Hekit offers them his right webbed hand and says, "One finger for each of you to hold and pull on."

"It's slimy," says Destiny.

"Very" replies Diablo with a frown.

"Pull on three," instructs Hekit. "One, two, three." They pull together, cracking Hekit's joints with pops, leaning back slightly. They leave their bodies there, seated, holding Hekit's hand. They fall back on the tatami. Slow. The room blurs into streaks of light, which fills their vision, before they hit the floor.

Down memory lane they fall. A visit of the other's life. All they remember seeing through their eyes, an experience not limited to visual impulse, but a study of the essence of every moment's emotion. Nothing recallable left untouched, however trivial or personal.

Destiny's does see Diablo's first snowball fight. On an early morning, in a pine forest where the warm sun seeped through many trees, adding a brash of rich gold to a white landscape. His father tutoring him how to tune in a snow fort. Diablo, at six, was adorably proud of a crude barricade. She witnesses his friendship blossom with Damon, a trusting pair, they rode on horseback through the many adventures the Academy had to offer. She burns a pinch to see him in the arms of the silent white spirit girl on a galleon anchored in a lake, in a room of Boulevard Amsterdam. She sees those memories and all in between. Easy to consume story capsules telling her the entirety of his life.

Hekit isn't there anymore, and beyond the table is Diablo. She holds all his experiences as people do dreams on waking. Fleetingly. The truth is plain; she loves him. Diablo's wide eyed gaze is comforting, but in them there is concern. A bother.

"What is it?" asks Destiny, afraid that the flavor of her life wasn't to Diablo's taste.

"Machiavelli tricked you."

Out of the Cauldron

It's dry and hot the way Machiavelli would have it. On his doorstep Diablo and Destiny suffer their first quarrel. "It isn't only you who has been wronged here. He kept me in the dark too. Luring me out on a false pretext. He threatened me, and the fate of the house of Daedalus. Is he not answerable for the psychological trauma he has caused?" argues Diablo.

"Daedalus and Icarus, I am so very eager to see them." Destiny deflates the anguish in their conversation. "You know of Icarus too?"

"I remember them from the dreams of you, the ones Hekit was kind enough to give me," smiles Destiny.

Diablo steps closer and takes her hand, "Then you are aware of their tragedy, and how severe their pain was Destiny. It isn't fair."

"You are right Diablo." Destiny is gentle as she would be to a child, "Yet, you do realize his misdeeds to me are far more unjust, don't you? I may lose my only friend, my partner, and perhaps my Bubble of Perfect Existence too, for I don't know how seamless the separation of Descartes' and my half of the bubble would be." Destiny is relieved to see Diablo's face soften. "I wish to cushion the blow to Descartes, and I want to be protected from his fits of pique that are bound to occur when he hears about us."

Diablo's resistance melts further, "Won't you need me in there? We could pounce on Machiavelli together, and force him to admit his crimes."

"I need to tackle this on my own Diablo. You won't be any further than an earshot away. Let us keep a safe word, if you hear me yelp, 'porcupine tits' rush in then."

"Porcupine tits?" Diablo laughs, all his seriousness evaporates, "Why them? How would you use that in a real conversation, won't it give us away?"

"It's the first thing that popped in my mind, don't overthink it. Won't you be there the instant I say the words?"

"Yes." Diablo is still trying to rein in his laugh.

"All right. Then I have nothing to fear, shall I go in?"

"All right." Diablo kisses her luck before she steps in. He turns around to find a pitcher of lemonade on the marble fence. He is certain it wasn't there on their arrival. A sign telling him that Machiavelli is aware of his presence.

"Oh! Such a pleasant coincidence, I was thinking of the two of you, and was wondering how you should be here anytime now." Diablo can hear Machiavelli's silky talk from beyond the door. Destiny doesn't reply. "Where is Diablo? Hope you didn't have a fallout."

"He is waiting outside."

"Pray, why? Let me invite him in, the etiquette of the Welcoming House demands I offer him refreshments."

"No, that won't be necessary, we won't be staying long."

There is silence. Diablo pours himself a glass of lemonade, and rests on a pillar. "What's wrong?" asks Machiavelli.

Diablo gnashes his teeth, certain Machiavelli is pretending. He can imagine Destiny's struggle to hold herself back. "Did you not know?" He overhears her, and mumbles, "Don't trust him Destiny! Say porcupine tits already."

"Know what?"

"How is it that you knew Diablo and I could help one another better nurture our created creatures?" Destiny says in a brusque manner.

"That's a silly question Destiny, what else is the business of

Elders?" Did Diablo catch a hint of nervousness in Machiavelli voice?

"That won't do, you will have to spell it out for me."

"Our motto is 'Maintaining Perfection' Destiny. We strive every day so you and all other children of Eutopia stay happy. Do give us some credit." His manner betrays his contempt for Destiny's line of questioning.

"I don't doubt your motive Machiavelli. I suspect your method." Destiny's voice cracks. Diablo gets closer to the door and holds its knob.

"The unity of the council of Elders is strong; every time we see trouble brewing in the lives of those we are responsible for, we seek guidance from one another and from the Observatory. That is not to say, I wasn't delighted when they recommended Diablo to fix you. I have known him for long and consider him a friend."

"If our meeting wasn't your idea, who then is responsible?" Diablo can barely catch her words.

"It wasn't anyone's per se. When I mentioned the matter at the last council, it was the High Mentor Ananta who reminded us that it's always better to let people solve their problems by themselves, or with the aid of their peers. Instead of the government's heavy hand intervening in their private affairs. He believes in the merits of self-education."

"You lie," Destiny screeches, and she blurts out, "Porcupine tits." She isn't letting Machiavelli shrug off the blame so easily.

"What?" Machiavelli is confused.

Diablo slams the doors open. "Tell her the truth Machiavelli. Tell her it was you who orchestrated our meeting, and falling for one another."

"Diablo? Oh! For Eutopia's sake, will you cut the theatrics and speak plainly? What is up with you two?"

"Long have you manipulated our lives Elder, it's our time to ask you questions. It's best if you cooperate." Diablo keeps his calm.

"Or else? What would you do?" Machiavelli calls their bluff. Destiny is the one who replies, "We shall leave."

"Leave, is it? And where shall you go?" Destiny exits their conversational circle and takes an ottoman chair along a pillar separating two arched renaissance windows. She covers her face in thought, in a bow. "We visited the Omniscient."

"Destiny!" cries Diablo. Letting on that they matched best among all other Newmans wasn't part of the plan. Well, not until they were certain that the entirety of the last thirty-two hours weren't part of a ploy geared to serve a cynical cause of Machiavelli.

"The Omniscient? Why would you go to him?"

"Her," Destiny corrects him. "Hekit is a mother." She flicks hair off her face, and Diablo notices the warm light caress her cheek and brighten her neck. She is pleasing to look on, even when perturbed.

"The Omniscient has many forms, the one revealed to me was of a bull. Hapis was his name. He is a proud father," says Machiavelli.

"Father or mother, whatever the sex of the parent, he showed us things."

"Yes, its function is to reconcile the couples who are drifting apart. He would do the same for anyone who visits him. I still don't see why the two of you would seek the Omniscient."

Diablo steps between the two, covering Destiny, "How did you get the idea of introducing the two of us to each other Machiavelli?"

"It was procedural," replies the Elder with a sigh of surrender. "When a couple needs aid from other Eutopians, we share their woes with the Oracle of the Observatory. It is she and her Observers who, with their bottomless data mines, suggest the individuals or other paired couples who the troubled can work with.

"It so happened to be that they suggested the two of you for one another. It made sense, considering how alike your problems were, and yet how well your skills complement each other. Even the High Mentor remarked that he should have seen this coming, and that he wasn't in the least surprised."

Diablo and Destiny exchange a glance. Machiavelli is relieved to see that the second mention of Ananta has given them a pause; he shall now dismiss their suspicions once and for all. "If the Omniscient granted you visions, he must have then taken you as a couple." Both Destiny and Diablo avoid his gaze. "Did you find them agreeable?" he asks them delicately. They don't respond, they look away. He asks again, a notch more sternly, "Were you convinced by the gift of the Omniscient?"

"Yes," they say together. Diablo turns to Machiavelli: "We are paired. We are a couple."

Machiavelli retreats, walking backwards to his desk acting shocked; he slumps down in his rococo fauteuil. He looks comical in his oversized furniture. A bead of sweat lingers on his chin, growing threateningly larger. He breathes audibly, "This should not be happening. Our intention was not to realign you. It is possible that Diablo suits you better Destiny, but how can you be certain without visiting the Omniscient along with Descartes too?

"One should not be hasty in such matters, you should weigh your options before you make a choice. Oh! Poor Descartes, he isn't even aware..." He trails off in murmurs.

Destiny approaches his desk, "The dreams Hekit has given us are waning, and one day they will all but disappear, but the knowledge he has left us with will always remain."

"Yes, yes. All isn't lost. Mayhap nothing needs to change. Hapis wouldn't have shared visions with you without telling you how to make sense of it." Machiavelli's glassy eyes stare at nothing in particular. "Let us call Descartes here as well, and we can see who fares better. We could compare, and learn which of the two relationships is stronger," Machiavelli pleads. Destiny stays quiet as doubt fills her up.

Diablo speaks up in an unfamiliar falsetto: one he didn't know he had in him, "We can't let that happen anymore." He feels his misstep the instant he catches their attention. They wait for him to elaborate but Diablo fumbles, "It's not my place to tell you what should be done. It's your choice to make Destiny."

The late afternoon light peers through the tall windows, its fall has a tendency to brighten up the movements of everyone in the room. Destiny nears Diablo and takes his hand in hers. Pressing it reassuringly, she declares, "There is no one awake in Eutopia who would do better with me than Diablo. That is the truth Hekit gave me."

"Is it so? And what did the Omniscient tell you Diablo?"

Diablo finds his true voice again, "She said it is Destiny for who I had waited for, to no avail, during my coupling season. It is she with whom I should share a Bubble of Perfect Existence. I know now that without her I would never know what it is to be Eutopian."

Machiavelli can feel them in his grip, he must be cautious from here on out, "Fortune not as much as smiles, but chuckles at you today. Fate plays a bittersweet game, and its Destiny's turn. Would she play?" Machiavelli grins, "If you choose to be with Diablo, you will break Descartes."

"Why can't I have them both?"

Silence.

Diablo delays leaving her hand, wishing he could un-hear Destiny. He looks away. Thoughts are hard to come by. His eyes fix on a layer of dust settled on the translucent glass of the coffee table, marked with wine stains of yesterdays.

"It's rare, but not unheard. There have been instances of Troikas being formed instead of Couples. Though I doubt Descartes would agree to such an arrangement."

Diablo hesitates before slashing down the keenness in Destiny's eyes, "A Bubble of Perfect Existence can't have a trinity for overlords. It will be very unstable. I have always lived alone, you can't expect me to permit a stranger to trespass through my home."

Destiny feels cornered, "I don't wish to be cruel, that's all. Descartes has done us no wrong Diablo, a modicum of kindness would save him much pain. Besides, he hasn't had anyone else but me in a long time. His parents took off for the Sleepy Suburbia abandoning him when he was merely nine."

"You may visit him whenever you may so please." Diablo takes a chair, crosses his legs, and says with much gesticulation, "Stay with him for days or even weeks. Why at times, I might come along too, but the three of us can't live together. We can't call the same bubble home."

Machiavelli had not expected such magnanimity from Diablo. He spots Destiny's lip curl in a smile before being eclipsed by a frown. She says, "Where will my Dwarkoids live? I am not leaving them behind with Descartes. He would restrict my access to them on the lightest slight, and he would have plenty of excuses once I don't reside in the sixteenth cell of the twenty-seventh hive. No, I can't take a chance with my children, I must keep them close."

Nothing would entertain Machiavelli more than watching them quarrel, the idea of seeing them turn against each other is enticing; but alas, he must be professional. "Take a deep breath both of you. Despair isn't going to get you anywhere." He is thrilled to find a beggar's hope in their eyes, "I assure you, nothing you face is new. The generations that have come before you and I: they have suffered every possible challenge."

Machiavelli gets up on his feet and begins to pace around, enjoying being in command once again. "The history books keep a record of them all, and we only need to refer to the past to get you out of this cauldron." The wall behind Machiavelli's desk is that of books. "A library of Eutopian history, present in all ninety-nine Welcoming Houses of the ninety-nine hives. They usually do little more than add to the decor of my hall."

He partially pulls a few hard bounds by their headbands at random. "Let us see, I think none of these have been of use for over half a year now." He draws one out and flings it up, running his bony index over its spine in midair. The book lands open, and the pages flutter to a hundred and two.

The text in the book leaps off the page like a hologram. They appear in steps, the way letters would on a set of transparent scrabble racks stacked on top of each other.

"Where is it? Where is it?" Machiavelli is skimming through the text, "You see before we perfected the practice of the coupling season, conflicts such as yours were common, but since then they have been few and far between. Ah! Here it is." Machiavelli reads aloud, "'As of today there have been twenty instances of the Academy's duos choosing a coupled life together on their graduation. The odds of such relationships succeeding are one in ten. Following is a list of eighteen relationships that failed.'" Machiavelli scrolls down the hologram.

"What happens when a relationship fails?" asks Diablo. Machiavelli looks up, but it's Destiny who answers, "Most of them have to live alone for the rest of their lives, and a few are introduced to their perfect partners by the Elders. They are the lucky ones, their supposed perfect counterparts refused the next best thing that was offered to them, or they get to be with those such as you, who weren't introduced to anyone at all."

"Here they are, Vixy and Elena, yes, it's remarkable how similar their tale is to yours." Machiavelli takes a pause to regard the new couple, "I remember it well, it was all of thirty-two years ago when Vixy sat here with me, very much as you do Destiny. I remember the incident well."

"The incident?" asks Destiny, "I hope their story isn't one of tragedy."

"No, no, not at all. Elena wasn't pleased but we took care of it. It helped that Vixy allowed us to deal with her problems, letting a party of Elders descend on her bubble.

"One has to be patient when delivering bad news. We sat in there with Elena for nearly a week, calming her down, holding her hand. Not leaving until we made her believe she would be better free of Vixy, that there are still pleasures for the likes of her, that Eutopia is full of experiences beyond that of a coupled life."

"Fabrications. False hope," accuses Destiny.

"No, it's true," says Diablo. "My life up until today might appear lonesome from the outside, but rarely have I felt lonely when by myself." Destiny nods, though unconvinced. Instead she finds herself agreeing with Machiavelli when he says, "A better analogy would be the life of the Elders. Most of us were coupled before we chose Elderhood. After centuries we don't tire of one another, but we ease with such comfort in our relationships that living apart, uncoupled, feels natural. We may see each other only once a year and that's enough."

"What then was the fate of Elena?" Diablo is concerned.

"She is well." Machiavelli smiles, "She is radiant, a jolly Elder in her own right, the Warden of the twelfth hive; you may call her careless, but she is a poet of innocence, and a dancer in the making."

"You intend to follow Vixy's and Elena's model with Descartes and I?"

"With your permission Destiny, it could avoid pints of tears."

"Will it not be dishonest? It would be cowardly, should I not face him by my own."

"You could, it will release you of guilt, but for a time. In the long run you would have added to his suffering."

Destiny feels herself let go of Descartes as she caves in, "Fine, you may do as you deem fit. My only plea to you is that you would let me see him at the earliest possible. The day you are certain he would not be hostile, and will be able to hold a calm conversation of reason."

"I can't peek in the inner working of his mind Destiny, but rest assured, he will seek you out when he is ready."

Fading Grove

Retraction to land felt no different from a sailor's homecoming after a long voyage. Descartes sinks into the comfort of having solid ground under his feet again, and wraps himself in the touch of a zephyr. Being an inhabitant of the ocean for years has left a residue order of the deep on him. Used to the sea, it takes days for Descartes to become aware of it.

He takes a bath in a freshwater body, landlocked in the middle of the forest where he had first met Destiny on the day she had introduced him to the Dwarkoids. He scrubs, overcoming his desire to avoid water, silencing the excuse that he has had enough of it for a long time to come. He needs to get the nasty smell off his skin. He must be presentable, for he is going to the City.

All has not been well in their bubble since Destiny's been gone. Her absence was never intended to stretch over a couple of days, but it's been a fortnight. Nor did Descartes' stay in Dwarka and the speeding up of time there has helped.

Their bubble is built in a bipolar manner and it needs the two of them to function smoothly. In absence of half of its life force many of its systems have begun to decay. Descartes' thoughts scramble back to the menacing signs that he has ignored, the tiny ones such as the rising of the sea level by a fraction of an inch. The speedier than necessary winds that shook the foundation of Destiny's bamboo shacks on the beach. Those in which he has been taking refuge since returning to land.

He repaired the tiny glitches, those easy to strengthen.

Preventing a few touches of change to take grip, such as the flooding of unsuspecting anthills by untimely rain. He could have soldiered on, ignoring the clouds of depression that form in his thoughts, if he had not stumbled on a fading grove with wilting leaves. One of palm, the only trees Destiny permitted him to plant on her side of the bubble. A gift by him to her, they line her beaches. Graced by the capacity of reading the mood of Destiny's palate, they would shed the day's fruit whenever she chose to rest in their shade.

Shabbier than naked electric poles, Descartes found all the members of the grove standing decapitated, their leafy heads making a pile of garbage at their feet. The sight triggered the unwilling Descartes into action.

Dipping down in water one last time, he beats himself for not being vigilant. He had let himself be too caught up in his effort not to miss Destiny, to notice the damage being caused by her absence. *"You have left me no choice but to come look for you love. You could have dropped me a line, and let me know why you are taking so long."*

A notification pops in his mind as he pulls himself out of the bath and onto the grass. He's got mail. *"It's you, I presume."* Descartes fights the urge to call in the letter here, and ask it to be read out to him as he gets dressed.

He waits in the sun, turning up its heat so his skin and hair may dry quicker. *"An excuse won't do Destiny, I am not changing my mind regardless of what you have to say; it's been long enough already."* In the grass by his side lie a rope and a couple of articles of clothing: A white shirt and a pair of harem pajamas.

He puts on the low v-shaped shirt with a bold rigid flaring collar; it's adorned with a pattern of leaves that are subjected to Descartes' will, and today takes the shape of shriveling trees. He is ready to get moving once his pajama is firmly held by the rope tied around his waist. Descartes sighs; the only thing he hates more than getting dressed is leaving his Bubble of Perfect Existence.

A leap and Descartes lands on the Yonder Land of nothing but grass. Here at the center of the triskelion, he is greeted by the Master Beetle, "I have a message from our lady Destiny, my lord."

"Yes I received the letter's notification in my mind; do read it out."

The beetle rubs his front two hands together, "Do you wish I read the letter first, or lady Destiny's message my lord." The beetle isn't a creature of real intelligence, but is a machine attempting to mimic thinking, much like Machiavelli's puppets.

Descartes gathers that the beetle is in possession of two messages. "You may read them chronologically."

The beetle stretches its palms apart, but between them is sticky elastic mucus, which doesn't permit them to be free. It eyes this fluid of green. "The first is fifteen days old, and reads: 'I am leaving Descartes.' Left by lady Destiny for when you come to the Yonder Land."

"Fine, and read the later."

"It's a letter by Elder Machiavelli my lord, and it reads:

Mr. Descartes

Hope you are doing well. We are sorry you have had to care for the perfection of your bubble all by yourself for nearly half a month. Nevertheless you would be pleased to learn that we have found a way to lessen your burden.

Three Elders will visit you on the morrow. They have been entrusted with instructions from Destiny, and will be more than glad to help you fix the varied issues you may be facing. The party shall include Elder Pax, Oracle Cassandra and I. We are all very excited to see you.

Until then, yours faithfully,

Elder Machiavelli
Maintaining Perfection"

"What? Hand me the letter." The beetle has trouble balancing the scroll in his tiny hands; it wobbles before Descartes snatches it. He reads the letter again, and then for good measure one time more. He is puzzled. The news of Destiny's failure to avoid government interference in their bubble doesn't bother him as much as the lack of any mention of her whereabouts. *"What kind of trouble are you in Destiny? They can't be keeping you from returning against your will."* A vision of a duel flashes in his mind between Destiny and a faceless Elder, but he ridicules the thought instantly.

"Play Destiny's message again."

The beetle repeats, "I am leaving Descartes."

A spark *"You have no desire to return."* turns into a raging fire. *"Why?"* He grimaces at the remembrance of the last exchange of words he had with Destiny, *"Did I wound you so very deeply Destiny? No it can't be, something far viler is at play here."*

Circle of Void

They gasp as Descartes bolts over them with a supersonic boom, heads turn, and many of his neighbors recognize him. "How rude!" he overhears a pedestrian say, but he has no cares for their criticisms today; it isn't as though he has ever thought favorably of them anyway. "Nosy low lives," he mumbles.

He knows his way around, and needs no help in finding the Welcoming House. The taxicabs that are lined up at the edge of the plaza would take him there quicker than flight. A trickery of the Elders intended to instill civility in all visitors of the City. His mood is ruinous enough not to let him suffer the bumpy, uncomfortable ride the automobiles have to offer. He would much rather take the smoothing notion of flying's speed there, even when he knows it would delay him.

Diving low Descartes enters the hedgerow gate of the Welcoming House. The folly structures of its garden sit there to remind visitors of the hardships and struggles of Humans on the Earth of Old. Descartes does not have the usual minute for their guessing game. It's very unlike him to brush them away from his thoughts with, *"Are we to be thankful that we are spared the pains of labor usual for our forefathers? What is it to be Eutopian, if I am not to be loved?"* His personal dialogue scares him, *"You better prove my doubts wrong Destiny."*

He lands at the foot of the doorsteps and makes his way up, the doors open by his will, and without a sound. The answering bell which is supposed to announce his arrival shatters in the attic above the portico. Its pieces turn feather light and land on the floor. On entering the house the voices that were to declare his presence to those inside bite their tongue, managing no more than a syllable. He won't permit Machiavelli the deceiver any warnings.

He enters Machiavelli's study, but all his deliberations in the hope to take the Elder off guard are in vain. "Calm down Descartes, don't denigrate thyself by being so indecorous," Machiavelli states with pressed lips.

"Where is she?" Descartes booms and the entire room rumbles with him. The furniture vibrates and shifts an inch away from Descartes; a few books on the wall behind Machiavelli remove themselves and fall, but Machiavelli remains unmoved. He keeps his brave face on and says, "She is safe. She is well, you need not worry."

An image of Destiny being restrained crosses his mind: hurdled by a group of Elders, they talk down to her, arguing she and Descartes aren't capable of nurturing the Dwarkoids; and in her goodness, she doesn't disregard them and leave.

Machiavelli rises up and comes forth. He decides to seize this moment of weakness in Descartes and suggests, "Why don't you settle down Descartes, I know you are teeming with questions. So much has happened in the last few days, come, I shall fill you in over a drink." Machiavelli moves to the lounge and picks up a crystal bottle filled with amber. "Here is some vintage whisky, I am certain you have never tried. Its make was only recently rediscovered, the blueprint of which was lying in the public library unheeded since the era of the first Newmans."

Descartes finds himself especially aware of the distance between him and Machiavelli. His offer seems too out-worldly for serious consideration. He is three paces away. Descartes glares and his head shakes in rage at the realization that this is an attempt to neutralize him.

He moves fast. His instinct is set free of his mind. The goblets on the table roll over and fall, and the bottle in Machiavelli's hand slips and shatters. A shard manages to slash and injure Descartes at his ankle. In a breath Descartes pins Machiavelli by his neck to the wall, their combined Absolute Defenses rendered useless against an old school physical attack.

"Do you keep her?" Descartes hisses in his ear.

Machiavelli croaks in the choke hold, "I can't... breathe." Descartes softens his grip, letting the Elder say, "No, she is free to do as she pleases." Descartes lets him go and backs away a step. Machiavelli can't tell whether he retreats because he is satisfied with the response or if Descartes has become aware of how out of control he is.

Machiavelli doesn't care, and says, "She has left you." Descartes withdraws further. Reassured by the effect he is having on him, Machiavelli presses on with the truth, "You cease to be a couple. She has found a better partner in Diablo." He regrets the slip of his tongue: Descartes wasn't to know of Diablo.

The floor shakes in a wave. The stone walls, which were to form and protect Machiavelli from Descartes' tuning, barely appear at the edges of him, before he is thrown to the ground.

Machiavelli will never be able to do justice in retelling what he is to witness today. Descartes pulsates with a sinus rhythm, as though every cell in his body is a heart. A beat and a second, but on the third his teal surface ruptures everywhere simultaneously. Torn pieces of skin twirl in the air, but his insides don't leak blood. His veins and muscle tissue shoot out of his torso in waves of red and blue. Then they return to him, being sucked in by a black hole where his heart was supposed to be.

His features smudge and sink in too. No more does his body hold a humanoid form. "Where is she?" a screech comes from the hole. Machiavelli crawls backwards, not taking his eyes off the thing that used to be Descartes. It has neither eyes, nor limbs, but the hole bears teeth. It's a bodeful mouth without lips. "WHERE IS SHE?" His voice is unpleasant, and forces Machiavelli to cover his ears.

He forms an ouroboros: all of Descartes' body pours into his black heart mouth, he is recycled, and in a shapeless pulp he reappears to fuel his appetite all over again. Wind fills the room, chests burst open and expel the gemstones of Machiavelli's collection. The drawers are drawn further than necessary; falling to the ground they spew out the checked socks and the bright ties the Elder wears. The paperweights and paper knives take off from the desk and land with a smash on the carpet. They don't stay down long: the broken articles begin to swirl anticlockwise in a whirlpool, whose center is Descartes.

A startled Machiavelli thinks of escape, mayhap that's the only way he can guard Diablo and Destiny. The thought is proven futile for the broken pieces that make the wind zoom toward the absence of Descartes. They vanish in him. Machiavelli, too, against his wishes, gravitates toward the circle of void Descartes has become. He resists, commanding a chaise longue to hurl itself at Descartes.

A bad idea, for the furniture disassembles in midair. Its upholstery unpins and the white webbing sheet floats free. The screws that kept its frame together come off, allowing its wooden body to zip into Descartes. The sofa turns to sawdust.

One after the other objects in the room fall in him and are devoured. Much as how a shredder works on paper, they lose all form. They are broken down to an insignificant size, as though all of entropy has occurred at once.

"Fine, I shall talk." Machiavelli gives in as a four foot tall candle stand disappears. It stops. All those things that have not yet been consumed by Descartes fall to the ground, but the suspended hole remains. Still pulsating, still sounding menacing.

The wind coming to a standstill is the only sign Machiavelli has of the real Descartes still being there. All shook up and panting, he hesitates, still unwilling to spill the beans, but he can't dare displease Descartes, he needs to get out of this fix alive. "She is with Diablo, in his Bubble of Perfect Existence, the 238th cell of the one seventy-third hive."

In a blink of an eye a cool healing breeze rushes the room, and before Machiavelli could panic, the room is returned to how Descartes had found it on arrival. "Thank you my Elder," says Descartes. His face doesn't betray distress. He smiles. "Tell me one more thing before I go, did you do this because Destiny and I weren't ready to procreate?" Descartes offers Machiavelli a helping hand to get up.

Machiavelli, however, isn't ready to trust him. No Newman should be able to do what Descartes has done today. Lying there he wonders if there's more to Descartes than meets the eye, if there was more to why the High Mentor Ananta had kept emphasizing how crucial this mission was, even though to Machiavelli it had seemed so very mundane.

"I don't know anymore." Machiavelli gives his honest reply.

Descartes nods, his anger has all but disappeared. His smile is genuine. "I do apologize for temporarily wrecking your room. My business here is done, and I shall be taking your leave."

"You are mad."

Descartes withdraws his hand, "Yes. The sane thing to do is burn everything." He turns around and walks out the backdoor which leads to the City.

Alone again, Machiavelli waits until he is certain Descartes has left his premises before getting up. He rushes back to his desk and is impressed by how well Descartes reorganized all his things after causing such disarray. He finds his inkpot and pen kept at their usual spots on his desktop. Reaching for a sheet of paper he writes quickly to Diablo.

Dear Diablo,

Descartes is on his way to you. Be prepared. Warn Destiny. He is mad.

Your loyal Elder
Machiavelli

Maybe she will

Bright white light blinds Descartes as he steps inside Diablo's bubble. A feature hard-set by the Architects of Eutopia for the Bubbles of Perfection. A tool to allow enough time to the owners of a home to dispel unwelcome callers. Descartes had half expected to be denied the visit altogether. He was prepared to knock or if need be break in, disregarding the damage to the insides of the bubble his force could have caused. Instead he has been let in.

His eyes take a while to adjust to the minimal lighting inside Diablo's bubble. At the behest of Destiny, Diablo's generosity has stretched to a frugal three-foot wide ledge, enough for Descartes to stand on, but there isn't anything separating him from the abyss. He takes a peep, and is startled. *"How could you choose this over the delightful home we built together? How can one think of living here?"*

Looking up it seems Descartes hasn't entered Diablo's bubble at sea level but is much higher. He can tell this by the clouds, for they hang so near that he can see what a few of them keep on their backs. They are prowling the heaven, the white fluffs are sailing away, and the menacing black ones march toward him, intending to blot out the setting sun.

Those who flee carry entire islands on themselves... floating bits of a rainforest. Tall tropical shades of green... did Descartes notice monkeys swinging between the trees? The songbirds, too, are off with the forest, flying with too many flutters as is peculiar to their species. Planked rope bridges network these celestial woods, connecting the cloud islands with one another. Descartes' last glimpse of the fairer clouds is of a stag galloping with ease across a treacherous bridge.

The darker ones come in position, casting night over the landscape. The sun doesn't fight back, but, instead, is an accomplice in the crime. It chooses to grow dimmer, as though its mood humors an ice age.

Descartes checks again the lay of the land, to make sure his eyes had not lied. They hadn't. It's a waste. A piss pale chlorine mist keeps it dead. It breaks at times to reveal pockets of deoxidized swamps covered in green algae, the kind that favors the breeding of winged parasites. There are signs of what was once a bush forest: leafless stems shoot up beyond the veil of yellow fog; eaten away by wasps, they now freeze.

Descartes is impressed. The landscape doesn't puzzle him anymore, for he can guess that this isn't the natural state of things here. The floating islands that have left are a better indication of how alive this Diablo's bubble must usually be. All of this cynicism and dystopia are projections being made to convey to him how unwelcome he is. They don't bother Descartes much, he isn't here to measure the nobility of Diablo or compare himself to him; he is here to hear from Destiny. He pushes off, taking to the air to find her.

They thunder and it rains. Black are the droplets of tar, the warning shots. "Turn back!" says a voice coming from space itself. It originates from every fiber of the bubble; the stone of the earth, the atoms of the air that float by Descartes' ears, they all speak in unison. "You aren't permitted to leave the ledge you have been granted."

Without rage Descartes is a reasonable man. He knows it would be folly to take to battle with his adversary on his home ground. Nor would he take orders from a stranger. In defiance he stays where he is, high above the ground, neither retreating, nor pushing on. The storm gathers strength, and the rudeness of the droplets that lash him is willful. Despite the heavy tar there is dust, visibility falls and Descartes has trouble seeing his very arms.

Under this onslaught Descartes' Absolute Defense activates and he is ablaze. He is protected by a ball of fire, which sizzles and dims at the spots where the tar makes contact, but it doesn't let the outsides in, keeping Descartes warm and clean.

"You cower in your Absolute Defense? Duel with me fair and square Descartes." Diablo breaks his cover, riding on a surfboard made of cloud fluff. Only here in his own bubble does he have the strength to crack open the firewall that keeps Descartes safe.

He can't pinpoint Diablo's position in the black, but he reckons Diablo spies him easily. It's his bubble after all. Descartes must act quickly; he can't let Diablo catch up to him, for he can render his shell of fire useless by a touch.

A provision is set by the Architects of Eutopia to protect residents from the ill willed tuning of others in their bubble if a visitor is out of line, is defying all requests, while choosing to hide behind their Absolute Defense. The host can break through their shield, and can then easily expel them out of their bubble.

Descartes can sense Diablo's approach: it's the radiation of his will that gives his location away – a heat signal, which tells Descartes he still has time, Diablo seems to be gathering all his might before he strikes. Assured of his invisibility Diablo wishes to end the duel in a single blow that would knock Descartes out.

Descartes isn't here to fight. He splits his consciousness in two. Half of him is dispatched to seek out Destiny. It's risky business: telepathy in the unfamiliarity of a hostile bubble. If caught he would fare ill: it could be fatal.

Moving free through the sky, his consciousness skids through the atmosphere in a zigzag manner, the way lightning does. He can't be seen, but can be felt; he treads softly, not to give himself away. He knows she is here, her presence faint and buried deep in the paint of Diablo, which fills the shell of this bubble.

The Descartes that remains in the cocooned inferno intends to distract Diablo. He rises up, gaining altitude, with Diablo, who hopes to drive Descartes away, in pursuit. He believes he is making progress as he chases Descartes toward a far corner of his sky. Diablo will burst him out once and for all, and to do so he scoops up all the moisture that he finds in his path. Leaping up from the tip of his boots it collects between his hands, a globe of tar and water that grows in density and size as he draws closer to Descartes.

Descartes has no more ground to give, but he can see beyond the curvature of the earth. He gets a glimpse of Diablo's bubble, and is taken aback by a strong sense of recognition.

In the west at the horizon is a crescent shaped mountain range, the highest peaks among them reach the stratosphere. Descending in size are the ones that make the two arms of the range. They extend in opposite directions at first: north and south, then together they move east, as though reaching out to Descartes, who remains speechless in his circle of fire, in awe of their resplendent majesty.

His exiled spirit finds her in the woods under a snow endowed Bo tree. Destiny can't see him, but she appears to be in waiting. On an island so cold it snows there in summers, she is working her wonders when Descartes finds her. Bent over a picnic bench, she contemplates an assortment of petals. She has changed; no longer does she dress in white, but wears silver and a hue that out-blues the sky.

She is trying leafs of different shades and compositions to see which will best survive winters, and breathe life in the snow. She picks one of teal, and twists it between her fingers. She holds her breath, and meanders back to the Bo tree. There is new elegance in her gait: it exhibits the keen intimacy she shares with these new grounds. She sits under its canopy. She closes her eyes, with no lines of uneasiness on her face. She takes a whiff of the leaf, and in it she can taste a future garden, but with that gulp of air she is made aware of Descartes.

Between him and the mountains is a planet-full of gravity-defying islands. Descartes can't see any logic in the pattern that they are scattered. Adrift, a few of them are adorned with clouds, where others are naked: proud to show their rocky pointy tails, which often dip in the ocean below.

Yes, in this jam-packed bubble there is an ocean too. The mountains don't keep a continent of plains in their crescent arms, but they give way to the sea. Pockets of white or rocky beaches line the places where the two meet.

A glimpse is enough for Descartes to imagine the life Destiny and Diablo might share here. He tries to think of himself in Diablo's shoes, he tries to conjure an image of himself living on these drifting landmasses, but the very thought is nauseating. He tries to place himself in a homely cave of the mountains, but the idea of waking up to such a crowded sight is repulsive. He considers taking to the beach, but he knows he never would, for if he could, he would have done so back at home, when Destiny was always a call away.

"Is this why you left me Destiny?" he asks her, knowing he shall get a reply.

Vivid is his image. Destiny and Descartes have tried telepathy a plenty in their better times, and she has always had the upper hand. When they meet they have done so in the eye of Descartes' mind, and not hers. Not meeting as equals has characterized the telepathic bridge between them as unstable and faint. In the past she has given in to the temptation of toying with him, but she has been careful to keep it playful and her intentions honest.

It's Descartes who is in command today; it is he who has taken Destiny by surprise, sweeping her away from reality. Watching him surpass her for the first time and project his will over her with such ease intimidates Destiny.

"It is him Descartes. There is nothing to be done. By ploy or coincidence I met Diablo, and I can't undo it."

Descartes can recognize the truth of the matter when stated plainly. He tries to accept it, but his inner intuitive self revolts against the thought of losing her. He protests, "I can be more like him. You could shape me to be who you want me to be." The resolve in his voice is weak, mirroring his argument.

Destiny eyes him with pity. She stays silent, in the hope that Descartes would realize how irrational he is being. Instead, he is encouraged to say, "Don't I deserve a reply?"

She is tactful, "For how long Descartes? Would you rather not be you, than be an actor until the end of days. Would you not one day have your fill of me, and then revert to your old ways. Won't it be cruel of me to hold you in chains as you do the same to me? We shall only delay the inevitable, being unhappy all that while."

In the darkness of her mind Descartes moves toward her. Fear fills her to the brim. He kneels, takes her hand, kisses it, and then vanishes.

He is one once more, all of him returned to his body with the knowledge: *"This isn't my home. I don't belong here."* Diablo catches up with him while he is still assimilating. Finding him off guard Diablo does not wait for Descartes to recover. "Get out of here!" is Diablo's war cry, as he releases the tar ball on Descartes' Absolute Defense.

He had not expected success; he could make do with inflicting a setback to Descartes, hoping Descartes would recognize Diablo's presence then, and be susceptible to reasoning. Instead, the fire protecting Descartes is extinguished. Diablo finds himself landing a hard punch into Descartes, taking the wind out of him.

Descartes is ejected out of the bubble, and his sight is momentarily eclipsed by darkness in the passage of the cell. He then breaks through its glass door and is airborne over the plaza of the 173rd hive, but he isn't flying. The last of the flames slips off his left hand: an independent spiral ripple without fuel or the will of Descartes, it flickers out. He falls.

The Secret of Helix

Machiavelli is among a chosen few who knows the whereabouts of Ananta's abode. He lives in space. His being is independent of all creature comforts. He lives alone, a recluse. Machiavelli suspects it is he who started the introversive trend that dominates the habits of most Eutopians. He rarely leaves to visit the City and his people, that too only on matters of business and governance.

Machiavelli is reminded of how old Mentor Ananta is on entering his nebula. Where newbies such as Descartes, Destiny and Diablo have covered an area no more than that of mid-sized islands of the Earth of Old such as Britain or Madagascar, Ananta has created thirteen life inhabiting planets in three dozen solar systems. All of them are the real deal with comets, asteroids, and gas giants with planetary rings, far surpassing the two-dimensional illusion of a sky the City and most Newman have in their bubbles.

Machiavelli looks around in the black of the outer space for Ananta. He could be anywhere in the vastness of his creation, but Machiavelli reckons Ananta shall reveal himself in the only form and place he always has, on an astronomical plate made of reflective dark metal zirconia. He calls out to his overlord, "Mentor Ananta! I have screwed it all up. The mission failed. I was careless my lord. It's my doing, and you may judge and punish me the way you deem fit."

He can feel Ananta's presence behind him; he turns around to find Ananta in a giant's form seated in a *padmasana*: with his legs folded underneath him in the style of Buddha's meditation.

Ananta towers over him with Machiavelli reaching no higher than his knee. His eyes are closed.

Machiavelli steps onto the black flat disc that flips around slowly, in the cosmos of Ananta's making, the way a coin does when tossed. He runs to his feet and kneels, "I tried, but I could not resist him. He forced me. I should not have deviated from your instruction, I should not have tried dealing with Descartes alone."

Ananta remains absorbed in himself. Machiavelli knows his silence is a sign of displeasure, he is aware he is pushing his luck, but he has no choice. Either ways it's certain he shall suffer Ananta's wrath, and the later it comes the more exacerbated it will be.

"There is something wrong with him Mentor, he is much too powerful, he is insane. I had to tell him, I had no choice, my life was at stake."

Ananta awakes with a jolt, alarm cascading over his face. He shrinks as he stands up, falling back into the absence away from Machiavelli. He calls out from a distance, "What did you tell him?"

Machiavelli takes heart in the absence of rage in Ananta's tone and he confesses, "The address of Diablo and Destiny."

A marble podium carrying a rotary telephone, similar to the one on the zeppelin Machiavelli steers about rises up from the zirconia floor. Ananta picks it up and says, "Give me the Observatory please." He waits. "May I speak with Oracle Cassandra, it's I, Ananta."

"Do you have any disturbances to report Cassandra? Yes, fine. Good to know they are safe. My, my! That's a pity, it could have been much worse." Machiavelli can hear Cassandra's muffled but panicked voice too, but he can't decipher her words. Ananta reassures her, "Don't you worry child, I shall look into this personally dear. Yes, I know, we could have handled this better, if not for Machiavelli here. Thanks, anyway. Keep your eyes on him. Report immediately if you see him out and about again." Ananta puts down the phone.

"I am sorry," is all Machiavelli is able to manage. Ananta takes a while before responding, caressing his flowing beard he says, "I shall spare you, for the fault lies with me as well. Not letting you in on the reason why this mission was crucial was a mistake. Otherwise you would have been compelled to take it seriously. You didn't see how Descartes was different from those you have dealt with in the past." Machiavelli can't believe he is being let off; he isn't going to jeopardize his position by saying something stupid, so he says nothing. Ananta continues, "It is I who should apologize, I prioritized secrecy, and didn't trust you with the true nature of Descartes."

"The true nature of Descartes, my Mentor?" Machiavelli asks, playing it safe.

"Yes. He was a star on the verge of going supernova." Machiavelli isn't able to grasp the metaphor in use here. Ananta waits for him to add the dots, but seeing him unable to, he gives him another clue, "Do you remember the incident of White?"

"Had you not forbidden us to speak of the unfortunate incident?" He begins to see hints of the picture, "You are not saying...?" The thought inspires genuine terror in Machiavelli. "So many beautiful ones were lost with White. It can't be happening again. Is Descartes similar to White? Is he too about to go..."

Ananta completes Machiavelli's sentence, "...Supernova, yes."

"You had reassured us that Scholar White was an anomaly, you had promised that no one such as her could ever exist."

Behind Ananta, in the black, shapes begin to appear. Tall as pillars that support nothing, they come in focus as the Mentor speaks on, "Despite all your faults Machiavelli, you are wise, and so I shall let you in on the problem at hand. Would you walk with me?" The politeness of Ananta is that of a man who knows he can't be refused.

It's a roofless cellar, the shapes turn out to be wine cabinets, but the slots don't hold in them bottles of wine, instead they keep cylinders of glass sealed in metal zirconia. Full of a flush red liquid within which floats spiraling strings of mystery. "It goes without saying that you shall not mention the existence of this place to anyone, not even your peers."

"As you wish my Mentor, but where are we?"

"You are in the heart of Eutopia my lad, this is where the magic happens. Can't you tell where you are Machiavelli?"

Machiavelli nods a witless no. Ananta picks up one of the glass cylinders of those that he refers to as urns and hands it over to Machiavelli, "Do you not see what's inside?"

"They spiral in the way DNA does, are these genetic samples?"

"Yes they are," says Ananta with a smile of approval. He turns away and walks further down the corridor, slow as his aged body allows. Machiavelli places back the urn in its spot and follows. "Here in this labyrinth of a library we keep a genetic impression of every Newman who has ever lived."

"A temple of knowledge," remarks Machiavelli in awe.

"Yes," replies Ananta. "It is by the combination of the data here in my keeping, and the records of their lives with the Observatory that Eutopia suggests who should be coupled with whom in the coupling season.

"Are we then to fix Descartes by a study of the qualities of his DNA?" Machiavelli sounds hopeful.

"How I wish we could." Ananta expresses his remorse. "Alas, Descartes is beyond fixing. He is far beyond the reach of the likes of you and I Machiavelli."

"I understand my being incapable High Mentor, but surely your infinite wisdom will be able to save Descartes from drowning."

"Here we are." Ananta pretends Machiavelli hadn't asked anything. He picks up an urn and smashes it on the ground. Machiavelli leaps away instinctively. The DNA sizzles out the way a genie does from its bottle. It stands as tall as a man in between Ananta and Machiavelli. It auto rotates at its spot, exhibiting to them its every detail. Its four components, the building blocks take the form of color-coded stone balls, the first of amber, the second of cyclamen pink topaz, the third of tawny orange citrine and the last of glass. "This, as you may have guessed, is Descartes'."

Machiavelli reaches into the inside pocket of his suit for a magnifying glass. He peers at the double helix structure to read and see if he may find any abnormalities. He takes a few minutes to hover around it in silence. Descartes' make up reveals nothing out of the usual. Machiavelli knows it's unlikely that he would stumble upon what makes the subject unique by chance.

Still absorbed in his study he asks, "What am I supposed to be looking at?"

A touch of Ananta's shaky hand stops the clockwise rotation of the helix. He points at a spot waist high; wiggling his index finger he brings the conversation to a segment starting at a particularly bright fruity Citrine and says, "Do you notice the Serotonin Transporter Gene."

"Yes, I don't see anything wrong with it."

"Do you notice how short it is?"

"Yes, but that isn't anything to be worked up about, the Serotonin Transporter Gene comes in pairs, and all Newman at least have one tall one. Working twice as hard to keep one's mind at ease."

"True, that is the rule, but where do you find the second half of the pair here?"

"Oh! Why, it should be right..." Machiavelli stops mid speech. It's not there. Neither a short one nor a tall one. It's simply missing. "That's impossible," he whispers. "What then is the purpose of the coupling season, and all the hassle of making sure people stay with their anointed partners when mutants such as he can still be conceived?" Machiavelli speaks quickly in his growing ill temper, but without letting his annoyance raise his voice.

"Don't doubt the merits of the system Machiavelli. Our dwindled numbers would not have bounced back without it. You were not there in the era of terror, when so many had stopped being enchanted by the gift of Eutopia. If we muster a little tact we can easily take care of the few and far mistakes such as Descartes."

Machiavelli is quick to regain his composure, "I pity him, that's all."

"As you should." Ananta smiles, pleased by the humane expression of compassion in Machiavelli.

"Yet, I can't help but ask! Why does he exist at all? Is it not for the discouragement of pairings that produce the likes of him that we hold the coupling season each year?"

Silence fills the space between them and stays there a while before Ananta admits, "I don't know. I had tried to probe Gaea after the White incident, and ask of her why a glitch such as White was ever born. All she said was that it was necessary. Eutopia needed White."

Machiavelli sighs, "Well, time is running out. A Newman whose innate nature is to keep sadness for company needs to be rescued from himself. What will you have me do Mentor."

"Nothing. There is nothing to be done."

"Please let me fix the damage my callousness has caused," Machiavelli pleads. "I have a plan; I could quarantine him, and then with your permission if I can tell him of his condition, it might still be possible to reason with him."

"It's too late Machiavelli." Ananta shakes his head in a no with disappointment. "Descartes is no more."

Guilt keeps Machiavelli tongue-tied: no more can he meet Ananta's eyes. He is no expert at handling news of untimely death – such things are not of Eutopia. He is relieved when Ananta gives him a simple actionable command, "It's time to wake Descartes' parents: Ixtab and Darko. Will you cross the Styx and find them in their halls of Sleepy Suburbia?"

Bruised Zapatista

Bruised. His skin peeled from his elbow to his wrist, letting the pink of the insides breathe. He welcomes the pain, it keeps the more troublesome thoughts at bay. A limp suits him fine. His twisted ankle demands deliberation for every step on the way back home. The discomfort is acute enough to keep him entirely occupied. He could have flown, he could have healed if he so wished in an instant, but he chooses a walk of inconvenience.

They stare. His return to the twenty-seventh hive is eventful enough for a crowd to gather around. They point at him. He makes his way through their whispers of criticism. "Poor chap, that must hurt," is the talk of the sympathizers, overshadowed by, "Only fools allow themselves to be in accidents," and, "Don't waste your kindness over those who inflict torment onto themselves."

A part of Descartes wishes to explain his wounds; he could shout out and say that they were caused by a duel he engaged in, but never fought back. He could, but he won't; a conversation with these nobodies isn't going to uplift his mood.

The Hive has elevators. They have always been subjected to mockery by Descartes. In the past he has had trouble fathoming why people would delay their exit from the plaza for the comforts of their home by choosing to get into such ancient contraptions of travel, but today he finds himself taking one as well.

His muscles relax, the touch of an alien breeze is preferable over returning to an empty home. The people of the plaza shrink away as the elevator rises. The birds, which leave a blur of color off their wings in their path of flight, keep him engaged even as the pain ensues.

He hesitates before opening the glass door of his cell, preparing himself to bring the sad news of abandonment to his bubble. He turns around and looks beyond one last time. *"You are out there. You will never again stand here, nor walk back through this door as I do now."* The thought isn't heartening.

In the habit of being pleased to return home, his mind tricks him into a smile. A mistake. Once inside, messages and alarms besiege him. Ill news has taken the zephyr from the far reaches of his bubble, and they crash onto his eardrums. They aren't unexpected, but their intensity was underestimated by Descartes.

His natural response is to calm them down, *"It will be all right. We will be fine. No, the southern sea board shall not drown. The lake shall not leak and empty itself into the crust. Yes, I shall fix the nitrogen cycle, how did you guys manage to bundle that up? I have barely been gone at all."* All the while he walks on toward the shore, intending to leave the Yonder Land. *"The pH level of the next shower will be a pleasant five."* He steps into sludge.

There aren't supposed to be any waves off the cost of Yonder Land, the sea here has standing instructions to stay ripple free and calm. It keeps the shoreline devoid of rock or sand, letting the grass here kiss the sea salt. Lately, though, there have been waves, made evident by the swampy muck in which Descartes' legs sink knee deep. *"Oh my! The damage has reached here as well."*

The notifications of distress keep popping up, the ecosystem is under pressure and its systems are failing. Descartes calls the invisible gondolier to carry him across. His wounds sizzle in the mud. Every stride is a struggle. *"No, for Eutopia's sake, the ground shall not shake."* Descartes silences the bubble. It is overly sensitive to undesired change, Destiny was too particular about many things, and she had to be updated about the slightest happenings of her home. Right now, though, its wails and complains are too much for Descartes. He turns off notifications altogether.

Descartes brings the sludge on board, he commands its residue to leave his skin, and lets it jade the blue linoleum floor. Next he undoes his pajamas and shirt and casts it in the sea. "Take me to the other side," he commands, and crawls inside the dark iron felze of the vessel.

It has pillows a plenty. An unsaid rule has only had him enter here before on invitation of Destiny. He shuts its mesh sliding windows, cutting himself from the rest of his home, letting only a handful of rays seep in through the decorative holes in the iron window. He notices his unkempt nails on the knob, overgrown with their crescent lined with muck. He suppresses an urge to cut them. *"I would have never dared let them get so unruly with you around. Fear of your contempt kept them in check. It matters none now."*

In his arms he takes a cushion as large as his torso, and clutches onto it as though it's the last remaining friend he has left. The physical distress he is in manifests sharply now that he isn't moving. He might have fractured his right collarbone, it sure hurts that way.

He will wait here until they have come and gone. The Observers of the Observatory, lead in all probability by Machiavelli. He hopes they will come soon, while he is asleep, when he is recovering, so he isn't able to put up a fight. Sleep is elusive, but he must, for he doesn't want to be awake when they take Destiny's things away.

It occurs on the Earth of Old, before Eutopia. The logic of dreams, however, does not bother to fix the era or the century of the setting. In these visions, too, Destiny is special to him. He is particularly aware of the tenderness in her cheeks when she says, "I must find them Descartes."

She seeks her family, they who live in the realm of King Jeremy. He releases her, permitting her to go. Here in his subconscious projections his permission seems to hold value. He lets her travel alone, the tyrant is in retreat and is said be in sleep, and their rebel 'friends' the Zapatista are winning.

She leaves their house, a cottage, and time passes too quickly.

He paces around in his cabin, squeezed between pinewoods and a banyan tree. He dreads the news, delivered by a flat-faced presenter on the curvy twelve-inch screen of a wood-framed television set. Underneath a pair of V-shaped radio antennas, and above a white embroidered tablecloth, the screen displays war.

Clashing of swords and spears, muffled sounds of snipers and torpedoes. A fleet of bombers laying to waste entire cities and countries. She isn't safe, for human troubles boil the world over. Descartes is able to keep his calm for there isn't any word from the Kingdom, until the announcer speaks, "King Jeremy the Wicked has awakened and he has spoken. I repeat, King Jeremy the Wicked is awake, and promises the use of biological weapons." Descartes' left hand easily finds the hilt of his claymore, he unhinges it off the wall, and walks out the door. He is off to rescue Destiny.

To the docks and a deal with pirates, a safe journey paid in solid gold rubles to take him across the Arabian Sea, through the Red and into the Adriatic. A scuffle and the pirates try to sell Descartes and the passengers as slaves, but he and the other travelers mutiny and take command of the ship. They blindfold and force their former captives to walk the plank.

In the battle for the ship he sees the use of laser guns, spring guns and good old gunpowder. It makes Descartes take a pause and wonder how all these weapons of different eras could be used at the same time. He wonders if anything around him is real. The answer he finds is *"Yes, I have always been me, and the world has been such, and I must rescue Destiny."*

To the east, on the shore, on a cliff stands a fort: The prison Palermo, in which are kept those rebels whose victory Descartes had trusted in and therefore allowed Destiny to make the trip to find her long lost family. His hope was that they would be able to take back Aleppo before King Jeremy's slumber breaks. Alas, the Wicked's wrath was swift, he caught them in the act, paratrooping in secret into his city; he swatted their Zapatista mischief, and now they fill his prisons.

A party of four: First, a recluse mechanic, second a nimble ninja of sixteen, she is an assassin with black hair and Asian eyes. Descartes, a heavy saber-wielding slow-body, and last, an old lady brimming with strategy. This unlikely team has taken the now deceased pirate captain's cabin, and they together hatch a plan to free first the prisoners and then, town by town, the kingdom. They will anchor south of the prison, the cover of the forest will allow them an element of surprise, and in the dead of the night they will storm the fort.

Descartes' faith in the mission doubles when by chance they are met at the beach by the last of the Zapatista resistance: a bunch of ragtag warriors with small firearms, bazookas and grenade launchers. Together in the shade of a black forest they creep up to the foot of the Palermo.

Battle is joined at dawn. Descartes is at a loss, his blade does not once touch an enemy, and neither do the bullets of the King's men ever touch him. To him it seems he isn't there at all; he contemplates if he is in someone else's story. There are explosions, white lights that fill his vision, obscuring the violence. When it recedes they have victory.

Descartes made no contribution to this win, he has strictly been a spectator. His hugs and cheers are those of pretense, he can't let them know he isn't real. His smiles and laughter are disingenuous.

They have stormed the keep in which his mechanic friend is delighted to find networked computers; there are a lot of hurrahs and high fives going around. "I shall be able to find the exact details of what's happening under King Jeremy's rule with these machines," he says, and everyone else gathers around the computer.

There is much buzz and excitement in the room, for every warrior here has someone dear to them trapped beyond the enemy lines. They find a projector and eagerly hook it up. The room conveniently has rows of desks, the way classrooms do, and a white curtain screen no different from those in theaters.

It's a horror. Demonic creatures, pets of the King, wargs with human limbs, with the torso of a boar and the face of a rodent plague the wastes of Aleppo at night. Their two front teeth are too large to hide behind lips so they protrude and shine menacingly. They can't stand upright, but have the asset of four fingers and a thumb and are armed with clubs and stones even as they crawl.

The computer operator zooms onto Destiny's house first. It is after all Descartes' dream. The lens stays there long enough to confirm Destiny is inside with her old granny, the one who she had come seeking here. The vision then shifts to the underground to the sewage system of Aleppo.

The royalist wargs are here. In their lobster-tailed pot helmets, they crawl about with murderous intent, positioning themselves underneath every dwelling of the city. The camera then shifts to the beloved of the others in the room, all unsuspecting civilians of Aleppo. It moves back underneath the manholes again. They are ready, the harbingers of death, they ascend, crawling up to the surface.

The wave of rage does not wait to confirm the fate of the innocent in the live stream. Triggering from the closest seats to the screen, it washes across every bench in the room. The Zapatista all rise, but the hate in them is so pure that they are unable to word their chant; instead they scream. It's anger, yes, but its intensity is enough to set aflame the dream dimension. They burn to a crisp in that room together.

A Broken Toy's Suspicion

He wakes up in a pool of sweat. Breathing heavily. A recap of his nightmare runs across his mind. He is relieved it wasn't true. Destiny is safe. Descartes looks around, he is in the White Pebble Room. His panting slows, he wishes to reach out to Destiny, to tell her all about the ridicules of his dream, but he grimaces at the remembrance of his meeting with her yesterday.

He shakes his head in disappointment, *"You discard me as though I am a broken toy, and all my night is filled with is worries and cares for you."* His better arm dispatches no warnings to Descartes before hurling itself in a punch onto the wall. Freshly formed scabs are shed on his knuckles' contact with the stone. He shakes the hurt away from his wrist. He is more taken aback by the very presence of such anger in him, than the pain. It lasted for no time at all, yet how beyond the control of his coherent mind it was.

He pulls away the sheets and gets onto his feet, but his sprained ankle has him sit back on the bed again. "How did I get here?" he wonders out loud. He remembers going to sleep in the Gondola. He isn't one to sleepwalk, but there have been times when he has woken in the night to quench his thirst, or to find a more comfortable bedding, or the company of Destiny, and in the morning not know how he got to the place of his waking, or have trouble recalling much of the happenings of the night before.

Today, however, isn't one such morning, his wounds are too severe to allow his memory to make light of mobility, especially in the groggy state he is usually in on his midnight strolls. He gets up, careful not to pressure the wrong spots as he wobbles to the cottage's door. The night's rest, albeit disturbed, did help his sprain a little.

"It's still here," Descartes says with regret, but also pleasure. The Observers didn't turn up in the night to collect Destiny's things. Descartes finds himself wishing that she doesn't appeal to those in charge at all, but comes herself to parley with him. "To what end?" he asks the part of him that seems so eager to suffer seeing her again. It starts to rain.

He appreciates the serenity brought by the shower, it invites Descartes to forget the troubles he is in and those of his home, but the recent darings of his bubble don't let him. The bubble moved him, it would not have acted on its own if not to protect Descartes, but the trouble is there is no one here for the bubble to protect Descartes from, except itself.

The design of the miniature world of the garden where he is has a film obstructing the rain, it is as high as his knees would have been if Descartes was life-sized. The droplets – they are able to break in through the film the way bullets would the surface of a pond with gushing fizz, but they quickly lose all momentum, far above Descartes' head. It's loud, much too loud for a drizzle and the sepia of the sky warns of the storm to come.

Leaning on the door, he takes a pause. His mind stays clear for a moment no longer than a breath. His inner voice begins to mumble her name in a chant again, but he hears away. He would rather hear the rain and the silence in the absence of thoughts. It takes awfully long for the first distinct clear idea to rise in his mind. "I shall write," he declares.

He limps to the chair with some difficulty, positioning his leg carefully on a wooden plank that acts as the footrest underneath his desk. He flips open the book, and dips the fountain pen in the inkpot. He gets to work.

Descartes hasn't visited Druce and Makoto in a while. He first finds himself refreshing his mind by reading, so he may get a better grip on where he had last left his characters. The elegance of his own style puts his mind at ease. It takes him away to a world full of faces, but too few smiles. He marvels at how his characters are able to find grace in the most cruel setting of Tokyo.

Written in the image of him and Destiny, he delights at being reminded of the moods they shared, in which entire acts of his play are draped. It's a delightful story. A chain of positive moments linked together, each inspired by a heart touching memory he has of Destiny. If anything, his characters are better than him and her. Makoto is a pinch more sensitive, despite keeping Destiny's upbeat rhythm. Druce isn't as reserved as Descartes, he has friends! And doesn't harbor contempt for all company.

It's fun to think how it would be in his shoes, to hold a job, to be late, and run after busses. To go to karaoke bars and have a gang. Would the constant challenge of competition with peers, and the limitations of never tuning be too much for Descartes? Imagining himself in the environment of the past is a daydream he doesn't mind revisiting often.

Descartes starts to get nervous as the stack of pages still left for him to read thins. He has been reading the play and visualizing the acting in his thoughts alone, choosing not to project programmed role players on the empty floor of the room.

Later, when his writing is complete, he hopes to convince real Newmans to play the part of Makato and Druce; he would direct them himself. It is not entirely beyond the realm of the possible. The more sociable of them at the plaza might agree if they see merit in his work.

The deeper in the pages he dwells, the clearer he sees the motives with which he has created the caricature of Druce. Intended to inspire Descartes to be more patient with Destiny, Druce is there for Makoto, helping her soldier through the troublesome visions that plight her. Today, however, the more Descartes reads, the further disheartened he gets.

Makato and Druce, after much debate in philosophy, manage

to interpret the visions for what they really are, that they are from a time yet to come, that they belong to the future. Makoto is able to get over her inhibitions and begins to use the visions for good. She paints them.

Druce nails a portrait of a bench on the wall behind it, in the bench's future its polished wooden frame is dry and dark. Its wood has patches of green moss, and where it used to seat bird feeding pedestrians, a mushroom troop grows. The depiction of the wall on which the painting hangs is sans its yellow color and at spots it's naked, unashamed of its bricks.

They make a habit of taking walks together at night, stopping and setting the canvas wherever Makato finds a ruin that interests her. This is where Descartes abruptly stops reading, he throws the stack away before reaching the end, or reminding himself of how Druce and Makato's partnership brought them fame and wealth: the vile incentives for humans.

He needs to get out of here. He gets up and exits the room without purpose. It was futile, his attempt to write in his present state of mind. In every previous sitting all he has had to do to pen a scene was to reflect on the highlights of the past week. There would usually be an instance to fuel his imagination, such as Destiny plucking the stars from the sky and using them as ice for her drink. *"I was writing of perfection, what is it that we are now Destiny?"* He looks about as though the object capable of giving him closure lies around him somewhere. He notices Toro, not swimming, but on the garden floor, breathing heavily through her gills.

He sets aside his troubles and rushes to Toro. He glances over its body to check for wounds, but spots none. He presses his open palms on its scales, and asks what impairs her. "Oh no! Oh no! You have been poisoned," Descartes discerns. "How? Is the air contaminated?" He looks up, and speaks to his bubble, "Who did this? I would be needing a report on all systems shortly, but let me fix my Toro first." He picks her up, one hand supporting her tail and the other underneath her gills. He peeps inside through her mouth, and wills the poison to leave her body.

Tearing through her insides, the liquid matter collects in a ball just off her lips on the outside. Descartes hopes there isn't too much of it, as the volume of the toxin grows. Black as oil, it collects as a bucket would from a tap from a full reservoir. He hopes it won't tear through her delicately designed brain, but her neurons bust, millions at once taking away whatever little memory the creature could hold.

"She is dead," Descartes whispers. "Death?" He keeps holding her. The venomous elevated ball falls and stains the ground. Descartes couldn't even save her. He knows necromancy is an option. He can with ease return life to Toro's body, but there are no records kept of her dreams and thoughts. Few they might have been, but it's a collection of them that makes the stuff responsible for her gifted catfish's personality. Lost forever. Dead.

Slumped. He stays still for a long while, the passing of time isn't of any consequence to him, he stays that way for well over an hour, or mayhap for the entirety of the early evening. He looks up then to find the storm in full swing. It keeps in its grip the atmosphere beyond the protective shield of the miniature world. "They are here."

His hands shoot up the way they would if being pulled up by strings. He levitates, bursting through the film, its surface pops open the way hot chocolate does when boiled.

Human sized again, he rises above the peaks of the Lying-Man Mountains in the blink of an eye. The air gets thinner as he flits across the clouds and gains altitude. The higher he goes, the weaker is the storm's capacity to cause harm, and the further he is able to see.

It's chaos. Typhoons rampage the landscape with no mercy. A wall in the sea, made of a wave moves toward the shore. The sky is red as blood, it spells out the prophecy of doom to all that's living in Descartes' bubble.

"Who dare trespasses my lands?" he shouts at the wave as it towers over the shacks of Destiny on her beach. His claymore forms in the grip of his wrist, he twists it once, but his will keeps its hilt rotating like a turbine. With a swing he chops off the crest of the wave. Descartes' broken collarbone gives way in the effort of wielding the hefty saber, forcing him to kneel and take the support of his blade to prevent himself from falling. His intention was to slam the top half of the wave back into the sea, but he isn't able to. It crashes as a tsunami and washes away all twelve of Destiny's places of residence.

"Reveal thyself!" he demands from his adversaries. He knows they are here, the cronies of the Observatory to do the bidding of the Council of Elders, not acting against the pleasures of Destiny. His anger, among other things, is born from their lack of courtesy. They could have announced themselves and their intentions, rather than playing foul and taking him by surprise. They have chosen force over diplomacy, they wish to wrestle Destiny's half of the bubble away from him.

Attacking him wasn't wise. Descartes was open to reason, but now they leave him with no choice but to fight and defend his home. They are mistaken if they think he shall relent easily.

He demands the bubble to tell him who the perpetrators are, how big is the invasion, and where do they hide. On opening his telepathic channel with the bubble he is beseeched by pleas of the Dwarkoids: "Save us our Lord." They pray at his altar, assembled in panic are hundreds, in the hall of Newmans – the one which he used as his courtroom when kinging over them.

Their despair is addressed to a humanoid statue that they have erected in the center of the hall. It sits on a human chair, which has replaced the device that made Descartes' Dwarkoidian throne. It's supposed to represent Descartes, but it isn't anything like him. Dwarkoids aren't capable of telling Newman faces apart, but they have built the image of their God to the best of their knowledge, and have given him a mouth, a nose, a pair of eyes, and ears.

Descartes' consciousness enters this statue and takes charge of its limbs and features. It isn't designed to move; bits of its stone body break away and fall at the joints, as Descartes tries to stand up, causing his devotees to scatter in fright.

"What's the matter?" he asks, in the tongue of the Dwarkoids. There's too much ruckus there for him to get an immediate response. Rubble is raining down, and on looking up Descartes finds the roof is about to fall. He holds the ceiling up, and his touch reveals deep cracks in its structure. If he releases his grip the building will surely fall. "What's happening here?"

It's Echo who answers, he is the one who has lead his people in the reciting of the hymns that have summoned Descartes. "It's Armageddon, oh Lord God. The ocean floor spits out lava, we are surrounded by purple fire, a flame so hot that it burns here as well. Our drowned city Dwarka is aflame. Only you can save us Lord. We call upon you to undo the apocalypse."

It's one thing to wreck a bunch of bamboo shacks held up on stilts, but he can't believe they have gone so far as to jeopardize the existence of an entire civilization. He leaves the statue there acting as the chief pillar for the hall, no different from the way Atlas holds up the globe or Krishna a mountain.

"I will make you pay for this, whoever you are!" Descartes screeches, once he is back in his physical body. He doubts now if it's the Observers who infiltrate his bubble. They won't disrespect the laws of Eutopia. Wasn't it the excuse to discuss the protection of the future of the Dwarkoids that Machiavelli had used to lure away Destiny?

"*Machiavelli! Is it he who you asked to handle your dirty business for you Destiny. It may so well be; all he had to do was to rush here when I was off to see you, or mayhap while I was sleeping, he could have very easily sneaked in then and succeeded in his evil will of disruptive change which plagues our home.*" Descartes' suspicion shifts. "Tell me of all the happenings here from when I left the day before, up until now," Descartes commands the bubble.

His eyes move rapidly behind their lids while replayed to them in time-lapse is the rising and setting of the sun twice over. First he sees himself exiting the bubble, and regrets his forgetfulness. Before leaving he should have frozen the bubble by suspending all its operations. He should have asked it to hibernate, waiting for Destiny or his return. Unfortunately, he got so worked up by the letters that the only objective he was able to hold was to find her.

"Is that how you and Machiavelli made a fool of me Destiny? Tricking me into leaving, making sure that I forget to put our bubble to sleep. An alarmist message to draw me out and then discreetly slipping inside to ruin everything?"

Leaving the bubble active, without the presence of a stabilizing Newman overlord is never a good idea. By his very being the clouds remember not to rain over the Attic, and the waves to not spoil the shoreline of the Yonder Land. Without him the elements of the bubble attempt to imitate their ancestors of the Earth of Old.

The specified zigzag path the sun has been asked to navigate across the sky so it may cast shadows of measured lengths at the spots that Destiny has taken a fancy to was promptly discarded in favor of a more natural but boring straight line.

The forest in his absence is able to see the truth of the two dimensional illuminative yellow sticker pinned on a domed ceiling. It switches off the tiny factories that manufacture oxygen in its greens, powering down to a strike.

"Ah! That explains the pH level, and such silly disparities which the bubble greeted me with on my return. If not when I was out, did you dare make your move while I slept? That's far too bold for someone such as Machiavelli."

No one visited his bubble while he was out. A long watch of the recording shows him leaving and returning to the bubble, and his crawling into the felze of the Gondola. *"He makes his move when I was out cold, isn't it Destiny? That conniving Machiavellian."*

Yet, a hunch has him forgo three-dimensional viewing in favor of keeping an eye on two different locations simultaneously. On his one retina the bubble feeds the recording of its gates on the Yonder Land, and on the other, that of Descartes sleeping. He is still confident Machiavelli will be bursting onto the scene at any moment.

Hours pass by but there is no sign of the Elder. The only point of interest is his restlessness in bed. Descartes twitches, his motions aren't smooth, but they flash in a blur, as though he isn't of flesh and blood but of clockwork.

He cries in his sleep. His precious tears don't inspire sympathy in Descartes. *"Weak."* He has no pity for himself. *"What of worth did you ever see in someone as fickle as I Destiny?"* "Stop crying, you nothing of a man." Descartes lashes out but to no avail. He can access the memory of the bubble, but he can't rewrite it. Newmans don't have the power to reverse the Arrow of Time. Nevertheless, he tries to wake himself up by shaking.

It isn't so, but it seems that in response to his touch Descartes turns away. "Wake up!" he shouts at himself through space-time, but his voice never reaches the other end of the line.

His sobs die down, but he continues to fidget under the sheets. His motion gets violent, repetitive and fast, his knees and elbows shoot up within the sheets to make hills. He tries to rise but isn't able to and his movements stop making sense. Concealed by the cloth, a dozen peaks rise and fall in succession, too narrow and quick to be considered human.

"Are you skin changing in there?" Descartes asks, before the covers slip. He had expected to see himself in his Dwarkoidian form, that would have explained the multitude of limbs playing with the quilt, but, instead, he finds a pile of bugs.

Doom's Clarity

Metal are their horns in their black crowns in shape of hooks. Ablaze, rich patterns grace their backs while they stay constantly on the move. They churn among themselves, crawling over one another. A biological machine. A stampede of bugs. A colony of beetles. The only trace of Descartes ever being there is the shape the insects are stacked up in. They keep a humanoid outline that resembles his dimensions.

Voices in his head, they scream in terror at the sight of the swarm, "What's happening to me?" He remembers nothing of this transformation in his sleep. It shakes him. If there is anything Descartes values more than Destiny, it's his sanity. His identity. The bugs make up their mind to break formation and move out. Descartes panics and he tries to hold them in place.

Defying the rules of time, his hand smudges through them, and he feels their insides. Their pulp is silver cool to the touch, but he isn't able to grasp them. "What's this?" he gasps.

The bugs envelop his hands, they march up toward his elbows. He tries to pull out but the beetles don't let go. His skin starts to simmer, the way tea in a cup would tremble at the first vibrations of an earthquake. The longer his arms remain stuck in the pile of bugs, the more volatile his composure becomes. He commands his skin to smooth out, and the bugs to release him, but they refuse.

They are all over him. Descartes attempts to mouth his wishes to his bubble, but he finds his voice missing. He isn't allowed to make a sound. There is no sound. Only the sinister squeaks and hisses of the insects.

His neck grows stiff, he can't turn or see how much of him is covered in bugs. To his relief, they stop moving. A silence in which Descartes can do little but anticipate. He is powerless. Despair sets in. He is scared.

They lift their husk hard hoods to reveal a pair of delicate translucent wings. They spread them apart and from within a green bio-illuminated, pulsating oval body beckons Descartes to come join them.

In this hour of horror, by their light an alien but amusing idea impresses his mind. "So it's time." He finds his voice again. His terror is eclipsed by endearment, and he sees the beetles in a new light.

If he had any cares for self-preservation he would have struggled on, and would be plotting how to free himself from their grip. He should be frightened at least, but instead, he yields to his fate. He shatters.

An explosion. He isn't one but many. Bits of him smear onto the pillows like sawdust. He thickens the air within the gondola's cabin. The bugs recognize Descartes' dissipation into dust as their cue to start feeding. They take flight, buzzing up the room.

Descartes delights at being so much lesser than a Newman. His thoughts are nil, clean and in bliss. Lighter than a feather, parts of him stay suspended, the rest of him settles down, and he latches onto any object that the countless bits of him may come by. He sees nothing, he hears nothing, but he can touch and feel all that's there in the felze.

It tickles when the bugs gobble him in, plucking him from the air, and feasting on him on the floor. They munch and they cricket, a party of the six-legged, with Descartes the only item on the menu.

It takes a while for the beetles to eat all of Descartes dust. It isn't unpleasant; his consciousness starts to club together, piece by piece, in the hive mind of the beetle colony, gracing Descartes with the sense of sight through the many compound eyes of every individual beetle. His new intelligence activates when all of him has been consumed. It's different from the old by lacking specifically the capacity to entertain high thoughts of philosophy and logic; rather it has an intuitive bent, and a novel moral certainty.

Once inside the belly of the many beetles, he is bestowed with the power to control them. He questions not his mission, and experiences a holy pleasure in directing the bugs out through the air holes in the windows of the gondola.

They shoot away in a circle from the boat in a shape of a single wave emitted from a radio tower. Transmitting Descartes' will, and with their destinations predetermined, in haste they take the shortest routes, those which can be drawn with straight lines on an aerial map.

To the nooks and corners, to the caves, to the Attic, to the undergrowth, within the trees. They swim down to the ocean floor, they slip in the cracks in the walls of the stone keeps and forts. They take his command everywhere they go. Their one word message is 'doom'. In the depths of their hive mind, Descartes speaks, *"I hear you call my destiny and here I come."*

He is in all of them at once. They shut their wings within their double-leafed hoods. The vivid patterns on their backs were meant to camouflage them with the surfaces on which they land. Quarts in the gravel of the beach, pink lines on limestone. The beetles melt. Descartes melts. They cease to be, so does he, becoming a part of the background, one with the very fabric of his bubble.

His mind changes again, no more is his thinking trapped by the limitations of the hive mind of the beetle colony, nor is he his former Newman self. Instead he is the ideal complete version of the persona Descartes. He can feel his bubble integrated within him. A part of him, as natural to him as his physical body had considered the two lobes of his brain.

He can once more entertain humane thoughts. Though without a body he knows not where they arise, *"Is this the delight you had kept in store for me? Is there more? How could that be?"* He is calm as the surface of a lake in serenity.

To this new Descartes is revealed the true guardian of Eutopia. Naked and tall she is flanked by her two younglings. They steal all the words from him but the ones reserved in their praise. Their very presence is ethereal, but they aren't a mystery to Descartes. He is in awe of them, and he knows who they are.

"Come closer," says the guardian, her voice delicate and young, but it carries a motherly authority. He complies, without limbs and without a body he is drawn toward them. "Don't worry," she encourages him. "I only want to see you more clearly." She beckons him with a gesture of her sharp eyebrows. "It's over now. You will be fine dear. You are free of your worldly pains," she promises. "Your troubles are a thing of the past." She spreads her arms, inviting him for a hug. "You will be one of us, you will be at peace."

Descartes believes her. Yet he hesitates. He knows if he accepts her invitation there is no going back. He contemplates his position, inching toward the three. Will he miss the world if he is one with Eutopia? He shall be the Omniscient. He shall be omnipresent. No knowledge will be kept from him, he shall be the very medium in which knowledge exists. It's tempting, and it's hard to see the fine print trade off unmentioned.

Breaking the spell, the youngling on the right, silver of straight hair, and plain of freckled face, shrieks, "STOP!" She never moved her lips. Yet her tone is severe, and ruffles the tranquility that is Descartes.

She turns to look at her guardian, who Descartes knows by name. She is Gaea. "He isn't yet ready to be one of us Mother Eutopia." Gaea looks at her with kindness, the way parents do when their children make honest mistakes in their attempts to learn the ropes of the world.

"Look at him White, he is nothing. No body, no thoughts. Besides, he has suffered so deeply. Don't you empathize with him?"

"Ask him; what is it that he is carrying."

Eutopia stares at White with suspicious eyes, and then she, Gaea Eutopia, asks Descartes to do something for her, "Descartes, child, show me what you carry." He can't restrain his urge to please her, and though he has nothing on his person – for he isn't a person – he is thrilled to present Gaea with a crystal globe.

Descartes is as surprised by the presence of the object as he is by the disappointment which shrouds Mother Eutopia's face. Looking at it carefully he finds in this globe a figure of Destiny, as he last remembers her. Divine under a Bo tree with a tulip in her hand. One look at her, and his will is berthed again; Descartes wishes to join her there under the canopy within the crystal globe. His Newman body begins to form next to her.

"NO STOP!" It's the girl called White again. Descartes obeys. He is uniquely malleable to the wishes of the three. "You can't carry your baggage and be one with us Descartes." Affection oozes from Gaea. "You need to let go of her," she tells him. "Do you understand?"

Descartes would have nodded in affirmation, if he had the luxury of a head. Nevertheless, his acknowledgement is received. "I will forget Destiny," he tells them. He lets go of the globe and demands of his mind to erase all memory of her. He glitches. His chain of thought disrupts.

"Take your time child. We aren't going anywhere. We shall wait for you here." The image of the three wanes and along with it the consciousness of Descartes breaks. Gaea says, "Go now, do what you must, and don't forget, we love you."

"Please no, don't send me back" is all he is able to muster before his intelligence is packaged in little boxes and placed once more in the tiny skulls of beetles. They re-emerge out from the spots where they had melted. The last that he sees of the three is Tetsuo, the youngling on the left of the Guardian Gaea Eutopia, spiky of hair,

with a Superman red cape on his back. He wishes Descartes luck
with a thumbs up and says, "Remember, rage is good."

That's when the beetles take off again, taking Descartes to the
White Pebble Room.

The Great Dying

The dreams that depict an altered personality of the dreamer are the ones that invite doubt onto themselves, and run the risk of turning lucid. A telepathic discourse with the Bubble of Perfect Existence works in the same way.

Descartes' out of world conversation with Gaea and the twice over disintegration of his consciousness and its coming back together are enough to break the spell, letting him remember where he is.

He had struggled hard to keep open the telepathic channels of his mind that allowed him to communicate with Eutopia via his bubble. Yet, despite all his will, his grip had loosened. No, please keep me, don't let me suffer anymore. I can't..." he had protested, but the vision of the three faded and was replaced by that of the beetles who had found their way to the White Pebble Room. There they formed his sweltering sleeping body from earlier in the day.

"Why was your memory concealed from me on my waking?" Descartes had witnessed his meeting with Gaea only in telepathy with his bubble. "Why instead did I have the nightmare of Aleppo?" are the questions that Descartes asks on hanging up the telepathic phone, and before he could readjust to where he physically is.

He is in the sky, and with a God's view he oversees the typhoons, which haven't in the least lost strength. He spots pages, bookshelves and cabinets in their whirlwind, proof that they have already trampled over the Attic.

Loud is the sound of the churning mantle deep underground.

It's an earthquake. Suspended in the air, he swirls once on the spot to take stock of what's happening all around. He watches without remorse the fracturing of his favorite keep built on a motte. It had often served as the site for the sighting of aurora lights on wintry nights. Not an ounce of sympathy moves Descartes to see it crumble to rubble and dust. "I get it now. If you had left our meeting as a residue of a dream, I would not have trusted in it."

"I don't need you anymore," Descartes screeches at his home. "This great dying is my doing." His outburst shocks his bubble, making it pause. Everything stands still, the mud color typhoons don't lose shape, but they halt in their gait. The furniture in their whirl don't start respecting gravity, but they stop moving, and stay stagnated in mid-flight. The tremors, they quiet down and so does the call of alerts of the beasts and birds in panic. His home comes to a standstill the way a playback of a three-dimensional video would when its operator strikes the pause key on their console.

Being at the mercy of Gaea Eutopia and her two younglings had made Descartes forget his powers of tuning. It comes as a surprise to him that all he had to do to achieve quiet was wish for it.

"I don't need you anymore," Descartes repeats, as much to the bubble as to himself. He tries to think away, but a flash remembrance of Destiny's embrace has him say, "How could she abandon me?"

He had always known that one such as Diablo existed somewhere in Eutopia. "She was never supposed to meet him. I should not have let her go to the City on her own. They tricked me." His Absolute Defense of fire activates. "I hate you all. I hate everything." His anger prevents him from being eloquent.

In his private circle of fire he hisses, "Be gone and never come back." He radiates heat, filling with energy the space between him and the outer rim of his protective flames. He shuts his eyes and shudders with determination, his body stiffens. "I don't need you anymore, go away and never come back." Descartes knows his words to be true. The atoms in the air that surrounds him start churning within the circle of fire, catching speed, and with each revolution their velocity doubles. He musters more and more of his will together. The lit up globe that he is in pulsates and grows. Outshining the pretend sun Destiny and Descartes had casted as the light bringer for their home.

The very ocean evaporates in this new warming, the sea-level depletes. The Dwarkoids in their drowned city intensify their efforts in prayer, as the room of their underwater world shrinks. In the face of certain death by surfacing, the oceanic beings have no one else to turn to but Descartes.

His kindness for his eight-limbed friends is limited to a word of reassurance, "You shall not suffer long, nor as severely as my ancestors had on the Earth of Old, when their ecosystem had collapsed."

Unaware of human history, they take his message to be the proclamation of Judgement Day. In despair, they plead to him to undo his decision. Unfortunately for them, their cries fall on deaf ears. Descartes finds only cacophony in their voices. If anything they disgust him. "I am not your savior. I am your doom. Pray to her, your beloved mother, let us see if she cares." Descartes dams them. He stops listening. He has no need of the Dwarkoids anymore, his only want is to be with Eutopia, and he can't afford to be distracted from his quest to search within himself a path to her.

He brings forth additional will from the depths of his being, from the mines in his core he didn't know existed. The revolving atoms in his circle of Absolute Defense are stripped of their electrons as they near light speed, turning into plasma, turning into the matter of stars. Descartes is unaware, but this is when his body loses its organic form.

He grows to fill half of the sky, and the heat that he gives off burns the earth. A summer so harsh, that it sparks a holocaust. Burning forest, melting stone, bringing an abrupt end to all who roam the lands.

The bubble doesn't resist him. In the absence of Destiny, the only will it has is a reflection of Descartes'. It makes no attempts to preserve itself. It does not activate its immune systems. There are no frantic commands for the clouds to gather and to rain down to stamp out the fire. The sea isn't asked to break its embankments to relieve the scorched land. Forewarned of the happenings of now by the beetles of yesterday, the bubble shall not resist the wishes of its master.

Beyond his rage Descartes can envision a landscape of peace. An unspoiled void. An empty canvas. A place without matter. He needs to get there. Fire doesn't burn him, but then again there is nothing left for it to burn. Descartes is no more Newman. He knows. He too is plasma.

Subatomic particles, the positively charged protons they rebound instead of crashing into one another. Six thousand degrees on the surface, fifteen million at the core. Descartes is nearly there, as promised he shall soon be part of Eutopia. He grows to cover the entirety of the cupped sky, horizon to horizon, east to west, north to south, to be a Sun which knows no boundaries; and then fusion occurs.

An outburst of energy, a flash of light, magnanimous and all encompassing. The red ever-moving sky turns into a continuous spotlight. Brightness floods his bubble to the brim. In the glow everything shreds.

The Red Giant

Ananta has never visited Descartes' home, but the records at the Observatory and the profiling of Destiny's and Descartes' personality gives him a fair idea of what to expect. His experience allows him to guess very closely the lifestyle the couple had shared together.

"I hope it isn't too late," Ananta prays to Eutopia, as he opens the glass door of their cell. *"Please tell me you haven't claimed him yet."* He talks to himself in a manner similar to the way Descartes does. He rushes across the passage that connects the City to the bubble.

A last second foreboding stops him from diving in. *"I know it's unlikely, but it would be unwise of me to take a chance."* In his thoughts he addresses his long passed daughter Gaea – a habit he keeps in her memory.

His automated Absolute Defense will not be enough to protect Ananta from a supernova event: The way the protection mechanisms of the victims of the Incident of White could do nothing for them. His shield needs to be akin to the celestial stuff of supernovas.

The lucky ones who survived the White were the ones who had the rare Absolute Defense of lightning. Ananta the High Mentor, the Architect, the Beloved of Eutopia has the special ability to bend its laws. He switches his Absolute Defense from his usual one of air, to that of lightning.

He steps in. On the other side, he leaks within the bubble as fluorescent plasma, in blooms of sprite lightning. A precautionary measure to avoid getting caught in the blast.

On his way in he considers the three possible states in which he may find Descartes. The best would be a troubled but alive Descartes, who hasn't yet succumbed to rage, nor embarked on the path of self-destruction.

The second would be the opposite, in which Descartes has passed on to Gaea, leaving behind only a shell of their Bubble of Perfect Existence. Made anew, the bubble would be plain and empty, the way Descartes and Destiny had received it when they had been coupled together and housed.

The worst, which he dreads and must be prepared for, is one in which Ananta is unlucky enough to catch Descartes midway into a Supernova. Ananta remembers well how terrible was the incident of White, and how hard it was for him to contain it. Thankfully, he was present there, otherwise the fallout would have claimed many more.

Eyes shut tight, Ananta's hopes halve by the absence of a pink glow that should have seeped onto his retina through his eyelids. His hosts are known to greet their guests with bright sunny days. Embedded in the very design of their bubble, it's required of the Yonder Land to always be of a pleasant disposition. The darkness is a sign of the changed mood here.

The revelation is not one of those that Ananta had anticipated. He does not find an empty canvas left behind by Descartes, nor is he received by violent fits of a dying star, but there is a star here and it's millions of years away from its end. It isn't a sun with a backdrop of blue skies, but is a red giant in the black of space. Ananta is in orbit of this massive star, as far from its surface as Jupiter is to the sun in the solar system of the Earth of Old.

Transfixed by the giant, Ananta can't look away. Confident in his ability, he does not duck away as a solar wind lashes hard on his magnetic shield. The star's radiations simmer on the outer surface of his shield, filling his sight with the magnificence of auroras. He is safe within the plasma of his Absolute Defense.

"Did you spare him? Is Descartes still here?" he asks his daughter, but doesn't wait for a reply. He shouts out into the void, "Is anybody home?" but there is no answer.

Ananta, out of habit, sits down in a *padmasana*. In a quest to solve the mystery of what transpired here, in the sixteenth cell of the twenty-seventh hive, he searches his ancient memory to deduce associations that will help him make sense of the red giant.

Twice before he has witnessed supernova events, the one of White and that of Tetsuo, both were identical in form: a flash of lightning, lasting only a fraction of a second, bringing a quick end to most of those caught in their blast radius.

A later slow motion playback showed that they had transformed into stars, and had quickly burned out their life cycles to Supernova. Descartes, it seems, had failed to do so, and is now stuck in the third stage of being a star, fusing helium.

Ananta contemplates what happens when a star fails to complete its natural life cycle. If he stays this way, his end will not be by a blinding supernova but a wimpier, in which the red giant will lend most of its mass and knowledge to the solar wind, sinking down to become a white dwarf.

This would be terrible for Descartes, for if his conciseness is still here within the star, he would be trapped in it forever, beyond help or rescue. Ananta cannot let this happen. He must gather more information. These are new grounds for him, never before has he attempted to communicate with one who has become a star. Unsure of what he may find, he reaches out in telepathy, to no one in particular.

If the circumstance was a pinch more normal, rationality would dictate that the first contact Ananta makes is with the bubble, the home of Descartes and Destiny, but that can't be, for its artificial intelligence has been consumed by the star. "Descartes, is that you. I only want to talk." Ananta attempts a civil conversation with the star. The response is a tsunami of incoherent will. Carried by solar waves, it crashes onto Ananta, muting his efforts of telepathic speech.

The most skilled among the Newman, Ananta too is no match to the brute force being radiated from the star. Luckily for him, the all-powerful will of the star isn't encrypted with specific commands. It has no intentions. It simply is.

A frustrated Ananta knows not what to do. Incapable of speaking up, he reaches inside, *"What would you have me do Gaea? How am I to be of aid to this poor soul?"* To his delight, she believes the predicament at hand is critical enough to speak back to him.

"She must let him go, if he is to be free to be with me."

Tinfoil Origins

Through the woods, in the night forest she runs, with Diablo at her heels. "What did the letter say Destiny?" he asks her again. She won't tell, all he knows is that they have been summoned by the Beloved of Eutopia to his court, and that the letter contains a map to it.

Scroll in hand, quick footed as a centaur, she paces on in leaps and bounds. She would halt at times, whenever she spots a change in the monotony of the woodlands, to refer again to the map, and then push on. Each time, Diablo would have only just reached her.

The urgency in her is real, the determination in her gait absolute. Worrisomely, she hadn't ceased smiling for this long before, unlike now she was bereft of frowns when over at Diablo's. She was bursting in kind laughter at his very gesture, and would grace the details of his home with bashful grins, as though all of his things share a joke with her, jests that he wasn't privy to.

Now her pensiveness deters him from bugging her. "We are here she announces," at a circular clearance that breaks open the density of the jungle. "This isn't a court." She states the obvious with disappointment. Diablo spots the fear in her when she looks at him.

"Yes, it's not a court, but at least it's a clear field." He reckons any optimism will help. "If the map says this is the place, then it is. I recall Mentor Zen back at the Academy told us that the position and the layout of Ananta's court keeps changing. That those summoned are provided with the route to the correct spot."

He slips his hand in hers, as they walk to the center of this clearance. It's an elevated platform covered in grass. A restless Destiny asks, "Can you spot any clues that confirm we aren't lost?"

"The boundaries of this field are too symmetrical for them not to have a deliberate social purpose." His words are hogwash, said only to keep Destiny's spirit from falling further. Thankfully, he soon spots a hint of something real. "What's that?" he points among the trees. "Those lights, do you see them Destiny?" She looks at where he intends, she might have seen a glitter, but she isn't certain, when a sound from the left makes them glance away. A rustle in the bushes, indicating the presence of a beast. Followed by footsteps.

Despite the rational knowledge of insured Newman immortality, a primal fear grips the couple. "Sharpen your senses," Diablo commands, standing firm with his legs apart, in fight or flight mode.

They carry staffs made of iron, on the heads of which burn steampunk Edison lamps. The first to appear is Machiavelli, followed by Ananta, who is aided in his elderly trot by two ladies, Daphne the green of skin, and Cassandra with a whip-like platinum pony tail. Diablo has never met Cassandra before, but he recognizes Ananta from his projection in the sky years earlier at his graduation convention.

Without warning, Daphne rushes from Ananta's side to Destiny and embraces her. This move of hers turns the mood somber; tears seem imminent. Machiavelli approaches her next. In his left hand he carries a bottle of pirate's rum, which he offers to Destiny, "Have a swig child." She takes it. Diablo considers advising her against it, but chooses not to voice his opinion.

"You may have a seat, if you so do please," says Ananta and by a movement of his hand, the grass on the central podium of the field grows backwards to reveal a pond walled in by stone. None of them take him up on his offer, and it is only he who takes the embankment of the pond for a chair. "Forgive my old bones, they aren't used to long walks anymore."

It is only now that Diablo notices how unhealthy Ananta looks. His skin sags, and flaps of it hang where there used to be chunks of muscle. "Why have you summoned us on such a short notice? Why the exigency?" Diablo is too preoccupied by his worries for Destiny to spare any sympathy for Ananta.

In contrast, Destiny's nature allows her a word of concern. "Are you unwell, my Mentor?" she asks.

"No not at all. You don't have to worry about me, my appearance is only a reflection of how tired I am, and lately I have been having far too many taxing conversations," the Mentor says with a sigh. "And yes, we do owe you an explanation for this Diablo, and for much more to Destiny."

"What happened to him?" she asks in a low voice, the first indication to Diablo that their gathering is to do with her ex-partner. He wishes Descartes isn't being more trouble than he already has been by merely existing.

"The tale is long, and you would have to be patient for its smooth telling," warns Ananta. "There is much about Descartes you don't know Destiny. It's not that he was keeping secrets from you. Do not rush to that conclusion. He didn't know them either, and once he did, there was no time available to him to convey the truth to you."

A dark dread takes hold of Destiny. A thought undeniably true, an unarguable hunch grips her. The news need not be spelled out to her. "He is dead," she whispers, and by her will the loaded question reaches only Ananta.

"It's not that simple Destiny," replies Ananta for all to hear. Machiavelli is able to discern from this exchange that it would be wise to allow the High Mentor and Destiny to speak privately.

"Ladies and gentlemen." Machiavelli addresses the rest of the party. "Let us not crowd their conversation, let us walk away a little, and hang under those pines, let the High Mentor have the space he needs to have his talk with Destiny."

Cassandra and Daphne show signs of compliance and willingness to get into motion, but Diablo hesitates. "You too, Diablo," adds Machiavelli. He still won't move, but waits for an indication from Destiny.

"I will be fine Diablo." He nods to her before turning around, enough to reassure her that he is very much with her.

"All was good in the beginning. We had saved humanity, and made real the promised land of science fiction. We had outdone ourselves, our Eutopia was full of surprises, and everyone was glad of it. The old celebrated their eternal youth, the young were enthralled in exploring their new powers, in much the same way that kids are fascinated by make-belief games in which they are superheroes. In this time of merrymaking, we, the architects, got to work." Ananta grows increasingly animated as he speaks on.

"We called parliaments and councils, passed laws and started to bring in place the institutions that govern our society today." His voice clears up, betraying his aged façade. "Spirits were high, and the grumpiest among us too kept light-hearted moods. It was splendid, those first nine months." He paces around. "We felt as though nothing could go wrong ever again, until the first child conceived in Eutopia was born."

He stops and regards Destiny, "You see, before the exodus, we toiled long and hard to find an apt way to incorporate children into the algorithm of Eutopia. They are by their very nature unstable, their emotions are erratic, and in theory there is nothing that prevents them from mustering as much will as an adult. If bestowed with the power of tuning, they can in a fit of cranky rage cause damaging, unpleasant incidents. Not knowing how to control themselves in Eutopia, they can be a threat to themselves, and those around them." He takes a pause.

"All of this had to be tackled before the mass transcendence, for our capacity to change the soul code of Eutopia from within was to be limited. Our former solution was simple, we taught Eutopia to recognize children, and allow them minimal tuning capacity, permitting them more as they grew up.

This in turn meant we would need an institution of learning. We planned in detail the scope of such a place, and were delighted to realize that it could be used not only to teach the young ones how to tune and control their will, but also to act as a vessel to pass down to them the rich culture we brought along with us from the Earth of Old. You know this institution today as the Academy."

At another time Destiny would have cherished a chance to discuss the early days of Newman civilization with the High Mentor. "What does any of this have to do with my Descartes? Why can't you get to the point?" She is annoyed.

A glimpse of disappointment visibly rises and wanes in Ananta. "Yes, I will be done in a matter of minutes. I apologize, but we must dwell on the details, if you wish to understand Descartes."

"Oh! Please tell me, what is it about Descartes that you know and I don't." Destiny takes offence.

Ananta rolls his eyes, an argument will not help his cause now. He sits down and continues with measured words; it's time for him to revisit his deepest regrets. Exhaling mist he admits: "Our projections were wrong. We were so preoccupied with designing the perfect world for ourselves, so taken by the act of building our utopia, that we didn't adequately study the response life would have to its new habitat." He stops and contemplates her in his eyes, "I have more hope explaining the matters of evolution to you, than to many experienced Elders." Despite herself, Destiny knows the Mentor to be correct. Troubleshooting evolution is second nature to her.

"You are aware that all living things share an intelligence, a quality as ancient as the formation of the Earth of Old. A living will, which functions without our cerebral consent, which has but one purpose, to help us adapt better to our environment."

"Yes that's Evolution 101. Pray, why do you reiterate it?"

"That's precisely what occurred when the first child conceived in Eutopia was born. We had failed to take into account the rapid change in our biological DNA triggered by our transcendence into the digital world. From the word go our biological memory exhibited a voracious appetite for this new digital environment. The first born was a mutant."

"How was he different?" Ananta's story has unavoidable hooks, the kind unravelling the very mysteries of life, universe and everything would have.

"Named Tetsuo, it was in the baby's ears: on their crescent was additional tissue, a minor mutation at first glance, easily excusable as a freak chance of nature. On further study it was revealed it wasn't accidental at all, it was a fully developed organ, dedicated to tuning. Brought into being by the will of life, in a matter of a generation! Do you believe that Destiny? The very first child to be conceived in Eutopia was altered." Ananta does not wait for Destiny's reply. "We panicked and banned having children altogether. Our decision wasn't popular, but emphasis on its temporary nature, and an appeal to the public's new found virtue of immorality allowed us to buy some time.

Tetsuo was quarantined, and his upbringing was closely monitored. Within the first five years it was clear that the safeguards we had built in for children in Eutopia's soul code didn't apply to him. His new organ lent him powers equal to that of three adults. It was tough work containing him as a toddler, and was only projected to get harder as he grew."

Ananta turns solemn, "We had to keep the young boy caged in glass made of the same rudimentary will as our individual Absolute Defenses are. A prison. A Tartarus. Believe me, the act was shameful, too similar to our barbaric past to sit comfortably in my heart. Yet it's the study of Tetsuo which let us project what would happen if we permitted evolution to go rampant."

Destiny interjects, "His symptoms would be magnified with every passing generation; in the end it shall completely transform our species." In distress too, it's no work for her to deduce the logic of evolution.

"Yes, our fate seemed sealed, it wasn't to be pleasant at all. Eventually, the coupling of our descendants would have ceased to produce beings of body and mind, but would instead birth pure will.

"It is hard to envision, I know, and yes it would have taken long, but in Eutopia time is an arbitrary concept, made all the more whimsical by our immortality. In the distant future what was once humanity would have evolved to be one with its digital environment. Our refuge, a place where we were meant to thrive for all eternity, would have turned inert, cold and empty. For the difference between the two, a) us: the Newman, the doers, the tuners, and b) the subject of our desire and work: Eutopia would have surely evaporated.

"We would have inevitably poured more and more of ourselves into Eutopia in the form of sheer will, our birth children, a will which in itself desires nothing, but merely exists.

"It felt as though all our efforts to preserve the essence of humanity from the doom brought by the decay of the Earth of Old was for naught. It seemed our ambitions only achieved a dimension where the heat death of the universe was expedited, for when enough of our race assimilated with Eutopia, it would no more consider itself bound to the desires of those who remained in physical form. A place free of order, Eutopia would have turned static, and perhaps choose to disintegrate into nothing."

He tells a fanciful tale, but Destiny sees through him. His words don't charm her, and she considers them spoken in narcissism. "But you didn't let any of these ghastly things happen did you Mentor? Newmanity is well and thriving. So why do you speak of them at such a crucial hour, when I am pleading with you for news of Descartes." Actual notes of despair ring out of Destiny.

"I burden you with my stories not only because I deem you worthy, but also because in them lie the reasons for Descartes' misery," Ananta states calmly. "We had to find a solution, a way to freeze evolution, so we may stay in charge of Eutopia, and it wasn't I who saved us, but my daughter."

In hushed whispers the myth of Ananta's child has been told so many times by fireplaces, and as bedtime stories that Destiny too has heard it before. Mired in misinformation, it's hard to tell which part of the fable is true and what's legend. "Gaea?" asks Destiny daringly. It's common knowledge that one does not speak to the High Mentor of his one true loss.

"Yes, Gaea," admits Ananta. "You were told of how she is one of the only recorded individuals who has ever managed to muster their own death." Ananta's pride in Gaea fails to conceal his underlying sorrow. "The rumors of her that you in all probability have heard must speak of how her strength had come from the pain of her being betrayed by her partner. Is it not?" He is full of disdain. "The one she was betrothed to before transcending into Eutopia, and had insisted to be coupled with once we were here."

Half of Destiny wants to scream, she can't believe that Ananta the wise would attempt so blatantly to hijack her moment of grief by seeking sympathy for himself. The rest of her is moved by the exhibition of emotions that the Mentor puts on display. "Yes that too, but I was fonder of the poetry recited in her praise." Her kinder self prevails.

"Those were crude misrepresentations of her, my daughter was no weakling, and she didn't succumb to self-loathing but, instead, sacrificed herself to ensure the continuity of our civilization.

"She gave her Newman form up, choosing to assimilate with Eutopia, she was my star who in secret went supernova. By being the first to be one with Eutopia, she gained much sway over its sole code. It is her work to deceive the will of life, tricking it into believing that our current form is apt for the habitat of Eutopia. Yet, she doesn't always win, and once in a while mutated ones come forth, such as Miss White. It's vital then that Gaea has them, so she may learn the ways by which the will of life is changing."

Only now is Destiny able to gather how any of this might relate to Descartes. "If she fixed it, why then do you need Descartes? How can he be of help? He isn't a mutant, nor is he an Architect who holds any true memories of the Earth of Old, or special knowledge as to how Eutopia came to be, the way Lady Gaea did."

"Gaea by her sacrifice had stalled the will of life, but it wasn't vanquished. It is in its very nature to try again, and so it still does, if not with every passing generation, in the least once in every millennia." Destiny is still but she feels as though she is falling, all things around her including Ananta slip and back away from her. "You always had a suspicion Destiny, you could tell by how fragile were his thoughts, how very sensitive he used to be, by his fluid temper; you had to know he was unstable, that he was different."

Tinfoil hocus-pocus rumors Destiny as a norm had disregarded the talk of supernovas, and the hearsay surrounding the incident of White, she never had patience for the cynics who took exodus-based conspiracies seriously. Even now when they crowd her, not allowing her space to breathe, a part of her has a hard time believing in them.

"I can't say if chance has been merciful to you or brutal, but Gaea failed to claim Descartes. His supernova fizzled instead of going full boom. It seems he can't let go of you Destiny."

Ixtab and Darko

"We keep him safe, but before we allow you to see him, there is someone else we want you to meet," says Ananta.

Destiny shuts down. No more is she able to grasp all that she is being told; she defaults to faith, and it assures her that Descartes shall never hurt her; harming himself too would count as doing her wrong, she rules it out.

Ananta rises up and signals Machiavelli with a nod, the implications of which seem predetermined to Destiny, for nothing else is said between them. The distance keeps her from hearing the conversation that follows between Machiavelli, the other Elders and Diablo on the far side of the field. She doesn't care.

She sits down by the pond. In her hand forms a goblet; she scoops up a fill for herself and by then Diablo is by her side once more. His hesitance to touch her makes it known that they weren't idling all this while, but that he too has been told much of what shocks her now. He creeps closer to her and sits by her side. She begins to cry. Diablo embraces her, presuming she wants to be held. She does.

Destiny isn't aware that Ananta and the other Elders have left the scene. "All will be good again Destiny, you will be fine." Diablo picks her chin on his index. "Look at me," gently making her face him, "You and I will be fine." She doesn't believe him yet, but she lets him console her.

Short-lived was their privacy and the absence of Elders. Machiavelli clears his throat, catching their attention. Diablo helps

Destiny up, she has resigned to whatever may come next, and doesn't react at all to the presence of two new individuals. "Destiny, meet Descartes' parents, Darko and Ixtab." Machiavelli introduces the father first, shorter than Descartes, but broader of chest, she can see Descartes in his features but not as much as she can in the mother. Ixtab and Descartes look identical, it explains the softness in Descartes. His skin too is hers, teal, with peppered black dots, which may not be there at all.

"Is this Destiny?" Ixtab asks to no one in particular. "See how pretty she is Darko, your son did well." She has no cares for Destiny's tears. "Come hear child, let us have a proper look at you."

It's hard for Destiny to keep herself from hurling a punch at Ixtab. It escapes her why Ananta would think it apt to have his parents here. "The fault lies in you," she mumbles with a new clarity. "If you had not abandoned him he wouldn't have gone astray at all. He could have been here with us." She raises her voice, still in tears.

Machiavelli and the other Elders exchange worried whispers, "This was to be expected, we know it's bad, it's worse than bad, and her tears are merely an omen that confirms it." Ananta's insensitivity carries to Destiny.

"Courtesy clearly isn't one of her virtues," remarks Ixtab, while Darko hangs his head in shame.

"We had no choice. How could a father be expected to conspire against his own son? It wasn't in me to partake in keeping him in the illusion of a false future of normality, knowing well that his fate was sealed in sorrow at birth." His mannerism and clear voice are distinctly Descartes'.

"When the High Mentor first came to bless the child he informed us that our Toplo had been picked by Gaea to be one with Eutopia. He asked us to be vigilant, to watch and report any discrepancy in his behavior.

"Toplo?" asks Destiny in-between sobs. "Why do you call him that?"

"That's the birth name we gave him. He might be Descartes to you, but to us he will always be Toplo." Newmans rename themselves in the Academy, in their teen years, choosing a word or a name that they feel better reflects their persona.

Darko continues, "They said it was vital that Toplo learned the nuance of what it was to be Newman. The more he experienced life the more knowledge he shall carry with him in his supernova. His passing shall then better sate the appetite of Eutopia, distancing further its next such meal. Sparing many families the tragedy that befell us."

"It was so very painful, knowing every time that I caught my son when he stumbled that it was for nothing," Ixtab disrupts his confessions. "At times such as these I wonder how it is that they reckoned you and I make a perfect couple. Why can't you ever accept that Toplo is gifted, that we won't lose him by his passing, but he shall be all around us. Supernova is not death Darko, it's enlightenment. It's nirvana. He shall be exempted from the burden of living forever, from hibernating a gazillion years only to wake up and find that nothing has changed. He shall never suffer like you and I."

She turns to Destiny, "You are young, you don't know yet, when you have seen enough in another thousand years, you too will see life as a burden. You should be happy for your Descartes, he gets the easy way out."

"You expect me to celebrate the fact that our son was robbed of a life?" Darko grinds his bitter words. "He has a right to get bored out of his wits, it was his experience to value as he may."

"Silence." Ananta steps into their quarrel, "You haven't been gathered here to debate what should or could have been done, but what is it that we must do now. Descartes is no more in the position to make his own decisions, and so the responsibility falls to you. His parents, and to Destiny, the only partner he has ever had. Do you grant him the only wish he seems to have, that to see Destiny, or do we leave him in his Tartarus to vegetate until he finds a way to be one with Eutopia."

Splendid Garbage

A universe in its own right, Eutopia has no edges. At its corner it tapers off, ending into a void. It spreads as far as how all things that are made by the will of those who inhabit it does. Similar to our minds its corners too are full of half-baked ideas.

Destiny is flanked by Cassandra and Daphne on the river side. "This is the Styx; it marks the end of the city of the Elders, and beyond it lies the suburbia of sleep," states Cassandra, the more knowledgeable of the two.

Crystals of water, a frozen river, but not a glacier. Unanchored masses of ice flow free of one another, majestic as a Saturn ring, in the darkness of space they revolve around the city the way the celestial arm of a galaxy does around its core.

"Its waters are decomposing bubbles, abandoned to the mercy of time. Left here by those who once tired of living, booked a ticket to cross over to suburbia. They cast their homes in the river, instead of freezing them in store rooms, in the hope that it shall strengthen their resolve not to return one day," she elaborates, and only now does Destiny notice the fossils flowing in the stream.

Ruptured and leaking are the once neatly capsuled Bubbles of Perfect Existence, unleashed from them is matter that made the abode of countless individuals and couples. It's mostly water and stone, peppered lightly by items of design, the first one that Destiny spies is an old school black umbrella with a polished silver handle. The next is a fever of stingrays, unconcerned that the ripples of their fins guides them not through the ocean, nor air, but vacuum. They are followed by stringed beads of pearls, each as large as a yoga ball, the utility of which is indeterminable by the onlookers.

In the mix of this splendid garbage an unmanned sail-less vessel, a Viking timber longboat of a light watercolor wooden shade floats toward them. "We can't accompany you any further Destiny," Daphne tells her. "The awake should resist bothering the sleeping, and we the Elders have many whom we miss."

A determined Destiny is certain she doesn't need them, "Am I to ferry across on this?"

"Yes." Daphne helps Destiny on board. "Will you be able to find him?" she asks Destiny, holding gently the dragon-faced prow of the boat.

It's the dragon that speaks for Destiny, "My folks shall show her the way." Mayhap not the sound but it's the movement of its lips that startle Daphne. She lets go of the prow. It's her first time at the gates of the sleepy suburbia.

Cassandra lets out a chuckle, "Do not be intimidated by what you may find on the other side Destiny, none of them wish you harm, but some might beg for your company. Ignore them. Do not waver from your mission."

Without a word Destiny turns away from them, and the boat starts moving. She allows her companions no goodbyes, nor good wishes made in pretense. A while later she looks back, but there is no one at the shore.

Alone. A dread ripples through her. It isn't to do with Descartes, but the fear of the unknown. She knows not how she would react when she sees him. "How wide is the Styx?" she asks the dragon, which for now is no more than an inanimate object. It does not respond.

The further the vessel travels the mistier it gets. On the surface of the river too hangs a fog, Destiny strikes her hand in, out of curiosity, and out comes a see-through frog, its matter not organic, but glass, with sharp edges and crystal eyes. It turns toward Destiny in her palm and attempts a croak, but manages only a faint hiss. She pities it, for it is lost. The Styx is not its home. She thinks unfavorably of its makers. It was selfish of them to deny their creatures the only home they knew, the bubble that they were born in. She would never let such a fate befall her creations. Her Dwarkoids shan't swim this river.

Hazy outlines of the buildings of Suburbia come in focus. They reveal nothing but broad foundations, and shadows of prominent eaves at the top of the buildings. Next come the twinkling lights, in appearance no different from those that usually reside in the sky, but their size grows as she gets closer to them, an indication they aren't stars, but city lights.

The gliding longboat comes to a bumpy stop, its hull hits land with the sound of shifting sand. The prow dragon twists around the way a rattle snake would. The boat lends him its wood, its neck stretches, twists in a swirl, and faces Destiny. "We are on the shores of the sleepy suburbia. Listen only to my kind, and pay no heed to any other." Its neck retracts, zipping up as a spring released, returning the borrowed wood, which made its length back to the boat.

Destiny leaps out of the boat; she isn't certain what the Dragon implied by its warnings, but she reckons she would know soon enough.

Sleepy Suburbia

The mountainside road is cobbled blue. The suburb is bathed in moonlight. It's silent, except for occasional mourns, the source of which is unknown. She ambles on with hesitation, waiting on a sign to tell her where to go. The main street runs straight a while, and then winds up, hugging the hill.

The street is lined on both sides with identical buildings made of turquoise bricks; the porticos aren't marked, and they make no effort to reveal their purpose. It's the castle on the mountain side, lit up in amber that beckons her. It's where the road ends. "Hello there," calls out a pedestrian from the shadows, with only his silhouette visible in the road-facing gallery of a building, among pillars with dragons for arches.

"Step into the light," she asks him. A hand shoots out from the shadows, gesturing her to follow. "I have been so lonely here, waiting for him to wake up. Do come sit by me, at his door, and give me company. I have words aplenty, well-crafted in poetry, in his memory. May I share them with you?"

Destiny takes an involuntary step toward the stranger; then she remembers the purpose of her presence, and not wanting to be rude, she flees. In her flight the voice of stone demons guarding the doors guide her, "Good choice, Destiny! Make haste to the peak, there in the last room before oblivion you shall find whom you seek."

She takes the advice, and even as she runs another voice calls out to her, "Who goes there? Don't scurry away, I have been here too long alone. She will be waking up any day now, do stay, and wait with me. Are you not here to hold vigil by your beloved's bed?"

Over a dry riverine is a bridge made of wood, covered on the top, the ceiling painted, depicting the varied abodes of Eutopia. Its very ink glows, the art is fine, as an Elder's should be, but Destiny doesn't have a minute to spare. Her footsteps are loud on the wooden planks.

On the other side, narrow is the mountain's path, and steep is its rock wall. Going higher, the rock wall of the mountain changes to a white castle stone. The slope of the road gives way to stairs. She hurries up through an arched door with the banner, "Hall of those who should never be woken." And a footnote, "Tread Softly."

Destiny is alone in the bailey of this castle. She swirls to have a look around, the windows of its turret towers are lit by diya lamps, small flickering naked inextinguishable drops of fire, fueled by a spot of oil fostered in terracotta vessels. The gallery and the living quarters of this institution are carved out caves in the mountain. She considers if Descartes could be in one of those room, but it can't be, for they aren't at the edge of oblivion.

Her curiosity is then summoned by the keep, a spike entrenched in the heart of the sky, a striking sight. Its chambers are high up in the clouds, their windows too far off for her to have a peek.

The diya lamps light the way up the spiral stairs. An endless flight, they demand much of Destiny; she pants, but she doesn't stop. It takes a while to reach the top, a single thin rotten wooden door, with a circular glass window in the middle. Dim moving shadows seep out. She presses her ear to its surface – she can hear sobs. It's Descartes.

The Tartarus

Incoherent whispers fill the room. Singular words seep out from the cacophony; "Deserter" is the first. It's damp, lit by a flickering fluorescent light, humming in its fight to keep functioning. He is on the floor, naked. His teal skin crumpled, only in patches keeping its original smooth texture.

Destiny is drawn to this shadow of Descartes. She moves closer, she kneels. Her dress gets drenched. He is bony enough for her to count his ribs. "Lier."

The Gatekeeper of his nightmares reveals itself in between the spasms of the room's light. Cloaked in ink, as a Rorschach blot card, he fills the wall on which Descartes rests. It towers over him. She sees it in stop-motion, inching toward him. From the chaos of the demon's being extends a solitary muscle-less arm of bone; it lingers by Descartes' head. A blink – and it's three-dimensional; erupting out of the wall, it wraps around his neck. It chokes him.

Descartes sees her, wide open, bloodshot, "Destiny save me!" The grip tightens.

"I am here," she says. Panicked by his desperate effort to free himself, she joins in. She pulls at Depression's grip, but to no avail. Descartes barfs.

Destiny shrieks, but isn't quick enough to duck away. The stuff is on her. Back on her feet, she looks down at herself, pellets of pink and flax grace her limbs. Filth greases the space between her fingers.

The wave of depression has passed. Head stooped, Descartes

breathes heavily, he shakes. Once calm he pulls himself up, a thread of drool connects his lips to his thighs. In a hoarse voice, he says, "You came." He smiles. He wipes his mouth with the back of his palm.

Pity is eclipsed by revulsion. Her face grows stern. Descartes attempts to rise, but can't stay standing – his legs refuse to cooperate. In his fall he reaches out to Destiny, but she backs away.

Back on the floor, he mumbles, "We can have it back, I remember the details of our home."

"Have it back?" She is confused.

"I deleted it." He isn't looking at her, his eyes are empty. "Gaia won't have me otherwise." Not an ounce of remorse in him.

She believes him completely. "You deleted our bubble," she reiterates. In the wake of ill news, breathing becomes a task. She calls upon an ottoman to appear as she sits. Railing in anxiety she moves back and forth. "Did you even think of me?" Her words are defeated.

Her melancholy is not lost upon the delirious. "I can fix it. Look..." For the first time, Descartes sounds as though he is the master of his own tongue. He crawls toward her. "Forgive me, Destiny." He sobs. "I will make our bubble anew." A teardrop drips off his chin and as it breaks on the ground the room transforms.

The circular window of its one door becomes the rising sun. The damp ground is a glen, and its four walls keep in them the colors of her forest. An illusion, for the nature of his Tartarus allows him limited space of no more than ten feet square. Yet the room fills with light, and for a moment Destiny feels at home.

"Don't touch me!" she yells, rising up, and Descartes withdraws, falling back. "I don't want your cardboard replica of my world. You don't own me, you never did." With her rebuff and Descartes' retreat, the room returns to as it was. Bleak.

"I love you..." he starts.

"I never loved you, Descartes and I never will."

"No don't say that Destiny."

Her name no more sounds safe on his lips. Her voice rises again, "Why are you here Descartes? You made your choice. You chose Supernova, Gaia and Eutopia over me."

He doesn't know what to say, "That's not true."

"You wouldn't have been able to go through with it if it wasn't. You would not have taken my home away from me." Destiny wishes to hurt him, but knows not how. She lashes out, "So why are you still here Descartes, what do you want of me?"

Descartes stands with a drunkard's grace, "If you won't have me back, then free me." He steps forward, she moves away, but has no more room to give, her back is to the door.

He presses something cold into her hands, it's a pepper box sized revolver, a gift he had made to her years ago. He makes her hold up its muzzle to his heart and says, "I can override the will of my Absolute Defense."

She can hurt him now.

THE END

2008 – 2017

Suyash lives in Bombay. He is twenty-nine and is a self-taught novelist. These days he prefers the company of old friends who tend to be mighty raconteurs and follow his artistic bent. He travels, but without consistency, taking writing sabbaticals which often outlast their intended period. *Eutopia* is his first novel.

Printed in Poland
by Amazon Fulfillment
Poland Sp. z o.o., Wrocław

52527950R00162